ANGEL
SONG

OTHER NOVELS BY SHEILA WALSH

Angel Song with Kathryn Cushman
Sweet Sanctuary with Cindy Martinusen Coloma

ANGEL
SONG

A NOVEL

SHEILA WALSH
AND KATHRYN CUSHMAN

THOMAS NELSON
Since 1798

NASHVILLE DALLAS MEXICO CITY RIO DE JANEIRO

Published in Nashville, Tennessee, by Thomas Nelson. Thomas Nelson is a registered trademark of Thomas Nelson, Inc.

The authors are represented by the literary agency of Alive Communications, Inc., 7680 Goddard Street, Suite 200, Colorado Springs, CO 80920, www.alivecommunications.com.

Thomas Nelson, Inc., titles may be purchased in bulk for educational, business, fund-raising, or sales promotional use. For information, e-mail SpecialMarkets@ThomasNelson.com.

Scripture quotations are taken from the HOLY BIBLE: NEW INTERNATIONAL VERSION®. © 1973, 1978, 1984 by International Bible Society. Used by permission of Zondervan Publishing House. All rights reserved.

This novel is a work of fiction. Any references to real events, businesses, organizations, and locales are intended only to give the fiction a sense of reality and authenticity. Any resemblance to actual persons, living or dead, is entirely coincidental.

ISBN 978-1-4016-8644-4 (DG edition)

Library of Congress Cataloging-in-Publication Data is available for this title.

Walsh, Sheila, 1956–
  Angel song : a novel / Sheila Walsh and Kathryn Cushman.
    p. cm.
  ISBN 978-1-59554-685-2 (trade paper)
  I. Cushman, Kathryn. II. Title.
  PS3623.A36615A8 2010b
  813'.6—dc22

2010020397

Printed in the United States of America
11 12 13 14 15 BTY 5 4 3 2 1

This book is dedicated with love to my friend
Eric Kuntz who helped me hear the angels' song.

—Sheila Walsh

To Caroline Cushman—you are a bright ray
of sunshine that warms our lives. This world
is a happier place because you are here.

—Kathryn Cushman

For he will command his angels

concerning you to guard you in all your ways.

PSALM 91:11 (ESV)

Prologue

The sun's first light crept across the wing. Ann leaned across
the empty seat beside her, moving close enough to the airplane's
window to watch the skyline she loved grow smaller and smaller.
Behind her lay the frenetic pace of millions of people, all trying
to succeed on the hard streets below. Only the best, or lucki-
est, would make it; the rest would become casualties in the meat
grinder that was New York City. Ann had proven she was strong
enough to survive there. She could make it without anyone's
help, on her own terms.

But now her plane sped closer to the polar opposite of all
that she was, to a city where antebellum homes lined the streets
and natives valued history and family bloodlines over modern
innovation. The place whose very existence was like a weight,
an anchor that should long ago have lost its chains. Somehow
Charleston never seemed to loosen its hold.

But her sister was there, the one person who made this trip
bearable. Probably at this very minute Sarah was frantically

cleaning the house, sweeping the front porch, and making some of her famous chocolate oatmeal cookies—and more than enough for just the two of them. She'd share them with the neighbors and anyone else who happened to drop by the house over the course of the weekend's festivities. Sarah was so much like Nana had been.

Ann quickly grabbed a copy of *Architectural Digest* from her portfolio bag and began leafing through the pages. *There.* A picture of a beach house somewhere on the Florida coast. Bright colors, seashell prints on the wall. It was tastefully done, but then again, it was all so . . . predictable. She pulled out her sketch pad and began redesigning the room.

First, the couch needed stronger edges, almost squared. And white would be perfect. She feathered in texture with her pencil, then added a row of pillows, shading a couple of them completely to black. She penciled in a table lamp like the one she'd seen just last week—uneven squares of black bamboo stacked on each other with a square shade on top—then added a piece of modern art above the couch, pale gray with streaks of black and white.

It still needed something. Monochromatic decorating required absolute precision in design, a challenge Ann savored. She compared the two rooms. Hers still needed work, but she was pleased with what she'd done.

"You've got a good eye." The man one row back was leaning across the aisle. He was casually dressed, short brown hair with just a touch of curl, probably in his late forties. Nice looking. And vaguely familiar.

Embarrassed to have been caught in her game, Ann shrugged. "Thanks."

"Are you a designer?"

"Yes. I work for a home staging company." She knew he probably had no idea what that meant, but she didn't really care. "Redesigning rooms from magazines helps keep the creative juices flowing."

"Do you work in Charleston?"

Ann shook her head. "The City."

"Now that's something I'm truly glad to hear." He leaned a little closer and offered a dazzling smile, complete with dimple on his left cheek. "Do you have a card?"

Ann looked at him dubiously. "Are you thinking of putting a home on the market?"

He smiled. "You could say that." He reached into the back pocket of his designer slacks, pulled out a leather wallet, and withdrew a business card. He dangled it by its corner, the print facing away from her. "Trade?"

What could it hurt? Ann's card didn't contain any of her personal information, just the office address and phone number. "Sure." She reached into her small purse and pulled out a card, and just for good measure, she removed one of the trifold brochures she always carried around with her.

After they made the exchange, Ann looked at his card. It almost fell from her hands. "Patrick Stinson?" She looked at him in surprise.

He smiled broadly, seeming pleased that he held so great a secret. "Guilty."

"What are you doing on this puddle jumper of a plane?"

"There's an event I need to get to in Charleston tonight. This is a nonstop flight. The Newark airport is much more convenient."

"I guess I expected you to be flying in private planes."

"When it's business and I'm taking a team with me, that's what I do. When it's just me, going to an event and back, well . . . trying to keep a small carbon footprint." He winked.

"Sir, we need you to sit back in your seat. We'll be landing soon."

"Oh, right. Thank you." He was all charm.

Ann couldn't believe how stupid she'd been. She had been sitting across from a major New York real estate developer and hadn't even known it. It didn't really matter. Marston Home Staging did work in some high-end residences, but the Stinson company was in another league altogether. He would probably have a good laugh with his associates over this whole episode.

But why should he? Ann's work was good. Good enough to be featured in last year's "100 Designers to Watch For" put out by New York City's *Design* magazine.

When the plane came to a stop at the gate, Ann threw her bag over her shoulder and descended the metal steps onto the tarmac. The humid morning air felt about ten degrees warmer than in the City. She made her way up another set of steps and began walking through the concourse. She debated about whether she should wait for Patrick Stinson, say something else to him, but then she saw Sarah standing just outside the security checkpoint, waiting for her.

Her blonde hair bounced with curls; her preppy outfit looked freshly pressed. "Annie, Annie. Over here."

Ann hurried to her sister's waiting embrace. "Well, if it isn't the graduate herself."

"That's me." Sarah squeezed tight. "Thank you so much for coming. Welcome home."

"I wouldn't miss this for anything."

They hugged for a moment before making their way toward baggage claim. Just then, Patrick Stinson breezed past them, casting a grin over his left shoulder. "Enjoy your stay in Charleston, Ann Fletcher. I'll be in touch." He disappeared through the exit with his leather carry-on dangling from his right hand.

"*Who* was that?" Sarah made no pretense of keeping the suggestive tone from her voice.

"Someone who definitely will *not* be in touch."

"Somehow I have the feeling you're wrong about that," Sarah said with a grin. "Let's get your luggage and get you home."

Chapter 1

Red and blue lights spun off broken glass and twisted metal, shooting cold barbs through the warm South Carolina night. Ann Fletcher sat on the curb, hugging her knees to her chest. *How could this have happened?* She closed her eyes, trying to regain some sense of equilibrium, but that only intensified the stench of hot rubber and engine fluid. She gave up and opened her eyes.

The multicolored strobes highlighted the scene around her. She glanced at a policeman in black barking orders into a walkie-talkie. Nearby, a fireman in yellow turnouts sprayed water over a steaming engine, and a duo in blue jumpsuits hovered over a gurney. She was staying out of the way, as she'd promised the EMS team. If sitting here would keep their attention fully on Sarah, then that's what she would do.

"Here, I'm thinking you could use this." A woman in a black pantsuit held out a bottle of water, which Ann reached for gratefully.

"Thanks." She took a long drink, and then another, surprised by how thirsty she was.

"Is there anything else I can do to help you?" The woman's hair shone like copper in the flashing lights, and her face looked vaguely familiar, like someone Ann knew a long time ago. "Anything at all?"

Ann simply shook her head and looked toward the medics. "There's nothing."

"That's your sister." The woman stated this as a fact, not a question, but she waited as if for confirmation.

"Yes." Ann watched a third jumpsuit emerge from somewhere behind the smoke. He walked over to the others, exchanged brief conversation, then hurried to the front of the ambulance.

The woman pointed toward it. "If you climb up into the back now, before anyone realizes what you're doing, they won't kick you out. On the ride to the hospital, she'll hear your voice and know she's not alone." She spoke with authority, as if she understood the situation completely.

Ann looked through the open double doors at all the sterile-looking equipment inside. How could Sarah not be terrified amid all that? "You're right." She pushed to her feet and stumbled toward the vehicle.

"Hey, you can't ride back there." The male voice sounded barely old enough to be past puberty—and completely lacking in authoritative confidence.

Ann started to ignore him altogether, putting one foot on the step-up, but then thought better of it. Keeping her foot firmly planted, she paused and turned. He and another jumpsuit were fastening straps around Sarah on the gurney, the sight of which fueled Ann's determination. "That's my sister. I'll stay out of the way, I'll keep my mouth shut, but I'm not going to leave her."

The female medic barely flicked a look in Ann's direction as she pulled the last strap into place. "Get in the far corner and sit against the wall."

Her young partner looked up. "Shouldn't we at least make her ride in the front?"

"Don't have time for that. We've got to move. Now. One, two, three."

Ann ducked quickly into the ambulance, the smell of antiseptic growing stronger as she moved into the back corner. The jumpsuits acted in sync, bringing Sarah toward her. Soon everyone was crowded inside, the back doors shut, and their little world was moving in a blaze of speed and blaring sirens.

With Sarah only inches away, Ann longed to hold her hand, to stroke her face, anything that might offer comfort and remind her that she was not alone. But with a long gash bleeding slowly across Sarah's left cheek, and her left shoulder standing up at an awkward angle, Ann was afraid to touch her. She didn't want to cause more pain, so she reached for a lock of Sarah's long blonde hair that was splayed across her pillow. Ann rubbed it between her fingers, desperately wishing she could transfer some of her strength through it. "Hang in there, Sarah. You've got to fight. Stay awake."

Sarah opened her eyes and looked toward Ann, blue eyes squinted in pain. "So sorry about this. Don't know . . . what happened."

Ann spoke as soothingly as she could. "Just a little accident, don't worry about a thing. Everything's going to be all right."

As the vehicle swayed, Sarah turned her face toward the coiled tubes, blinking monitors, and cabinets full of things that people don't like to think about. Her eyes remained open, something for which Ann was grateful, even as her breathing became labored. Ann focused on the sound of each breath, each gasp, each wheeze. As long as she heard these things, her sister was still alive and breathing. If nothing else, she would keep Sarah's lungs moving by sheer willpower.

"Ooooh."

Ann leaned forward. She reached toward her sister but somehow stopped her hands less than an inch before she touched her. What was she doing? She had no medical training. In fact, she'd barely passed health in high school. But she had to do something.

She grabbed the shoulder of the female medic, wondering why this woman was ignoring the obvious. "Help her! She's choking."

The medic shrugged off Ann's hand and continued uncoiling some sort of tubing, her face barely registering a reaction to either Sarah's gasping or Ann's outburst. "She's not choking. She's humming."

"What?" Ann looked down at her sister.

Sarah's face was not locked in the expected contortion of pain. Her mouth was open; her eyes were wide and focused past her right shoulder, above the tools and gadgets. "*Glorious.*" She drew another ragged breath, but her lips curved into a smile. She lifted her right hand until the restraints of the gurney stopped her, then stretched her fingers up as if reaching for something. "Colors so brilliant, oh my . . ." The string of words was little more than a strangled whisper. "Song . . . Pure joy." A choking sound gurgled up from her throat and she gasped for breath, but still she managed to hum through it.

The male EMT was wrapping tape around the IV line, but he looked up. "The morphine must be kicking in."

"You gave her morphine?" The woman's persona of cool control slipped with the crackle of anger in her voice.

"I . . . uh, no. I thought you must have."

"You don't give narcotics to a multisystem trauma without explicit instructions. Especially with a falling BP, shallow respirations, and a short ride to the hospital. Got it?"

"Yeah, I know. It's just, when she started singing and talking to people who aren't here, I guess . . . I just sort of assumed she had narcotics on board." He looked at Sarah, whose eyes closed while she continued to hum, then went back to his work with the tape.

Desperate for a way to help, Ann began to listen to the song. Maybe it would comfort Sarah if she hummed along. Perhaps the sound of a familiar voice could give her the strength to fight, help keep her here. Except Ann didn't recognize the tune. She focused all her concentration on listening, hoping to pick out something familiar. But there was nothing. Still, even with Sarah's strangled voice, the melody was beautiful.

"I've seen things like this before," the female medic said. "Awed whispers, peaceful expressions when there shouldn't be one, and almost always a song. Once I even thought I heard the tune. Makes you wonder what's out there."

With a final lurch, the ambulance screeched to a stop. The back doors clattered open, and a barrage of light, sound, and white coats stood waiting. Ann leaned forward and kissed the lock of hair. "Sarah, you stay strong. Don't you dare leave me. Not now."

Sarah didn't acknowledge her at all, just continued to look above her right side. "Help. Annie. Please."

Ann leaned forward, prepared to do whatever her sister asked. "How can I help you, Sarah? What do you need me to do?"

The gurney was lifted and a sea of personnel parted, taking Sarah with them. "No. Wait!" Ann jumped out. "Sarah, what do you need? Tell me what I can do!"

A behemoth nurse in pink scrubs jumped between Ann and the emergency room doors. "I'm sorry. You're not allowed to go in there."

Ann sidestepped the bouncer-nurse. "Just try and keep me out. She asked me for help, and I'm going to help her." Even at a skinny five feet five, she was sure her determination would more than make up for the size difference.

The nurse grabbed her arm, clamping so tight that it almost jerked Ann backward. "They're taking her straight into surgery. We're going to do everything we can for her, but we need you to stay out of the way."

Ann tried to yank her arm away, but the woman held fast. "Let me go."

"Your sister wasn't the only one in that car. We've got to get you in a back room and take a look at you too." Her calm voice carried that oh-so-concerned tone that didn't at all match the I'll-take-you-in-a-smackdown look on her face. But Ann would take Bouncer Nurse on in a heartbeat if it meant helping Sarah.

Then she saw a couple of uniformed officers heading their general direction and decided to try a calmer approach. The last thing she wanted was to get kicked out of here. "I'm fine. All you can do for me is take care of my sister."

"Let's let the doctors be the judge of that, honey!"

It occurred to Ann that if she was inside the ER, rather than in the waiting room, she might overhear things that were happening, find out about Sarah a lot sooner. In truth, her left arm did ache a little, and her hand and left cheek stung. It was worth the chance. "Okay, where do I need to go?"

"Just come with me." The syrup that now dripped from the nurse's voice could clog arteries, but she didn't loosen her grip in the slightest. She simply began to move slowly toward the doors labeled Emergency Room Entrance.

Ann was soon ensconced in a cubicle of curtains furnished only with a bed and two small chairs. Bouncer Nurse dropped a folded piece of pale blue fabric on the bed. "Put that on, and one of the doctors will be with you soon."

"Get him in here fast. I need some answers."

"Don't we all?" The nurse didn't bother to look back as she pulled the curtains shut behind her.

Ann put her arms through the oversized holes and was attempting to tie the back side together when she heard a male voice just outside the curtains. "Ms. Fletcher?"

Ann pulled the back edges of her gown together as best she could and sat on the bed. "Yeah, I'm ready." She looked down at the cuts on her left arm. They didn't look that deep—at least not to her. "I'm really fine. I do not want stitches in my arm, it will be . . ." Ann looked up at the doctor—except it wasn't the doctor at all. It was one of the uniformed policemen she'd seen out front.

"I'm sorry to do this now, but I really need to ask you a few questions."

Ann nodded once. "Okay."

He sat in one of the chairs, pen and paper in hand. "Can you tell me what happened tonight?"

"I . . . we . . . had just gone out for dinner. Sarah, my sister, is getting her master's degree on Friday. Social work. She wants to help inner-city kids." Ann didn't know why she was giving him all these details. She knew it was not the kind of information he was looking for, but somehow it was important to her that he understood who Sarah really was, to see that she was not just another statistic.

"Sounds like she's an amazing person." His voice was gentle.

"Yes, she is." Which is why everyone loved Sarah so much.

The officer cleared his throat. "What do you remember about the accident?"

"We were on our way home from dinner downtown. We'd stopped at the light on Calhoun, where it meets Rutledge. I was teasing her about some guy who'd been flirting with her. The light turned green, I looked over to say something, and all of a sudden there were these headlights right over her shoulder, coming fast. The light was so bright." Ann rubbed her eyes, trying to erase the image. "I don't know if Sarah ever saw it coming."

The officer wrote something on his pad, nodding slightly as if he understood. Then he looked up and in a matter-of-fact voice asked, "Had your sister been drinking at dinner?"

"What?" Ann jumped off the bed and pointed toward the curtain. "Get out of here."

"Look, I'm sorry to have to ask this. In fact, I'm sorry that events occurred that make this conversation necessary. I know this is very difficult for you, but the more answers I get, the better we can piece this puzzle together."

"That other car ran the red light and hit us. Why should

you care whether or not Sarah had a drink? Why should it matter if she was shnockered, as far as that goes?"

He didn't look offended by this outburst. "Just trying to get the whole story."

"No." Ann slowly lowered her hand and sank back onto the bed. "No, she didn't have anything to drink other than tea."

He nodded and wrote something on his notepad. "Are there any other details you can give me?"

"We were stopped at the light, first car in line, so I know it was green when we went through. The other car just came out of nowhere. It was moving so fast, right over Sarah's shoulder. It just kept coming, so fast, so fast . . ." Ann rubbed her eyes again. "There's not much else I can tell you."

"Do you have a number where I can reach you in case there are more questions in the next few days?"

After Ann wrote down her cell number, the officer stood. "Thank you for your help."

Ann looked up. "The other driver, did you ask him if he'd been drinking? That's what happened, isn't it? He was so drunk or high he never saw the light, never saw our car." The memory of fast-approaching headlights burned Ann's eyes. "Tell me you'll never give him the chance to do this to someone else. Tell me you're going to lock him up and keep him there."

"I'm afraid not." He put the pen in his pocket, then tugged one side of the curtains open. He waited the space of a heartbeat before he turned. "He died on impact."

"Oh." Ann shook her head and started to cry again. "Somehow that never even occurred to me."

"I'll call you if I have any further questions." He disappeared through the curtains, pulling them closed behind him.

Chapter 2

"Other than a few cuts and bruises, you appear to be just fine. I'm sure you'll be sore for the next few days, but let us know if you develop difficulty breathing, severe abdominal pain, or blurry vision." The bone-thin brunette in the white coat had the bleary look of someone who hadn't slept in a few days. The exhaustion sounded with each word—or maybe it was just boredom.

"Yeah. Sure. Now, what's going on with my sister?" Ann's plans to eavesdrop had failed miserably. Other than the occasional moan from the person in the cubicle next door, and the sound of retching from farther down the hall, she'd heard absolutely nothing. She needed to know how the surgery was going. She needed to know if Sarah's blood pressure was still falling and if her respiration was still shallow. She needed to know that Sarah was going to make it. "Is she all right?"

"After you get dressed, there is a waiting room just down the hall and through the door. Have a seat, and you'll be notified as soon as we know something." The doctor pushed through the curtain dividers and was gone.

Ann reached for her white button-up shirt, but what she saw made her stop short. The left side was mottled with the claret splatter of her sister's blood.

How had this happened? This was supposed to be a weekend of rejoicing, of celebration. Not this. No, nothing like this.

Why hadn't the other driver stopped? Why had he done this to himself, and to them?

It took all of her determination, but after a few seconds of deep breathing, Ann managed to pick up the shirt, put it on, and slog to the waiting room. A woman with bright red hair and too much makeup sat behind the counter window. "Miz Fletcher, if you don't mind, we've got a little bit of paperwork we need you to fill out."

If I don't mind? "What is it?"

"Oh, just the usual forms. You poor darling, I know you don't feel like dealing with all this right now, but I don't suppose you'd have your sister's insurance information, would you?"

Ann glared. "No, I don't have it. We were in a *car wreck*; her purse was in the *car*. I don't have mine either. It was in the same *car*, the one that was wrecked." Ann felt her hand tremble as she rubbed the back of her neck. She was going to lose it if she had to answer one more stupid question.

Another woman, sitting far enough to the left of the window that Ann hadn't seen her before, rolled her chair into view. "Wait, somebody brought your things in." She pulled out a key from the desk and went to a cabinet against the back wall. A moment later she handed Ann two purses. One was sleek black leather, the other a neon pink tote covered in white polka dots.

"How did these get here?"

She shrugged. "Someone from the accident site brought them in."

Ann dug through the tote until she found Sarah's wallet. It was jammed with membership discount cards to the Piggly Wiggly, bookstores, and video rental places. Finally, she found what appeared to be an insurance card, handed it to the woman, and answered the necessary questions to the extent that she could.

"Okay, sweetie, I'll let you know as soon as there's something to know. You can have a seat in here if you want. Or, if you prefer, there's a chapel on the fourth floor."

"I'll wait here, thanks." Ann didn't plan to go anywhere until she knew that Sarah was out of surgery.

The room was lined with brown vinyl-covered seats. The right half of the space was filled by a couple dozen people who seemed to be together. Ann took a seat on the far left and studied them, wondering what kind of tragedy had brought them here.

At the center of the group was a couple who looked to be in their forties. The woman was clearly at her breaking point, tears pouring down her face while her husband held her. Those poor people were fellow sufferers in tragedy. Ann had the most peculiar desire to run over and hug them.

A few other adults stood with them, but most of the group were teenagers. The boys all looked beefy and moved with the cockiness of athletes; the girls were all pretty—long hair and makeup, dressed to draw attention.

The back doors swung open, and a gray-haired man in a white coat came in. Ann jumped to her feet and rushed toward him, but he ignored her and walked toward the large group.

The low hum of conversation was swallowed by silence as they gathered around him.

Ann returned to her seat, but she didn't bother to pretend she wasn't listening. They were all in this together, and it mattered very much to her how her compatriots fared in their journey. The doctor looked at the mother when he spoke. "There are multiple compound fractures. We're prepping him for surgery right now, and it's going to be quite a long procedure."

Surgery. Compound fractures. Ann wondered if the young man in question had been in an accident too. Had his poor mother ridden in the back of the ambulance with him while he hummed and talked to people who weren't there? Fresh tears stung Ann's eyes.

"Will he be okay?" The mother sobbed through each word.

"He'll be laid up for a while, lots of physical therapy, but he'll be fine."

Ann almost shouted with the relief of it. There was good news coming through this place. She felt her own hope buoyed as she waited to hear the mother rejoice.

The woman sniffed and wiped her eyes with a tissue. "He's coming up on his senior year, and football means everything to him. Will he be able to play this fall?"

Ann's goodwill crashed down around her ankles. *What?* All this commotion was from a woman who was concerned her son might miss a season of football? Did she have no concept of true pain? Everything inside of Ann wanted to walk across the room and tell this woman exactly how much worse things could be—about Sarah, who was supposed to graduate in less than forty-eight hours, about the people she wanted to help, about the crash that was threatening to take it all away.

Ann leaned forward and wrapped her hands around her head. *One, two, three, four. Don't do anything you'll regret. Keep your mouth shut. Five, six, seven—*

"Is there something I can do to help you?" The masculine voice directly to Ann's left side startled her into looking up. She recognized him as one of the adults from the other group. About her age maybe. He could have been a surfer—sun-streaked hair that fell to his shoulders, dark tan, Billabong T-shirt, and flip-flops.

"No." The word barely came across Ann's quickly closing throat, so she shook her head. She stared at the double doors that Sarah had gone through just an hour ago. How was it possible that two hours ago she'd been laughing with Sarah over dinner?

"You were in an accident?" His voice grew softer.

Ann nodded. "My sister, Sarah, is in surgery right now."

"Sarah. I was afraid of that." He said her name in almost a gasp, as if he too shared Ann's grief. He looked silently toward the double doors, and Ann supposed he would return to his group. Instead, he remained seated beside her in awkward silence, shaking his head and mumbling. He jumped suddenly to his feet. "I know what I can do." He dashed out the door without a backward glance.

Ann looked toward the others and noticed that several of the teenagers, the boys in particular, were looking her way. She grew uneasy under their continued scrutiny, although she wasn't sure why. Why should she care what a bunch of southern fried teenagers looked at?

The blue sign on the wall said Chapel—Fourth Floor. Ann supposed there was no spiritual prerequisite for sitting in the hospital chapel. Maybe she could find some quiet there.

SHEILA WALSH & KATHRYN CUSHMAN

She approached the redhead at the counter. "I'm going up to the chapel for a while, but I need to be notified immediately if my sister's doctor comes out."

The woman nodded. "Don't you worry one little bit about that. Write your cell phone number right here." She handed Ann a piece of paper. "Make sure you have the ring tone turned off, though, okay? And if anybody comes looking for you, I'll make 'em stay right here and call you to come down. You go spend a little time with the Lord. We could all use a little more of that."

"Sure." Ann scrawled her cell number on the piece of paper, then looked for the stairwell. It required more than her limit of patience to wait for an elevator right now, and the four-story climb would help work off some of her anxiety. She ran up the stairs two at a time.

By the time she reached the fourth floor, she was breathing hard, which only seemed to aggravate the crushing weight that pushed against her chest. She shoved open the door to the chapel and found the first bit of relief she'd had all night. The place was empty. Finally something was working in her favor.

The inside of the chapel was not what she'd expected. It didn't look *holy*, or at least not what Ann pictured holy to look like. No polished oak pews, stained glass, or burning candles. Only a wooden altar of sorts that looked more like a buffet table or sideboard. On top of it sat a small potted plant and what Ann assumed was a Bible. The kneeling cushion below it could have been an artfully displayed throw pillow. A few wooden chairs were scattered around, and on the far side of the room, a fountain gurgled on top of a small cabinet. The ripple of water falling against the rocks reminded Ann of her occasional visits to day spas. Yes, all in all, a very Zen-like chapel.

She dropped into the chair closest to the waterfall and farthest from the altar, relieved to be alone. For a long time she sat and did nothing but focus on breathing in and breathing out. Finally, she turned her attention back to the room. When her eyes came to rest on the Bible, she looked toward the acoustic tile on the ceiling and spoke aloud. "You know, now would be a good time to show Yourself and help Sarah." Even atheists had been known to pray when in desperate trouble. But Ann knew that they were wasted words. God had never come through before—why should He start now?

A single piano note silenced her thoughts. She hadn't noticed any music in here. A second note added to another and another, until a melody began to form. The piano went on, playing the same song but no longer one key at a time. The music became multifaceted, rich, harmonious. She found herself wanting to move toward it, to blend with the liquid sound that stirred so deep she almost heard color in its notes. She leaned her head back and closed her eyes, simply listening, drinking it in.

The unusual rhythm of the water-music swells washed through her until it seemed the song was part of her—as if every cell in her body pulsed with the sound. A feeling of utter peace grew with each new note and she wanted to stay here and listen forever. Right now, in this moment, she knew that everything was going to be all right. The feeling—the song—was unlike anything she'd ever experienced before. Except . . . this music had the same soothing rhythm as Sarah's humming from the ambulance.

It took her a moment to realize that it didn't just have the same rhythm. It had the same tune.

Exactly.

The room began to feel small and stuffy, almost suffocating. Ann pushed to her feet and yanked open the door. She took a step out, drew a deep breath, and prepared to flee. She made it only one more step, though, because the surfer from downstairs was right in front of her, apparently pacing the hallway. He blushed when he saw her. "I'm sorry, but they told me you came up here, and well, I didn't want to come into the chapel and disturb you, but I thought you might want this." He thrust a bright green cloth toward her.

Ann stared at the item in his hand.

"It's a shirt. I . . . uh . . ." He nodded toward her stained left side. "Well, I thought you might feel better if you . . . you know . . ." He swallowed loud enough that she heard him. "I thought of Sarah—and you just looked so sad, and I just felt in my spirit that I was supposed to help you, and I remembered this shirt that I had in the truck. It's brand new, never worn. I got it last week and for some reason I just haven't bothered to take it out of my truck yet. And well, this is really awkward, and I can see that you probably would prefer that I go away, and I'll just go, but I just—"

"Thanks." Ann thought it best to interrupt him because she had no idea how much longer he might go on. "This was really thoughtful." She took the shirt.

"Good." He looked at the ground between their feet.

Some of what he'd said caught up with her brain. "You know Sarah?"

"And you." He paused. "Well, I think. You're Annie, right?"

She nodded. "Ann."

"I thought so. I'm Ethan." He looked at her as if this explained everything, which it didn't. After a few seconds of silence, he continued. "McKinney. I live in the neighborhood with Sarah . . . and used to live near you. My family moved in my senior year of high school, back when you were still living there with your grandmother."

"Oh, right." Ann had a vague memory of a new guy in the area. Still, she'd avoided her childhood memories for so long, she wasn't certain.

"Is Sarah . . . gonna be all right?"

Was she? Ann wanted to give an optimistic response, or even a flip one, but the words wouldn't come. "I don't know." The words took great effort.

Ethan dipped his head so slightly Ann thought she might have imagined it. The silence grew awkward. Finally, he nodded toward the chapel. "I'll go say a prayer for her."

"Thanks." Ann started to walk away but stopped, unexpectedly not ready to end the conversation. "The music in there is very unusual."

He looked surprised. "Music? There's no music in the chapel."

"Yes, there is." The flare of irritation felt good; it provided temporary distraction from the fear. She wanted to hold on to this relief for as long as she could. "Open the door and see."

"All right." Ethan pulled open the chapel door and leaned inside.

She waited for his concession but heard nothing. At all. Including any music. She strained her ears and moved closer to the room. Nothing but silence.

Ethan studied the ceiling. "Are you sure you heard music in here? I did some volunteer work on the remodel last year, and I know we didn't put in speakers. In fact, we put extra soundproofing around this room to make sure it was quiet. Just like it is now."

What's going on here?

Ann stood still, listening with every fiber in her being. She focused her attention on the gurgling water at the end of the room, waiting to hear the song. No music came, not a single piano note. "That's really strange. I don't know what I heard." But that was a lie. She *did* know.

She'd heard music, the same tune her sister had hummed in the ambulance. The kind of music that becomes one with your being so that you can never, ever forget it. And she'd heard it in a room with no piano, no speakers, and soundproof walls.

Chapter 3

Ann stood in the bathroom stall changing shirts, trying not to think about why she needed to. She rolled her white button-up into a tight ball and looked at her small purse. It would never fit. For the first time ever, she felt appreciation for Sarah's gaudy pink tote with its brass buckles and warren of pockets. The same handbag she'd made fun of earlier. Had it really been a couple of hours ago that she'd told Sarah she could swipe a whole place setting from the restaurant, load it into that bag, and still have room to spare? She tucked the shirt inside, looking forward to the day they could joke about the irony in that.

The refrain of the water-music tune remained firmly stuck in her head, and it unnerved her. She'd heard of auditory hallucinations. Was the accident making her hear her sister's song in places where the song wasn't? She was finally losing her mind, which perhaps wasn't that big of a surprise. Maybe she should walk back to the chapel to listen one more time, but just the thought made the air around her seem heavy. Time to get back downstairs.

Ann unlocked the door to the stall but hesitated when she remembered the mother of the football player. She looked at her watch: 8:15. Twenty minutes had passed; surely the woman had calmed down sufficiently that it should be safe to return now.

When Ann pushed open the stall door and looked into the mirror, she almost burst out laughing. Not only was she going crazy, but now she looked the part. The oversized green T-shirt had a sketch on the front of an antebellum home in bright yellow, and it said *The Charleston Historical Home Preservation Society*. This would get an interesting reaction from her coworkers back in Manhattan. Ann's designs featured clean lines of glass and chrome and small proportions. She made it a rule to avoid antiques, draperies, and T-shirts with writing. Especially writing that reeked of the past.

Before she could do anything about her new look, her cell phone vibrated in her pocket. Without another thought to decorating, or clothes, or melodies, she flipped it open. "I'm on my way." She slapped the phone shut, ran out the door, and started down the stairs before she realized that she'd never even looked to see who was calling. If no one was there when she got to the waiting room, then she would look at her cell's recent missed calls. Until then, it just didn't matter.

Ann skidded to a stop in the waiting room, now empty except for a fair-skinned, dark-haired man in a white coat. He didn't look much older than the EMT from the ambulance, but the name on his coat said Fred Zurlinden, MD.

"I'm Ann Fletcher. Are you looking for me?" Ann thrust a hand toward him, which he didn't seem to see.

His gaze never reached her face as he gestured toward the chairs in the corner. "Let's take a seat, shall we?"

Ann didn't want to sit, she wanted to stand, but she complied without hesitation. Whatever it took to get some answers quickly, that's what she was going to do.

"Ms. Fletcher, I'm sorry to have to tell you this, but at approximately 8:10, Sarah went into cardiac arrest. We were not able to bring her back." He recited these details like he was reading from a cue card. He still hadn't looked at her.

"What?" Ann heard his voice, but she couldn't comprehend the words. Didn't want to comprehend. "What are you saying? That Sarah's . . . gone?"

He nodded and pasted on a sympathetic frown. "Yes, I'm afraid so."

"But . . . she made it here, she was conscious, she was talking. They took her into surgery to save her." Ann's voice grew louder with each word, but she didn't care. Something was wrong, and everyone needed to know it.

Fred Zurlinden, MD, glanced toward his watch, as if he had work to do and this was keeping him from it. "We did all that we could, but her injuries were just too severe." He looked toward the double doors, seeming to wish he were behind them. "Would you like for me to call the chaplain, or someone else for you to talk to?"

"No, I don't want you to call somebody. I want you to get back there and save my sister. This is a mistake. I—"

"Annie?" Ann turned to see a woman leaning toward her, arms outstretched. Somewhere in the fog of her brain, Ann understood that this woman wanted to hug her. She looked at the woman's curly blonde hair pulled into a ponytail, tied with a red bow that matched her sleeveless shirt. She was not the football player's mother. She had called her Annie. Only Sarah did that.

"Hi, Annie." A round-faced boy who looked to be about twelve years old peered from behind the woman, clutching her shirt hem. When Ann saw the almond-shaped eyes behind the wire-rimmed glasses, she made the connection. Sarah's neighbors. A vague memory surfaced that they'd been introduced earlier in the day, although she couldn't summon any of the details from her mind. Sarah had been talking about the boy with Down syndrome and his mother ever since they moved in a few years ago. What were their names?

The woman finally dropped the arms she'd been holding out and reached back to stroke her son's fine hair. "I'm Tammy. This is Keith. We met this afternoon. Remember? We live next door to Sarah."

Ann nodded. These details didn't matter. They couldn't make the doctor change what he was saying about Sarah, couldn't change anything that had happened. Ann turned back to him, but Dr. Zurlinden had already stood. "I can see that your friends are here to help you. The ladies at the desk can help you with the necessary procedures." He walked crisply away, leaving Ann alone with a stranger of a woman, that woman's son, and the knowledge that she was now the only living member of her family.

Thirty years old and completely alone. What was she supposed to do with that?

She quickly shifted her mind away from the thought and brought herself back to the present, to the pressing needs of the moment.

She turned toward Tammy. "How did you know I was here?"

"Ethan called me and told me there had been an accident. I hurried over as fast as I could, but we walked in just as the doctor was giving you the news. Oh, Annie, I am so sorry." Tammy threw her arms around Ann and cried into her shoulder. "I loved her so much."

Ann tried to pat Tammy on the shoulder in some semblance of comfort, but mostly she concentrated on taking deep breaths and pretending she was somewhere else. She'd never been comfortable with demonstrative strangers, even when she'd lived in the South. Now, after almost a decade in New York, the gesture completely unnerved her. She tried to focus on details in an effort to keep her sanity intact and to steer the conversation in a direction that did not encourage physical contact.

"Ethan? Why would he call you?"

"Well, I guess he was here because a kid he knows was in a motorcycle wreck, and while he was waiting, he recognized you. He's my cousin and he knows how much Sarah means to me. He knows I'd want to be here for her. And for you."

"Hmm. Okay." Ann stared at the ceiling tiles, thankful for the numbness that had settled on her.

Tammy sniffed, straightened her posture, and wiped her eyes. Ann had the distinct impression that her lack of emotional display made Tammy as uneasy as Tammy's hugs made Ann. "Come on, let's get through the paperwork, and then I'll drive you home."

Home. Ann's home—well, her current apartment—was almost a thousand miles away. But she nodded without comment. "Bring out the forms and let's get this done." Ann didn't want to stay here another minute.

By the time they walked out of the emergency room an hour later, Ann felt . . . disconnected. She'd only partly noticed the goings-on of Keith, who had hugged everyone who sat near him. He'd also done an impersonation of Elvis—or was it Johnny Cash?—for the entire waiting area, stopping only when Tammy sat him down with a firm talking-to. Then he'd finally turned his attention to an *American Idol* rerun playing on the wall-mounted television, occasionally blurting out, "That Simon man is mean." Keith's over-the-top behavior only added to the surrealness of the whole evening.

She followed Tammy and Keith to a black Saturn that had to be a dozen years old. She climbed into the passenger's seat and hoped for a silent ride.

"You sad, Annie?" Keith's speech was slow and somewhat difficult to understand. He leaned forward from the backseat and began to rub her arm. Ann flinched away from the un-expected touch.

Tammy very gently took his hand and reached back to put it in his lap. "Let's give Ann some space, okay, Keith?"

"Okay."

They rode for several minutes in silence before Tammy tried again. "You know, Annie, if you'd rather not be alone, you're welcome to stay at our house tonight."

Ann did appreciate the gesture, but it did not tempt her. Alone was something she was used to. Something she was going to have to get even more used to. "No, I'll be all right."

"Well, if you change your mind, you just come on over. Doesn't matter how late, you just ring the bell."

"Sure."

Tammy didn't seem to get the hint from her short responses.

"And we'll be over in the morning to help you start making the arrangements, okay?"

Ann nodded. "Thanks." She hadn't even considered that it would be up to her to plan a funeral.

When Tammy turned onto the oak-lined street, she slowed the car and looked toward Ann. "Do you have a key to the house?"

"I've got a key." Ann had had a key for the last twenty years, but there was no reason to say that now.

The song from the chapel kept playing through her mind. Ann suddenly wondered what it was and if it had lyrics and if maybe it had special significance for Sarah. One way or the other, it was the most powerful music she'd ever heard. Maybe they should play it at the . . . *No!* This was all just a bad dream, and there was no reason to be thinking about songs to play at Sarah's funeral.

All she needed to do was to have a few stiff drinks, fall into a deep sleep, and wake up in New York to realize none of this had really happened. Yep, that was the plan.

Keith, who had been silent the last few minutes, leaned forward and began to rub Ann's arm again. "I like that song."

His words jolted her around. "What song?" Had she been humming aloud? The radio was not on.

"They sing that to me sometimes. When they help me. They help you too?" His eyes were bright with innocent hope.

"Who sings to you?"

"My angels."

Ann had no idea what she'd been expecting Keith to say, what logical response he could give in the midst of the illogical things that had happened. She looked at Tammy. "Angels?"

Tammy shrugged. "Keith seems to be able to see and hear angels from time to time." She said it with a hint of weariness in her voice, but not even a trace of doubt. She pulled into the driveway and turned off the car

"Okay." There was nothing else to say. Ann climbed from the car, wondering how long it would take to find something to drink around here.

Chapter 4

Sarah writhed in pain. Ann held the antidote in her hand, but no matter how fast she ran, she couldn't get any closer. "Hang on, Sarah. I'm coming."

Sarah stared up at a blank wall. "Help. Annie. Please." With each word, the music in the background grew louder and louder until it was difficult to hear Sarah's voice at all.

"Sarah, I'm here, I'm here." But Sarah didn't seem to hear her. She kept her gaze focused on the blank wall over her shoulder. "Help. Annie. Please." She drew a final gasping breath and then fell back on the pillow, her face suddenly blank.

Ann jerked awake, her whole body covered in sweat. The music faded away more slowly than the dream, but note by note it, too, disappeared. She took a deep breath and tried to clear her head, but her brain felt hammered in. The sun shone directly into her eyes, the glare pounding against her skull. Her whole body ached from sleeping on the love seat, but she hadn't been able to bring herself to go to the bedroom. It made things feel so final. The thought of returning to that room—a room where she had once shared a bunk bed with Sarah—well, it wasn't something Ann was prepared to do. Not now. Not ever. She would finish out her time here parked on the small sofa.

She rolled over to get away from the glare, but the movement made her stomach lurch. Before she had time to think about it, she ran to the bathroom, where she retched the remains of too much vodka and last night's celebration feast into the toilet. The irony was not lost on her, even in the throes of the worst hangover she'd ever had. Nothing good about this visit could be allowed to remain, even the remnants of last night's dinner.

The faucet was easily fifty years old, and it squeaked with enough volume that it hurt her head. She splashed cold water on her face, fumbled for the toothbrush she'd laid on this shelf just yesterday. In a different life. In a life where there was rejoicing for the future in spite of a painful past, a life with hope, and the radiant smile of her sister.

She stood in the only bathroom of the little bungalow that had been in her family for longer than she cared to remember. Now this little house and Ann were all that remained. She walked out of the bathroom where the two bedrooms flanked her on each side. If she turned left, she would be inside the room she'd shared with Sarah during most of their growing-up years. If she turned right, she would be in Nana's room. She knew it was the room Sarah had used for the last six years, since Nana died, but it would always be Nana's room to Ann. She couldn't stand the thought of either room at the moment, so she pulled both doors firmly shut, making certain the latches caught. If only she could shut out the memory of her dream so easily. And the music.

She walked across the room and dropped onto the same red-and-tan-striped love seat she'd just slept on, propped her feet on the beige armchair, and looked around. It was Nana's old furniture, she knew, but Sarah had recovered it in the last few years. It still sagged, but at least it looked better than the floral chintz pattern that used to be here. Beside her was Nana's oval coffee table. It hadn't changed. The imitation maple had a glass top, with dozens of old photos underneath. Nana had always put Sarah's and Ann's school pictures in there alongside candid snapshots of them. After Nana died Sarah had never touched them—said she didn't have the heart.

Ann scanned the tabletop and stopped at a picture of her mother, standing in front of Nana's Christmas tree, holding a three-year-old Sarah and smiling. Ann was in the background, a skinny eight-year-old with brown pigtails peeking around the branches and looking toward her mother from what seemed a long distance away. Ann removed the glass oval and placed it on the carpet beside her. Then she picked up the photo and turned it upside down. She looked at the next picture, this one of Sarah and Ann, bare feet sticking off the end of the porch swing, Nana behind them, smiling. Ann touched the photo with her finger, certain she could almost hear the squeals of delight and Nana's quiet laughter, smell the magnolias, and . . . remember the question that had invaded every part of her childhood—why didn't her mother want her?

Ann put her palm in the center of the table and moved it in a circular motion until all the photos were askew and overlapping. She put the glass back onto the table. It didn't lay quite flat now, but she didn't care. At least the pictures weren't staring up at her anymore. Her head was pounding with the effort.

She shuffled into the kitchen and opened the cabinet above the refrigerator, hoping it was where Sarah kept her medicine. Bingo. Sarah was not one to overmedicate, that much was

certain, because there were only three items: Neosporin oint-
ment, Visine eye drops, and Advil. Ann was truly thankful for
this last item as she popped four tablets into her mouth and
swallowed them without water. She doubted it would help
much, but she at least needed to try. The vodka bottle still sat
on the counter, offering another way to dull this morning's pain.
Ann was just about to reach for it when she heard the screech of
the screen door as it opened, followed by a brief knock on the
kitchen door.

The lace curtains that covered the window were thin
enough that Ann could see Tammy's outline. She considered
walking away and pretending she saw and heard nothing—
leave her outside and, along with her, the reality her presence
brought.

Instead, she swung the door open slowly and held it for
Tammy to come inside. Tammy patted her on the arm as she
entered; then Keith appeared from behind her and did the same.
"Hi, Annie." He smiled and stood right next to her, even though
his mother had continued to the kitchen. "I made somethin' for
you," he said.

He pulled a piece of paper out of his pocket and began to
unfold it. Ann watched his glasses slide down his nose. He pushed
them back up, then unfolded the next flap, then the next. The
process seemed to take an eternity. Meanwhile, she prepared
herself to say something complimentary about the cat or the dog
or the sunshine he'd drawn for her, but when the final fold
opened, Ann just stared, wondering how to respond.

"Thanks, Keith, it's beautiful," was what she finally managed, though it was less an overstatement and more a lie.

He smiled shyly and pointed at a stick figure with long

brown hair. "That's you." Then he pointed at another stick figure wearing hoop earrings, arms reaching up toward a blob of golden paint. "That's Sarah."

Ann pointed at the yellow octopuslike blob. "What is that?"

"Sarah's angel. He sings to make her feel better."

Keith and his mother hadn't even been at the hospital until after Sarah died. He certainly had no way of knowing there was any sort of music in the ambulance. "What makes you think that Sarah's angel sang to her?"

He shrugged, looking embarrassed, and walked toward his mother. "I'm not supposed to say. I just know, that's all."

Tammy drew him into the circle of her arms. "It's okay, honey." She rested her chin on the top of his head and looked up. Her gaze lingered to Ann's right, exactly where Ann knew the partially drained bottle of vodka sat on the kitchen counter.

In an effort to shift the focus elsewhere, Ann said, "Why aren't you supposed to say?"

Keith turned around to look at her, wiping a tear from beneath his wire-rimmed glasses. "They don't like it."

"Who doesn't like it? The angels, you mean? Is it supposed to be a secret?"

"Not the angels, the people."

Ann looked at Tammy, who was rubbing Keith's hair with her left hand. She shrugged. "Some of the people at our church have"—she paused long enough that Ann wasn't certain she was going to continue—"*requested* that Keith not talk about seeing or hearing angels."

"Really?" Ann thought about this for a minute. She personally could understand how Keith's declarations might make people uncomfortable, but somehow in this context, it didn't make sense. "Isn't that what people at church are supposed to do? Talk about God and angels, and all those kinds of things?"

Tammy shrugged again and kissed the top of Keith's head. "Apparently not about angels so much."

"Really? Why?"

Keith leaned close to his mother and whispered. She whispered back, and then he said something else.

Tammy looked up at Ann, her smile apologetic. "Could we possibly use your bathroom?"

Ann nodded in the general direction of the bathroom. "Do you know where it is, or should I show you?"

"Believe me, we know." Tammy smiled. "Thank you."

As the duo made their way toward the bathroom, Ann pulled a glass from the cupboard and stuck it under the faucet. Maybe a glass of cold water would help her feel better. She heard the sound of a car out front and pulled back the curtain over the kitchen sink just in time to see a silver Corvette glide into the driveway.

Seconds later, a heavyset woman with short gray hair emerged, carrying a large basket in her hand. She walked down the driveway then opened the gate to the half wall that surrounded part of the front of the house. But instead of proceeding across the courtyard to the front portico, the woman stopped. Ann had to lean way over to see what the woman was doing. After setting her box on a chair, she began to unfold a tablecloth and arrange it on the round table.

Ann scrambled to open the front door but held fast to the door handle in case this woman was deranged and Ann needed to rush back inside. But she suspected there was just a mix-up of addresses. "Can I help you?"

"No, honey. I'm the helper here." She spoke in a loud voice with a thick southern accent and wore no visible makeup beneath her small rectangular glasses.

"I think you must have the wrong house."

"Oh, Annie darling, I'm sorry, I do forget myself. I'm Danielle, and I loved your sweet sister. I'm here to help you in any way that I can."

"Right on time, as always, Danielle." Tammy walked past Ann onto the covered porch. "And she likes to be called 'Ann'."

On time? "Can I ask what this is all about?"

Tammy looked confused. "Well, I told you last night that we'd be here at eight to help you start planning, didn't I?"

Through the hazy memories of last night, Ann did remember her saying something like that. "Yeah, that's right." Ann combed her fingers through her disheveled mop of hair. "I guess I just assumed that *we* meant you and Keith."

"I'm here, Annie. I came to help." Keith reached out from behind his mother and touched Ann's arm.

"Uh." Ann took an involuntary step away from him. "I . . ."

"Yes, you did come to help, didn't you?" Tammy gently pulled Keith's hand away. "I'm sorry I wasn't more specific. I'm so used to Danielle being a part of us that I forgot that you wouldn't necessarily know that."

Danielle had begun setting plates around the table. "I brought muffins and fruit—oh, and I noticed the Hot Now sign lit at Krispy Kreme and just couldn't help but stop and get some. I hope that works for you."

"Sure," Tammy said.

Ann looked at Tammy. The shock of last night's events and the fog of this morning's hangover left her too weak to comprehend what was happening, much less voice a protest. Yet. "So, what are we doing again?"

"Right now we're eating our breakfast—I thought it'd be nice to eat outside. Hope you don't mind." Danielle set her basket on the ground, then sat in the closest chair and looked up expectantly. "Tammy, it's your turn to bless the food. Let's get going. We've got lots to do."

Tammy took a seat, and Ann did too, glad there was someone else here to do the thinking.

"I'll sit by you, Annie." Keith pulled his chair close to hers and took hold of her left hand as they all bowed their heads. Everyone except Ann.

She looked around the group, finally settling on Tammy's face, as Tammy said, "Dear Father, thank You for providing us with this food and with each other. Thank You for sharing Sarah with us for the time that You did. Thank You that she's basking in the warmth of Your love right now. Help Annie feel your peace and presence and give us all wisdom in the days ahead. Amen."

"Amen," the group responded in unison.

Keith squeezed Ann's hand before he let go. "Amen."

"There now, let's get down to business." Danielle looked toward Ann. "Would you prefer to have the after-funeral meal here or at the church?"

"I hadn't really thought about . . ."

"There's been a lot of remodeling at the church; the fellowship hall looks awful right now. I think we should just do it here, don't you?" Tammy looked at Ann, waiting for a response.

"Sure, sounds good." As much as Ann hated to be bossed around, today she was downright thankful for it.

"I'm glad you agree. I've already taken the liberty to make

some phone calls. Food should start arriving here by Sunday afternoon so that it'll be ready for Monday." Danielle made this statement matter-of-factly, then took another bite of muffin.

"Danielle, whatever would you have done if she had said she wanted it at the church?" Tammy looked toward the older woman, an expression somewhere between amusement and annoyance on her face.

"You know, Tammy, I keep telling you and telling you, there's absolutely no reason to worry about things that could have happened but didn't." Her pale green eyes twinkled as she spoke. "But to answer your question, it's simple. I would have called them back and said there'd been a change of venue. Not a big deal. But since that didn't happen, let's get on with business."

Danielle looked back at the pad of paper. "We need to pick out an outfit for Sarah, and Annie, you'll need to go pick out a casket. Tammy, you go with her. I'll take the clothes over to the funeral home after we get them ready. Okay?"

"Of course."

"Where's Sarah?" Keith popped the last of his muffin in his mouth. "I go get her." He started toward the door.

Tammy jumped up and took him by the arm. "Sarah's not here, darling. Remember? She's with the angels now."

Keith looked around, confused. "When is she coming back?"

It was all Ann could do to keep her composure. Keith's question—no, that question's answer—was too much to take. Sarah was never coming back.

"We'll be with her again someday. For now, why don't you color her a picture?"

"Okay." Keith wandered over to the far side of the porch

and began to sketch on a pad of paper that his mother handed him.

Danielle rattled off a list with complete efficiency, and in no time, everyone knew her assigned tasks for the day.

"Thank you both"—Ann could barely form the words—"for organizing all this. I don't know how I would have done it without your help." She was so numb from everything—from the accident to this overwhelming show of support from women she didn't even know.

Danielle looked surprised by this statement. "Well, of course I organized all this. That's my special gift. That and giving orders—I'm particularly good at that one."

"Got that right." Tammy rolled her eyes but smiled. "And since my particular gift seems to be taking orders, we get along just fine."

"Yep, that's why I let you hang out with me. I admire smart women—and the fact that you listen to me shows your brilliance." Danielle rubbed the back of the empty seat beside her and her face suddenly went solemn. "I don't know what we're going to do without Sarah. We need her to make the group complete."

A choking wave of grief washed over Ann; she needed to control it. "What was Sarah's gift?"

"Compassion." Danielle rubbed her forehead and leaned forward until her elbow rested on the table. "How many times have we sat at this very table and talked things over, prayed until there was nothing left to pray?"

Tammy reached over and put an arm on Danielle's shoulder. "She'd want us to carry on as best we can—you know that."

"I know, but how can we?" Danielle looked up then, wiped at a tear, and said, "Besides that, she has the best garden patio around. Where's she think we're going to carry on?" She began to laugh and cry at the same time, and soon Tammy followed suit. They were wiping their eyes, sobbing, laughing, and hugging each other.

Keith walked over. "You okay, Mama?"

Tammy patted his hand. "I'm fine, sweetie."

Danielle leaned toward Ann. "Looks like the only thing for us to do is to adopt Annie into our midst. Annie Fletcher, welcome to our little misfit family. We may be a bunch of loons, but at least we're in this together." Tammy came and put her arms around Ann, then so did Keith.

Ann wasn't sure how she felt about being adopted. But it didn't appear she had a choice in the matter.

Sarah's old desktop computer sat on a small desk on the opposite wall of the living room. A momentary escape was exactly what Ann needed after this morning of sorting through Sarah's clothes. She needed something to clear her mind.

Yes, she would sit down, surf the Web. Maybe she'd even do a little research about nonexistent music, figure out what might have happened to her yesterday. After she loaded herself up with facts, she could at least leave this part of the memories behind.

She typed "auditory hallucinations" into the Google search engine. Dozens of links popped up. She clicked on one.

A study back in 1894 concluded that 10 percent of the population has experienced a hallucination at some point. Interesting. Ten percent was a large number. If it was a hallucination of some sort, maybe Ann wasn't so out there after all.

She scanned and clicked on a few more links.

As she skimmed site after site, she repeatedly noticed the phrase "quite common in psychotic conditions, usually manifesting as voices." At least she hadn't gone the creepy-voice route. She supposed she should be thankful for that. And she wasn't, to her knowledge, psychotic, another reason to be grateful. But the fact remained that she'd still heard something that wasn't there.

She kept reading, determined to find something concrete that explained the song she'd heard. Finally, she found an article about *paracusia*. This was the scientific name for someone who hears things that aren't there. To Ann, it sounded a lot better than *hallucination*, especially when it involved her. Even better, it said that this paracusia—such as whistles, claps, and *music*—is often brought on by extreme conditions.

Ta-da!

Conditions didn't get much more extreme than they were yesterday. Obviously the whole episode was brought on by the stress of the accident. The fact that the nonexistent music in the chapel sounded like Sarah's song was because Sarah's injury from the accident was at the heart of her stress. Of course that was it. And the dream this morning was just her mind trying to sort through the trauma of losing Sarah. As the reality of what had happened sank in, the paracusia would diminish. She wouldn't hear it in her dreams, wouldn't wake up with the sound seemingly in her room, and she would soon forget how she'd heard those notes in every cell of her body. At least she hoped it would be that simple.

Chapter 5

By four o'clock that afternoon, Ann's head was still pounding, but at least she was alone. For the time being. She drew the curtains shut because she had other things to deal with now, things that had nothing to do with the accident or Sarah or funeral plans. It was not going to be any more pleasant, but at least it was familiar. She pushed the number two button on her speed dial.

"Marston Home Staging, this is Jen, may I help you?" Jen's perky phone voice felt soothing through the distance.

"Hi, Jen, it's me."

"Ann, I can't believe it's taken you this long to return my calls." She said the words in a singsong, teasing voice. "I'm guessing you stayed out a little too late last night? Mmm-hmm. Got your straight-laced sister out for a little pre-graduation celebration, didn't you? I told you that you could corrupt her if you just tried hard enough. Yep, the more you went on about what a goody-goody she is, the more I knew you would break her down. Score one for the bad girls. Way to go, Ann." She gave a quick laugh. "And don't worry about a thing here. Of course Margaret's been going crazy trying to reach you, but I told her the cell reception was spotty in parts of Charleston and that's why you weren't calling back. As usual, I've got your back."

"Return your calls?" Ann's cell had been turned off all day, but she hadn't been expecting to hear from anyone. "Why have you been calling?"

"Not so fast. Before we start talking business, you've got to tell me what's on the list of celebrations for tonight. Dinner? Late-night dancing? Wine? Tequila shots? Exactly how far off the straight and narrow can you push your little sister? It's Friday night! Details, I need details." She paused, obviously waiting for a witty response, or at least Ann's typical sarcastic one.

Ann could think of absolutely nothing to say. She took a deep breath, then concentrated on proper diction with each word. "There's been a little change of plans. Sarah's not going to graduate tomorrow after all."

"What? You flew all the way down there, and she flunked her last semester of grad school? You've got to be kidding me."

"No, she didn't flunk. There was . . . an accident."

"Accident?" Her voice took a serious tone, but she was obviously still waiting for the punch line. "What happened?"

"A car ran a red light. It crashed right into the driver's side. Sarah . . ." Just saying the words brought back pictures of Sarah's pale face against the sheets, the blood, the humming. "She didn't make it."

Jen gasped. "No."

Ann took another breath to make certain she could speak before she tried again. "The funeral is Monday. I don't think I'll be back to the office until Wednesday afternoon sometime."

Funny, once the focus of the conversation turned from the accident itself to getting things done, it became easier to speak.

"Oh, Ann." Jen's voice was quiet now. "I'm so sorry."

Ann looked toward the counters piled high with food and said, "Me too."

There was a full minute of silence. Even the ever-bubbly Jen had been shut down by this news. Finally, Ann said, "Now, back to business. Why did you say you were trying to reach me?"

"Oh, right. It seems that you, Miss Fletcher, received a phone call from none other than Mr. Patrick Stinson himself."

"You're kidding me." Ann thought back to the surprise of meeting him on the airplane. It felt like a lifetime ago. "What did he say?"

"Not much. He didn't want to talk to anyone but you. I'm gathering you had some sort of an encounter?"

"I don't think it would qualify as an encounter exactly."

"You must have impressed him during whatever it was. He asked for your cell number. I told him I wasn't allowed to give out personal information. Margaret almost killed me when she found out I did that, but hey, I'm not going to be the one to give your number to some stalker, right?"

"Thanks, Jen, I feel much safer knowing you're on my team."

"I know, right? I've got your back. Margaret got all freaked and I honestly thought she was going to stroke out right here in the office. Then"—she began to speak so softly Ann could barely hear her—"I noticed she'd been back in her office with the door closed for a while, so I made up an excuse and went in there 'looking for a file.' Guess who she was talking to?"

"Jen, you sneak."

"Hey, a girl's got to do what she's got to do. I walked in just in time to hear her say that Marston would be *very* interested in pitching the staging for his newest building. She was glaring at me and motioning with her head for me to get out of there, but I stalled as long as I could. So long, in fact, that as I was walking out the door, I heard her say, 'Only Ann?' in that screechy voice she uses when she's stressed. I'm betting he told her he would only work with you."

"Really?"

"Yep. And if Margaret's looks could kill, I'd be a dead woman right now, but she hasn't said anything about it yet."

"Jen! What if she'd come out and fired you on the spot?"

"Oh, she's so engrossed in the idea of getting a project from Patrick Stinson that she's already forgotten about me. Hey . . . just an FYI . . . The rumor I've heard is that he can get a little, uh . . . aggressively friendly with the females he works around, and he works around a lot of females. I'm sure you can handle him, but just so you know."

"Thanks for the down low. If I end up working with him, I'll be sure to keep him in line."

"No doubt." Jen laughed. "Anyway, Margaret's been practically dancing around since he called, in spite of everything else."

The thought of Margaret dancing would have made Ann laugh at any other time. Today, it didn't. "In spite of what else?"

"Well, you know, the Beka thing." Jen paused for just a second. "I mean, Beka called you, right? I assumed that she would have called you already."

"What Beka thing?"

"Margaret called Beka into her office first thing this morning, before all this, and told her that as of the end of the month, she was being laid off."

"She did what?" Ann jumped to her feet. "Transfer me back to Margaret." Beka had been Ann's best friend since their days as classmates at Parsons. Unfortunately, Beka's relationship with Margaret had always been tense, making her an easy target.

"Don't tell her I told you *anything*, okay?" Jen's voice dropped even lower. "You know how she gets."

"Not a word, I promise."

"Right. Hold on just a minute." There was a long, classical-music-filled pause, during which time Ann was sure that Jen was filling Margaret in on what had happened to Sarah. She was equally certain that Margaret wouldn't mention it. The line clicked.

"Ann, amazing news. Patrick Stinson called here and he wants Marston Staging to pitch Stinson Towers. I've already started preparing for the meeting. I want you to be the lead designer on the project."

She wanted Ann to be the lead designer. Right. Did she really think Ann wouldn't find out that Patrick Stinson had asked for her specifically? Well, two could play this game. "All right. Of course, I'll want Beka working on the presentation with me."

"I'm afraid that won't be possible." She offered a dramatic sigh. "Beka, unfortunately, will be leaving us in a few weeks. She'll need to be working on her own projects until then, getting them finished. But I'll work alongside you every step of the way."

"Beka's leaving? Did she find another job or something? She hadn't told me she was leaving."

"Times are hard, and I've had to make some hard decisions."

"Margaret, if you'll remember, I took a significant pay cut last month to keep something like this from happening. Beka does amazing work, and you know that she needs this job; she

needs the insurance more than anyone else in the company."
Beka's daughter had juvenile rheumatoid arthritis and the treatment costs alone were staggering. Margaret knew this well
enough, but as usual, Margaret acted on Margaret's best interest.

"Look, I don't want to cut Beka loose any more than you
want me to. Last month I thought I'd found an investor, someone who would act as a silent business partner, but that fell
through. Now I'm faced with the hard reality of today's econ-
omy. Unfortunately, Beka is a casualty."

"What if we land the Stinson job?"

"Then we would reevaluate, of course." She paused a moment,
letting that one sink in. "I'm sure you'll do whatever it takes to
make sure we get it. In fact, I've already found some photos of
their most recent project. I'll e-mail them over to you so you can
take a look. I want you to take what's been done and do it two
steps better."

"Two steps better. Definitely." Ann spit out the words,
hardly even knowing what she was agreeing to.

"I expect no less, even though I understand that you've had
some, *issues*, there. I know it's very difficult, and I know you're
overwhelmed, but this is important." Margaret paused for a
split second, and Ann almost thought she was going to offer
condolences. Then she said, "I'll leave you to get to your work,"
and the phone went dead.

Okay then.

Ann punched in Beka's cell number, barely waiting until
Beka answered before she said, "Why didn't you call me?"

"Oh, honey." Beka was speaking softly, obviously to keep
from being overheard in the office, but also just as obviously
choked with emotion. "How could I burden you with this right

now? It's been less than twelve hours since you called to tell me about Sarah. I couldn't dump this on you too."

"That's what friends are for."

"You just take care of yourself, okay? I'd give anything if I could be there; you know that, right?"

"Yeah, I know." And she did know. She also knew that she needed to do something for Beka, and she would, no matter what it took.

Tammy stroked her son's hair and sang softly long after he'd cried himself to sleep. Only now was he starting to understand the truth—that Sarah was gone and was never coming back. The realization had come slowly, then hit hard. He'd sobbed until his strength failed and he could do nothing but whimper as sleep finally claimed him. "Rest well, my sweet darlin'," she whispered, then leaned forward to kiss the top of his head. Still, she didn't leave his bedside.

How could they go on without Sarah? She had been like the third member of their family, her life so much a part of theirs that things would surely implode without her.

Tammy thought back to a cold winter's night just last year. Sarah had poured hot chocolate for the three of them from a beautiful hand-painted cloisonné pitcher. Tammy had run her finger along the graceful curve of the handle. "This is beautiful."

"Thanks. It was my great-great-grandmother's. Her father painted china back in the old country. It was the only thing she brought with her when she moved here."

Keith took a sip of his hot chocolate. "It makes good hot chocolate too."

Sarah smiled at him. "I think so too, Keith. It makes the best hot chocolate." She used a napkin to wipe a drip from the spout. "It's not worth anything really, but I love the history behind it."

A moment later Keith stood up from the table, stumbled on the leg of his chair, and knocked the pitcher to the floor with a crash that echoed through the kitchen. Fragments of china lay in a pool of cocoa at his feet. Sarah gasped and threw her hand over her mouth. Her eyes were wide with the horror of it.

Keith bent over the mess on the floor. "I'm so stupid. So stupid. I ruin everything."

Sarah walked over to him, the hint of tears glistening in her eyes. She knelt on the floor beside him and enveloped him in her arms. "Thank you, Keith."

He looked up at her, the surprise of her words enough to temporarily stop the meltdown. "What for? It was pretty and special and I broke it."

"Well, you're right about the pretty and special part." She took a deep breath, and Tammy knew she was fighting for control. "And I've been thinking for a long time now that something so beautiful shouldn't be kept up on a shelf where no one ever sees it except on those rare occasions when we drink hot chocolate. I've been thinking about breaking it and taking it to an artist friend of mine who makes mosaic tiles. That way I could put it somewhere that I'd see it all the time. It could make me happy every day."

"Really?" Keith wiped his eyes. "Do you mean it?"

"Absolutely." Sarah gave a firm nod of the head. Tammy suspected she was trying to convince herself. "Now, you go wash the sticky off your hands while I gather the pieces. Just you wait and see—it will be beautiful."

Two weeks later Sarah brought over a small mosaic tile and presented it to Keith. She had a similar one on her kitchen counter at home, but Keith's had the teapot handle, intact, sticking out from it. "Keith, I want you to put this someplace where you can always remember. Even something that appears broken, in the hands of a master artist, can be made into something more beautiful than the original."

"Like Jesus does for us," he'd said in his unique and simple faith, then set the tile on his dresser in the display stand that Sarah had brought him. Even now in the dark, Tammy could see its outline on Keith's dresser. He rubbed his fingers across that tile on days when things were going wrong. "It reminds me," he would say.

"I need that reminder too," Tammy whispered as she walked from the room. She wasn't certain how she could face the next few days bearing the weight of her grief. And Keith, well, he was going to be so difficult as he continued to work through all this. Today he had vacillated between asking her, "Why you sad?" and all-out wailing because he missed Sarah. It was likely to be relived over and over in the next few days. Tammy didn't feel like she had the strength to face it.

She made her way to the kitchen and began unloading the dishwasher, flashes of Sarah playing through her mind. The image that seemed to hover in her mind the most was of Sarah at her kitchen table, her blonde hair sticking out in all directions from her messy bun, wearing a T-shirt, sweatpants, and glasses that looked like Sarah Palin's. Large textbooks were spread out all around her on the table, and she had a pencil in her mouth, another in her hand, and a third behind her ear. She always looked so tired during finals or when she had a paper due. How often had Tammy envied her? What would it be like to work yourself to the point of exhaustion and actually move toward a goal in the process?

With Keith, homeschooling was the best option, which made working from home her only means of income. She enjoyed her sewing business, but she had no hopes of a better education, of a better job, or of ever having money left over at the end of the month.

She parted the curtains that looked toward Sarah's house. There was a light on in the kitchen and the dim glow of the television in the living room. Poor Annie. Suddenly Tammy felt selfish for feeling so sorry for herself. She still had Keith. And Ethan. Ann was left alone with no family at all. Tammy couldn't begin to imagine it.

She needed to do something to help Ann, but what? She thought of the pillows she'd been making for Sarah and decided she would make them for Ann now, just so she would know that there were still people here for her, people who would help her in any way they could. Tammy knew she wouldn't sleep tonight until she finished them.

In her sewing room, she looked at all the alterations she needed to finish by tomorrow afternoon. They would have to wait. For now, she pulled out the fabric she'd chosen just a few weeks ago. At the time, the bright colors had seemed so appropriate. Sarah was graduating; her sister was coming to visit for the first time in years. It held all the colors of new starts and happy beginnings. Now they seemed so wrong. But they would have to move past that, because Sarah would want them to be

happy. Maybe, by this one little gesture, Annie would get a measure of cheer.

It was after one in the morning when Tammy finally stood
up and walked through the kitchen to the laundry area. She
started a load of darks, then walked over to the stack of Keith's
crayon drawings.

The first was a drawing of Sarah—Tammy could identify
Sarah's stick figure by the large hoop earrings—throwing a ball
to the Keith stick figure in his wire-rimmed glasses. Tammy
couldn't decide if she wanted to laugh or cry at the sight of it. At
least she supposed it was a healthy way for Keith to work through
his grief.

The next drawing was the dark-haired Ann hugging Sarah,
big blue tears falling from both of their faces, and the yellow
glow that could only be an angel looking down on them. The
last showed Sarah, a huge smile on her face, in the clouds with
angels all around her. The sun had a smiley face in this particular
picture, and even the clouds had happy faces. Keith had written,
"Brokken made butiful."

This time the tears flowed unabated as Tammy closed her
eyes. "Thank You, Lord, for giving him to me."

"Mama, Mama!" Keith's panicked voice came from his
room. "Mama!"

Tammy ran down the hallway and into her son's room. "I'm
here, honey, what do you need?"

"Sarah. Will the angels bring her back?"

"No, darlin'. No, they won't."

"Please, please. Make them bring her back." A new wave
of tears, a new wave of grief, another day in the life that was
Tammy's.

She hugged her son close and once again whispered, "Thank you, Lord. Thank you."

Ann looked out the side window toward Tammy's house. She didn't know how she would have made it through the day without her help, yet something about Tammy made her uneasy. And Keith . . . well, he made her downright uncomfortable.

His talk about angels and his pictures of angels, they fed into her hallucinations—her paracusias—until the song played over and over and over in her mind, making it all seem so real. Not something she wanted to reinforce.

She walked over to the computer, typed in her account information, and found an e-mail from Margaret. She opened the photos of the last designs for Stinson, and her skin seemed to tighten around her body, squeezing against her face, her neck, her chest. It cranked tighter and tighter with each successive picture. The first room had two gray leather sofas—one two-armed, the other one-armed—and a black rug against a black tile floor. A blue handblown glass vase added a touch of color and contrasted perfectly against the room's structured geometry. Serene and sophisticated. These designs were amazing. How was she supposed to go two steps better than this?

Ann enjoyed creating new ways to show off spaces, to spotlight the positive features of an area, but she never seemed to reach perfection. She remembered the James's living room. How many times had she adjusted the side tables, rearranged the art, moved the chairs just an inch or two? She knew that, even now, if she walked back into that room, she'd find something to move. She looked at the photo on her screen and guessed that the designer who'd done this room never had to move anything a second time.

Well, Ann needed to get busy, be prepared to do her very best work. She pulled out her sketch pad, prepared to rework the room. Her pencil remained poised, ready . . . and unmoving. The problem was, for Ann, creativity required heart. At this moment, she couldn't even feel hers.

At just after midnight, with her cursor hovering over the power button, the thought that had been nagging at the back of her mind turned into an insistent demand. Maybe it was because she was tired, or more likely the grief just caused her to slip from reality for a moment. Whatever the reason, she pulled up the Google screen and typed in "angels."

The first two links had to do with the baseball team in California. Ann laughed aloud. Only then did she realize how tense she'd been while waiting for the answer, as if she expected "People who lose their minds and hear angels singing" to be first and foremost on the list. Time to get a grip.

She looked farther down and clicked on another link. The site offered a "personalized angel print." After you filled out a form to indicate the physical traits you'd like your angel to have, an artist would paint it for you and send it to you, "all for the low price of $29.99."

Changing tactics, she googled "angels' songs," which netted a link to a YouTube video of a group of five-year-olds wearing gold tinsel halos and singing "Joy to the World." Ann smiled. This search was obviously a ridiculous waste of time.

In a last effort to close this chapter for good, she typed in "angel water sound." This search provided a list of sites selling angel snow globes or angel statues for outdoor gardens, but one link intrigued her enough that she clicked on it. It opened with a picture of an angel and these words:

When the creatures moved, I heard the sound of their wings, like the roar of rushing waters, like the voice of the Almighty, like the tumult of an army. When they stood still, they lowered their wings. Ezekiel 1:24

Ann knew it was a Bible verse, but it had nothing to do with music at all—and was it really about angels? It simply referred to them as "creatures." Yet somehow, it *was* connected.

Long after she went to bed that night, the music continued to ebb and flow through her mind. She'd fallen asleep remembering the words from the verse . . . *"the sound of their wings"* . . . *"like the roar of rushing waters"* . . . while the memory of the song flowed through her mind, the notes playing in her brain like water crashing onto the beach.

The music had lost none of its power, showed no sign of letting up. Ann hoped she could keep her sanity through the long days ahead.

Chapter 6

The smell of damp soil and freshly cut grass lingered, perhaps anchored in place by the humidity that saturated the early afternoon air. Everything about this day felt . . . heavy. Even the clouds seemed less like fluff and more like mush. With May's heat beating off hundreds of headstones, Ann watched the last of the well-wishers return to their cars—back to their families and their lives. Now, for one last time, she could be alone with her sister.

"I'll stay with you." Tammy put her arm around Ann's shoulder.

"Me too," Keith said and squeezed himself between the two women, one arm around each. "I'm staying too."

Ann took a deep breath, doing her best to keep her voice gentle, although it took great effort. She didn't want to upset Keith, who had cried openly and loudly throughout the funeral and the graveside service. Half of her had wanted to tell Tammy to take him away; the other half envied the lack of restraint. As for her, she willed herself to hold it together—at least until tonight when she was alone. "I'd really like a few minutes alone with her."

"Oh, of course you would, honey. I'm sorry, I didn't even think of that. I'll just go back to the house and help get the meal set up. I'll see you there."

"You want me to stay with you, Annie?" Keith looked up at Ann, his eyes red and puffy. "I'll be real quiet if you want me to."

"Keith, honey, we'll see Annie at the house. Right now she needs some time to herself."

"But what if she needs me?" Keith's voice gained volume as his agitation grew. "She might need me. I can't leave her."

Ann saw that another wave of hysterics was coming on, and she wanted Keith away from her before it hit full force. She leaned forward so that she was almost eye to eye with him. "It's okay, Keith. I'll be right there. I just want to talk to Sarah one last time. You go and help your mother now, okay?" She hoped her voice sounded reassuring rather than agitated.

Keith nodded his head and wiped his hand beneath his glasses. "Okay. Promise you'll call if you need me."

"Count on it." Ann turned away from them and took a step toward Sarah's grave. "I'll be just a few minutes behind you."

"Okay. Come on, Keith."

"Bye, Annie. Bye-bye. Bye."

"Good-bye." In spite of herself, Ann turned. Tammy was holding Keith's hand and all but pulling him toward the car. Thank goodness!

Keith walked with his head turned toward Ann, and he continued to watch her even as he climbed into the car. Just as Tammy was closing the door, Keith sprang up and began waving wildly at Ann. Even from a distance, Ann could see the excitement in his huge smile. "The angels are here, they're with you now. You'll be okay. Bye, Annie. You okay." He sat back into his seat, readjusted his glasses, and continued waving as the car pulled from the drive.

"Angels. Right." As the sound of the tires crunching against the gravel faded, Ann focused on reality. She turned her attention back to the casket, hanging by dark blue straps over the open grave. The funeral director stood several yards away. He looked at her, his face solemn. "You can have a few minutes if you'd like. I'll just go make a quick call."

"Thanks."

Ann was wearing the same sleeveless black dress that she'd planned to wear to Sarah's graduation. It felt so wrong to be wearing it now, for this. "Oh, Say-say." Ann spoke the nickname she'd not used in fifteen years. Just the sound of it brought on a fresh wave of grief. She trailed her fingers across the steel of Sarah's casket, surprised by the coolness on such a hot and humid day. "This was supposed to be such a happy time. Your master's degree, what a great accomplishment. How many families would you have helped? How many children might you have saved from a lifetime of abuse? All that study, all that compassion. Wasted.

"I know you believe in God, and I hope for your sake that He's real and you're in heaven right now. But how could He be? If He were real, wouldn't He have let you do all your good works? Everyone who's ever met you talked about how perfect you were. Surely an all-powerful Being wouldn't have failed to notice that. Why would He have taken *you* and left someone like me here?"

Ann remembered Keith's insistence that the angels were here now. With her. Watching at this very minute. She shuddered as she looked at her grandmother's headstone beside the hole in the ground that would soon be Sarah's home. "Nana believed too, and look what it got her: a worthless daughter, a painful death, and her only decent grandchild killed in a car wreck the day before she graduated. There's no power in that kind of belief. The only person I can count on is me, and I'm going to achieve my dreams my own way."

Her dreams. Her own way. Everything inside her consolidated in this moment, and with absolute clarity, she saw what needed to be done.

"Sarah, Nana, you were the only ones who ever believed in me, and I want to thank you for that. I know I haven't always earned that faith, but that's about to change. I promise you both right now that I will do my utmost to live up to all that you thought I could be, to succeed in every possible way." She looked toward Nana's headstone. "Something you never got the chance to do because you were taking care of us." Then at Sarah's casket. "You were so close, so close. I promise the both of you that I will make the most of my life. Starting right now."

The funeral director walked toward her. "Ma'am, we really need to get started now, if you don't mind."

She kissed her fingertips, then pressed them against the casket. "Good-bye, Say-say. I love you." Ann backed away and watched them lower her sister slowly into the ground. The heavenly doves adorning the corners of the casket had seemed so garish just days ago but now felt comforting as the last earthly view of Sarah she would ever have. She was glad then that she'd let Tammy talk her into them. Tammy had been right. They were what Sarah would have wanted.

Ann walked back to her rental car, dreading what lay ahead. She was quite certain that if she had to hear one more "She's with the Lord," "She's in heaven," or "She's so happy now," she would lose her mind completely. She knew people meant well, and she didn't want to dishonor Sarah by being rude. So she had begun reciting the lyrics of every Beatles song she could remember, trying to keep her mind occupied. She could say, "Thank you so much for coming," while thinking about "Yellow Submarine" and "Sgt. Pepper's Lonely Hearts Club Band." In attendance, yet not present. This was a talent she'd perfected over the years.

She sat in the car and locked the door, not yet bothering to put the key in the ignition. With the taste of the promise she'd made to her grandmother and sister still fresh on her lips, she opened her purse and pulled out the business card she'd placed there just a few days ago. She dialed the number. "This is Ann Fletcher. Is Mr. Stinson available, please?"

Ethan's past few nights had been plagued with nightmares. Annie was screaming for help, drowning in choppy surf, and no one else seemed to hear her at all. It was up to him to reach her, but his arms and legs felt so heavy. Too heavy. He just couldn't make it. The expression on her face before she went under was always the same. Hollow. Empty. Alone.

Now, as he looked at all the cars lining the street, listened to the quiet murmurs of the dozens of people inside the house, he realized he had seen the same expression on her face during the funeral today. As far as he could tell, no other family members had been at the funeral, no one from New York had come down, and no other friends had come to be with her. Did she have no one? Why did he feel like he was the only one who could help her?

He made an excuse to wander outside, and more or less loitered there until he saw her car pull up in the driveway. He wanted to do something to help. But what?

He walked over to the garage and waited for her to gather her things and climb out of the car. What could he possibly say that would mean anything to her?

"Hey," he said.

She looked surprised to see him, even though she'd driven right past him. "Hey." She folded her arms across her chest. "What are you doing out here?"

"Well, I'm not going to ask how you're doing, because that's a stupid question, but I just wanted to see if I could do anything, anything at all, to help you. Is there anything you need? I know that's sort of a stupid question too, but I'd just really like to do something. Anything."

Ann shook her head at first, but then she looked toward the cars lining the street and nodded. "Get everyone out of here so I can collapse in peace." She sort of smiled at him, perhaps attempting to make it seem as if it had been a lighthearted joke. Ethan was pretty certain he knew better.

He winked at her, trying his best to look conspiratorial. "Tell you what I will do. I'll go inside, hang around, do the socializing thing. Then I'll make a big production about leaving, being sure to mention how tired I'm sure you are, how you probably need some time alone, those kinds of things. I'll see how many of the others I can suck into my wake as I go." She did look exhausted, so it shouldn't be that hard to pull off.

"That would be much appreciated."

"Consider it done, then."

The two of them walked to the kitchen entrance. Ethan

hurried forward, opened the screen door, and reached for the doorknob. "Shall we?"

She paused before walking through the door and looked at him. "Really. Thank you."

"Not a problem." Ethan held the door until she walked through, then followed just in time to see Danielle put an arm around Annie.

"There you are. Come right over here and get something to drink and a bite to eat." She pulled Annie in the direction of the modified buffet assembled on the kitchen counter.

"I don't really—"

"Bah! Don't even start with that. You need to keep up your strength. Let's see, how about some finger sandwiches and sweet tea? No one goes hungry when I'm in charge. Besides, you've never lived until you've tried my famous wild mushroom grits. Right, Cindy?"

Old Mrs. Edwards looked up from her post at the buffet table. "Let the poor kid choose her own food, Danielle. Honestly." She nodded toward Ethan. "Looks like young Ethan's already offering his assistance. She don't need any from us old women. Don't you remember your youth at all?"

Ethan held his breath. Mrs. Edwards had spent the last five years determined to get him "married off." Surely she wouldn't start that at a time like this. He let out the breath he'd been holding when she reached across the table and squeezed Annie's arm. "How you holding up, sweetie?"

"She'll be holding up better when we get some food in her. Now tell me what you want on here." Danielle grabbed a plate and started filling it while Annie looked on, mouth slightly agape.

Ethan smiled, thankful for these women who had loved

Sarah and would do anything they could to help her sister. Now it was time for him to start working the crowd and helping in his own way.

Group after group, he'd join the circle and agree with the conversations about what a wonderful person Sarah had been. And she had been. So wonderful. He thought of all the ways she'd helped Tammy and Keith over these last few years, the way her smile could brighten anyone's day. The loss to them all was almost unbearable. It just didn't make sense, and there could be no denying that. But Ethan's current concern was Sarah's older sister; he just couldn't shake the compulsion that he had to help her. So he'd say his bit about Sarah and then add, "Poor Annie looks absolutely exhausted." Just planting the thought in everyone's mind.

He saw Ann talking to Mrs. Williams, an eightyish-year-old woman with gray hair and large trifocals. He walked over just in time to hear Mrs. Williams say, "Sarah was such a giver. She was always taking care of people, driving me places after I broke my hip, bringing the groceries by. And not just for me, for a lot of other people too. Heaven has gained the most beautiful flower yet in the garden of the saints."

Ann choked on the coffee she'd just sipped and started coughing. "Garden of the saints?" she said.

"The place where her Maker can always delight in her, just like we did while she was here on earth."

Something about the look on Ann's face made Ethan fairly sure she was reaching the point of hysteria. He needed to do something—and fast. "Mrs. Williams, could you help me with something for just a minute?"

She looked up at him, her face eager. "Why, of course."

"Right this way." Ethan led her away from Annie, then leaned down and whispered, "Ann looks so exhausted. I'm wondering, do you think we should start hinting that it's maybe time for people to go on home so she can get some rest?"

Mrs. Williams nodded briskly. "Exactly right. I was just thinking the same thing. I'm going right over to Mildred and Ethel and tell them they're about to overstay their welcome."

Ethan was almost positive that she had not been thinking the same thing, but she was his ally now, and he wasn't going to question her. "Thanks, I'll get the Seidls and the Langmos."

"Right." Mrs. Williams walked faster than Ethan had seen her move in some time—a woman on a mission.

Ethan walked up to Elli Seidl. "This has been such a sad day, hasn't it? Sarah was such a wonderful person." He scrubbed his hands across his face and nodded in Ann's direction. "I think I'll be leaving now. I know it's been a long day for Annie, and she's got lots of things to take care of. The poor kid must be worn out. I think I'll leave her to get some rest."

"Oh yes, you're probably right. We probably should get moving."

Five minutes later a mass exodus had begun. Ethan walked past Ann, who was saying her good-byes to a group of guests. She looked his way, and he nodded, just barely. She reached back to rub her neck and dipped her head slightly in response. It seemed as though a silent friendship had been formed.

The garden of the saints? This was the comment that almost started the inevitable breakdown—complete with screaming and tears, Ann was sure—but she knew she needed to avoid that, at least

SHEILA WALSH & KATHRYN CUSHMAN

until after these people left and she could be alone. So she tried to remember the words to "Eleanor Rigby." How did that song start? Something about Eleanor at the church? The words wouldn't come to her, but the process of trying to remember had granted her at least temporary self-control.

Ethan had been like the pied piper of the crowd, because almost everyone began their good-byes right after his. Ann had never been so grateful to anyone.

Now she was alone, except for Danielle, Tammy, and Keith. "These casseroles all go back to the church." Tammy towel dried the last of the rectangular dishes and set it beside the other six or seven. "All the rest have names on the bottom."

"Right." Danielle looked up from the notepad she was writing on. "I'll drop those by tomorrow." She looked toward Ann then and nodded toward the counter. "Those are the cards from flowers, et cetera, which I'm sure you'll want to acknowledge." She looked around the room. "All done?"

"All finished here." Tammy wiped the counter. "You've got our phone numbers, right? You know you can call either of us day or night, and we'll be here for you."

"I've got 'em." Ann looked toward the typed list that Danielle had hung on the refrigerator. "Thanks. For everything."

"That's what we're here for." Danielle hugged her, and she, Tammy, and Keith walked her out to the driveway and bade her farewell.

Ann was pretty confident that Tammy was going to stay until told to leave, and since she was ready to be alone, she set about doing just that. "Bless your heart, thank you so much for all you've done." The "bless your heart" had been an intentional addition, as Ann had learned long ago that preceding even the bluntest comment with this phrase seemed to make it accept-able in southern society. Too bad Sarah wasn't here to see this. She'd spent the last few years complaining about Ann's increas-ing New York–ishness. What was it she'd said once when Ann was recounting the story of a conflict at work? *"Annie, you're getting downright Yankee-fied."* Yeah, that was it. And she'd said it in a per-fectly horrified voice, as if declaring Ann had the plague.

Sarah.

The thought almost knocked her to her knees. Sarah. She was gone.

"Oh, no problem at all. I'm just so happy I could do some-thing to help. Sarah loved you so much. I know she'd want me to look after you." Tammy reached out and grasped Ann's hands. "I bet Sarah is watching down on us and smiling right now. I'm sure she's happy to see that we've become friends." Tammy released her grip and started back toward Sarah's house.

Hmm . . . it might take some New York bluntness to get this one out of here. But Ann remained determined, at least for these couple of days, to be as polite as she was capable of being, for Sarah. "You know, Tammy, I'm really tired. I think I'm going to take a hot bath and call it an early night, okay?"

"Oh, of course you're tired. You go soak in a hot tub and relax. Get to bed early. That's what you should do. Do you need me to stay for a while?"

"No!" It came out harsh, but Ann couldn't control it. "You've done . . . so much already. I think a little alone time might do me good."

Tammy looked doubtful but stopped walking and looked toward her own home. "Okay then, but you've got to promise you'll call me if you need anything."

Ann held up two fingers, which she thought was like a Scout's honor kind of thing, but having never been a Girl Scout, she wasn't sure. "Promise."

"Well, I'll see you in the morning, then. I'll bring something over for breakfast."

Breakfast? Time for another round of diplomacy. "You know, I'm not much of a breakfast eater. How about I'll just see you around, okay?"

"Oh . . . well . . . sure. Sure. I'll come by tomorrow afternoon, then. Come on, Keith. We need to get home."

"Bye, Annie." Keith threw his arms around Ann and hugged tight. "I love you."

The words stunned Ann all the way to the bone. "I . . ." No other words would come. She hugged him tight, but when the urge to cry on his shoulder became almost overwhelming, she pulled away. They needed to leave, and fast, or she was going to break down right here in front of them. Ann focused on deep breathing.

"Come on, baby, we've got to go home now." Tammy took Keith's hand but looked toward Ann. "You call me if you need anything. I'll be over here quicker than you can get the phone hung up. I did give you my number, right?"

"Definitely. Completely covered."

"Right. Well, come on, Keith. We'll be back to see Ann tomorrow. Okay?"

"Bye," he said again, then turned to follow his mother.

Ann walked back into the house and closed the front door behind her. That's when the breakdown began.

Chapter 7

Ann floated through a balmy sea, completely enveloped in its warmth. She couldn't remember when she'd felt so peaceful, so happy, so loved. As she continued to float, she became aware of a vibration around her that seemed to ebb and flow with the rhythm of waves crashing in the distance—but no, it wasn't waves. It sounded like . . . wings. Each beat whooshed in rhythm with the next, creating a music all its own. Peaceful. Filled with a love so amazing it penetrated to her very marrow. She wanted to stay here forever.

A dull ache in her back began to pull her from the scene, but she still heard the faint hint of the music. It wasn't loud—it seemed to be coming from a great distance—but the tune was unmistakable. Ann couldn't tell if she was awake or asleep, so she forced her body to an upright position, then flipped on the table lamp at the end of the sofa. Finally, the music faded and disappeared.

Obviously it had been a dream. Again. Her current situation was nightmarish enough without all this nonexistent tripe messing with her mind. These dreams, this music, they needed to stop. Right now. According to the clock on the wall, it was just after 2:00 a.m. She stretched her cramped muscles, picked up the remote, and spent the rest of the night mindlessly pushing buttons, never pausing long enough on any single channel to really know what was on. She couldn't relax enough to even consider sleep—although whether it was from grief or fear of dreaming unearthly music, she wasn't certain.

It was Keith; he was the one who was doing this to her. He was the one who had her thinking about angels and wings and songs—paracusias—that were best forgotten. Perhaps it would be better if she avoided him altogether today.

As the rising sun began to blaze through the lace curtains, she stood up to stretch. After a few nights sleeping on this too-short and too-sagging sofa, she could feel all thirty of her years, and she thought maybe she even felt a few she hadn't lived yet.

Tomorrow afternoon, she was flying home. If she could just make it through another day and a half here, she would be away from these constant reminders of what she'd just lost. The confusing blur of faces and names that Ann could never recall. Sad smiles, tight hugs, words spoken in hushed tones. And flowers, endless deliveries of flowers. This in spite of the fact that Ann had requested donations to charity in lieu of them. She began to thumb through the stack of cards Danielle had left for her.

One card in particular drew her attention:

With sympathy, Patrick Stinson

It infuriated her that Margaret had told him. He'd known all about it when Ann had called his office yesterday, and whether Margaret's motive in telling was to convince him to work directly with her instead, or to gain sympathy and secure the contract, Ann didn't know. Somehow she suspected that Patrick Stinson was a man not much given to sympathy when it came to business matters. But at least this was a reminder that she had another life, with dreams within her reach, in another place, away from all this.

Sometime during the rush of yesterday's grief she'd formulated a plan. Now she was in the driver's seat, and now was the time to make the call to put it all into motion.

She smiled as she hit the speed dial on her cell phone, the rush of adrenaline making her feel better than she'd felt in days. "Marston Home Staging, this is Jen, may I help you?"

"Hi, Jen, I need to speak to Margaret."

"Well, well, I always thought people spent time in the South to slow down and remember their manners. Didn't know it worked in reverse and some people actually got uptight and rude."

"Sorry. Not thinking. Please and thank you."

Jen laughed. "That's better, not particularly heartwarming, but better nonetheless. You okay?"

"Really, Jen, thank you. I'm fine."

"Oh sure, sure. Like I'm supposed to accept that as genuine right about now. Just one second and I'll patch you through."

The phone clicked almost instantly. "Ann. So good to hear from you. Are you making progress on the Stinson presentation?"

"That's actually what I'm calling to talk to you about. Margaret . . ." Ann took a deep breath. "Here's the thing. I've been working for Marston Staging for six years now. I've worked my tail off, and I'm the one who has brought in the opportunity for the biggest job we've ever had."

"You've worked hard, yes. You did meet Patrick Stinson, yes, but I hardly think that alone brought him to Marston Staging."

"Funny, because when I talked to him on the phone yesterday, he implied that it *was* me who brought him there." Ann paused just long enough to let that one sink in. "Did he imply something different to you?"

"I really don't see—"

"Look, it doesn't matter. You said you were looking for an investor, a silent partner. Why can't I become a partner that isn't silent?"

"What do you have in mind?"

"I'll be selling the house here in the next year; I could use that money to buy in. But in the meantime"—Ann licked her lips and took her last breath of courage—"I want a 50 percent share in the Stinson job, and I want Beka to remain on staff."

"I see." Margaret remained silent for several seconds. This type of ultimatum likely would have meant termination at any other time, but with the promise of Stinson Towers out there, Margaret would not be so hasty. "Here's what I'm willing to concede. *If* we land the Stinson account, since you did play a role in bringing that to us, I would be willing to agree to your having a 30 percent share. And *if* you can come up with the money within the next twelve months, then I would agree to allowing you to start buying in to the company, not to ever exceed a 45 percent share. I still retain controlling interest; I still retain ultimate control."

Ann thought about that for a moment. "Okay, done."

"As for Beka, we really don't have the resources to keep her. Of course, the Stinson job would change that immediately. I'll agree to keep her on until we know whether or not we get Stinson Towers. The day we find out that we don't, she'll be let go immediately."

"Margaret, that's—"

"That's more than she would have had otherwise, and I simply can't afford to offer more."

"All right then. Deal."

"Now, get busy and do what you have to do to get that job."

"That's my plan." Ann hung up the phone, quite pleased with herself. She had taken the first steps toward achieving her goals. "See, Nana and Sarah? I'm already on my way. What do you think of that?"

The only answer was the roar of a lawn mower a couple of houses down, which was plenty enough for Ann. Now that she was focused on a concrete goal, she planned to crowd everything else out of her mind for good.

She padded to the kitchen and poured herself a bowl of corn flakes, slicing up a banana and adding it to the bowl before she splashed it all with milk. She took a few bites, then put the coffee in the filter and got the morning's brew going. There were some errands that needed running today, and her plan was to leave after breakfast but before lunch, hopefully timing it just right so that she would be gone when Tammy came over to make her neighborly call.

The doorbell chimed at that very moment. Apparently she was already too late.

Ann was wearing a ratty Boston Celtics T-shirt and a pair of black sweatpants that were easily ten years old and two sizes too large, and she knew without looking that her hair was its usual first-thing-in-the-morning explosion. Hopefully Tammy would take one look, come to the conclusion that she'd woken Ann up, and feel so guilty she'd disappear for a while—taking Keith and his dream-inducing angel talk with her. Yep, this ought to scare her off.

It wasn't until Ann had already started to pull the door open that she realized her mistake. Tammy never rang the doorbell, because she never came to the front door; she always went straight to the kitchen door. Ann found herself face-to-face with Ethan McKinney.

There was something like a grin on his face as he rubbed his chin against his shoulder and averted his gaze. "Look, I'm sorry, I didn't mean to wake you up. I just remembered another stop I've got to make for work, but there is something that I wanted to talk to you about, so maybe I'll come by later this afternoon if that's okay with you." He was already backing away as he spoke, still not looking at her.

"You didn't actually wake me up. I was just eating breakfast."

He had stepped from the portico onto the patio, so Ann had to lean out of the doorway to keep him in view.

"Oh, good. Well, like I said, maybe I'll stop by later, maybe I'll call first, but I'll just go run some errands now. There're some things I've got to do, don't know why I didn't think about it until now."

For the first time since the accident, Ann felt a real smile emerge from somewhere inside her. Ethan and his run-on sentences could be quite entertaining—a refreshing change from the clipped and direct style she often encountered in New York. Ethan finally reached the wrought-iron gate at the side of the enclosed courtyard. He pulled at the latch, which clanked and clanked but did not open. "This thing always sticks. I don't know why Sarah wouldn't let me replace this stinking latch," he mumbled, more or less to himself as he pushed and pulled and pushed some more.

Ann began to wonder if she should walk out and help him, but thought it would likely embarrass him more than he was already. Finally, the gate swung open and Ethan chanced a backward look.

Ann waved at him, one finger at a time. He nodded once, his face now a dark crimson, and hurried toward his truck.

Ann actually giggled as she closed the door behind her. She turned her attention back to the task of coffee making, but when she heard the sound of Ethan's truck moving down the driveway, she had the strangest urge to pull back the curtains and peek. The fear of being caught in the act was enough to restrain her.

She finished her breakfast, then took a long hot shower. It did little to ease the strain, but at least she'd tried.

When she was ready to leave the house, she determined to do so without encountering Keith or Tammy. She slowly pulled back the curtains, just a few inches, and looked toward Tammy's house, searching for any sign of an impending visit. Nothing seemed to be moving in that general direction, so she dashed out the kitchen door, resisting the urge to duck and roll. She hustled through the side door of the garage, then locked it behind her. So far so good. She climbed into the car, locked those doors too, and started the engine before she pushed the button on the garage door remote. Her escape must have looked like something from a grade-B spy movie, but so far, it had worked. While the door creaked open, she held her breath—uncertain if she was doing this from fear of a surprise Keith appearance, or fear of carbon monoxide poisoning—until it opened enough to reveal an empty driveway. Whew. She'd made it. This time.

Ethan parked his truck in the driveway again, a man on a mission. Today, right now, he was going to find something he could do to help Ann, do it as quickly as possible, then get on with his life. The dreams, the overwhelming compulsion that she needed his help, and his complete lack of clear thought around her ended here. Right now. He climbed from the truck and hurried forward.

It was almost two o'clock; surely Ann was up and going by now. Even though he was relatively certain she would be, it took every bit of his courage to press the doorbell. How many times could he mess up with her? He listened for the telltale sound of footsteps approaching the door but heard nothing. He turned his attention to the golden oak surface of the door. It was worn and scraped. Definitely needed a good refinishing. He rang the bell one last time and followed it up with a loud knock. Still nothing.

He'd just have to stop by later. He turned to leave and saw Annie's rental car parked on the street and Ann walking up the driveway carrying a large box. She was leaning back, arms stretched taut, face flushed with exertion. He ran out to meet her. "Oh, there you are. Oh man, did I block your driveway with my truck? I'm sorry, I wasn't thinking, I just assumed you would be parked in the garage. It never occurred to me that you weren't here, and that you would come home and then couldn't get into your garage, and that you would be carrying something heavy—"

"Not. A. Problem."

"Here, let me get that," Ethan said, already reaching for the box. Apparently there were still a few ways he could mess up.

"It's fine. Really, you don't have to do this."

"Of course I do." When the full weight transferred to his hands, he grunted. "Man, this is heavy. Now I feel really bad. I wouldn't have blocked you out if I'd known, because the last thing I want to do is make things harder for you."

"I know." She sort of sighed when she said it. What did that mean? That she was tired? Or tired of him? Or just sad?

She led him to the kitchen door and unlocked it. "You can just set it on the counter."

"Yes, ma'am." He followed her inside, taking in the scene around him. There were piles of paper in neat stacks all over the kitchen table. He put the box down, then nodded toward the papers. "This looks like a lot of work."

Ann nodded. "Yeah, I guess it's going to be. Apparently you don't have to have a lot of money to have lots of estate things to sort through."

Ethan looked toward the box he'd just set on the counter. It was some sort of fireproof, flood-proof, earthquake-proof file holder. He almost laughed at the overkill, but he supposed that after all that had happened to her, Ann wasn't willing to take chances with anything. He needed to help her in some way, he just had to. "Actually, that is one of the reasons I was stopping by. Is there anything I can do for you? I'm glad to pitch in."

"I've got it covered." She shrugged. "Most of the paperwork is something I've got to do, as the last survivor of the family." The words sounded so final, so heavy, in Ethan's ears.

This wasn't getting him anywhere. "What about your front door?"

"My front door?" She said each word slowly as if clarifying she'd heard him correctly.

"It . . . needs refinishing. I could do it for you, fix it up nice."

Ann stared at him, her mouth slightly agape. "My front door." Then she kind of smiled and started pulling the tape loose from the box on the counter. "It probably does need some work, but I can do it next time I'm in town."

"The floors need refinishing too." What was he getting himself into here? "The walls could use a fresh coat of paint."

79

"All of which I'm perfectly capable of doing myself."

Man, this girl is stubborn. Independent way beyond the point of sensible. "Capable, no doubt. But don't you have more important things to do with your time?"

She stopped what she was doing and looked up from the box. "Now that I think about it, I have lots of work to do on this place before I can put it on the market. If you know a reputable local handyman who could help with some things around here, that would probably be a good thing."

Ethan put his hand over his heart and tried to assume an offended expression. "How could you even ask that question? A local handyman you can hire? That has gone to the edge of insulting. I think that I might be wounded beyond repair. How can I bear to even have that question asked of me?"

Ann leaned back on the counter, arms folded, an almost smile on her face. "What's wrong with that question?"

"I, dear madam, am a contractor extraordinaire. I would never dream of allowing a friend of mine to hire a handyman for assistance."

"Well, I don't know if I can afford a contractor's rate."

He put his hand to his forehead and threw his head back in an imitation of a damsel in distress. "Now I am downright offended." He raised his voice an octave and thickened his accent. "In a situation like this, I would never be for hire. I shall likely swoon if this conversation continues."

Ann actually smiled at this, but it quickly faded as she crossed her arms and leaned back against the counter. "Well, I'm not taking charity."

"Your sister always said the same thing. In fact, some manual labor was going to be my graduation gift to her; that way she would have to graciously accept. I kept telling her, and now I'm telling you, helping a friend is not charity. Helping a friend is what makes a friend a friend. In fact, what kind of friends would we be, if we couldn't even help each other? That's what friends do, after all, help other friends, just because they're friends." Ethan began to wonder how much longer he was going to have to continue before she would interrupt him. It was coming—it always did, but he was fast running out of friend-isms to say. Still, he was determined to push on until she cracked. "What would be the point of the friendship? Friends are—"

"Even if it's a friend you haven't even seen for ten years?"

He tried hard to keep a straight face after his hard-earned victory. "Well, all right then, you're an interior decorator, right?"

Ann shrugged. "Yes."

"Well, how about a barter deal? If you'll help me put the best face on a property or two, then I'll help you in turn. It'll be an even trade, your specialty for mine."

"Could be fair enough. Are they your properties or someone else's?"

"Oh, they belong to other people. Most of the houses I work on have had a previous owner or two . . . sometime over the last hundred years or so." He smiled. "I'd like your opinion on a couple of places that I'm renovating so the owners can sell."

"How would I be helping you? You get paid for your work whether or not someone buys the place, right?"

"Well, sure, but I like to help as much as I can." Ann started to shake her head, and Ethan realized he'd backed himself into the taking charity trap. "I mean, after all, it's in my best interest if the homes I work on sell quickly. It gets the word out that my work makes a difference. Know what I mean?"

Ann's eyes lit up with that last part. "That makes sense. It's the same with my business. But old houses? Hmm . . ." She rolled her eyes. "Definitely not my specialty."

"But you can still do it, right?"

"And I don't have any firm plans for when I'll be back in town. It may not be for a few months."

Victory. Time to seal the deal before she comes up with another argument. "Well, you look like an honest sort, and specialty or not, I think I'll take my chances. Should we shake hands on it or draw up an official contract? 'Cause here in the South, a man's handshake is his word, but if you don't think I look all that honest, well then, we could do it the New York way. I know in the big city you have to be more careful about these—"

Ann stuck out her hand. "All right then, sounds good."

Her hand felt so fragile in his. Tan against pale, large against small. "Looks like we've got ourselves a deal." He released her hand and nodded toward the door. "You want to discuss it over dinner? Magnolia's still makes the best she-crab soup in town." The invitation came out before he knew he planned to offer it.

Ann stood perfectly still for the space of two heartbeats. Finally, she said, "Can I take a rain check? I've got lots of paperwork to get filed before I leave tomorrow, and besides, there's a bunch of leftover food from yesterday."

"All right, a rain check. I'll hold you to that." He kept the words short this time. He wanted her to know he meant it.

Ann turned back to untaping the box and briefly looked over her shoulder. "Well, I'd better get back to this paperwork."

"All right then. I'll see you next time." He walked out the door, hoping their next visit would be soon.

Chapter 8

Ann needed to go for a walk. After several hours of sorting through paperwork, she thought her head might explode from too much information. Yes, a quick walk around the block might clear her brain some.

However, there was little chance she could make it around the block without alerting Tammy and Keith. Yet somehow, as much as she'd avoided them today, she found herself almost hoping to run into them.

She changed into a pair of gym shorts and a lavender T-shirt, laced up her running shoes, and made a point of walking out the kitchen door instead of the front. Tammy's house sat on the corner, so the back of it faced the side of Sarah's. Ann wanted to allow ample time for them to see her, if they wanted to come out and talk. She knew this was silly. Tammy would be more than happy for Ann to stop by, but somehow she couldn't bring herself to go over there, and no one came out. Looked like she was going to have to go it alone.

At the end of the driveway, she turned right, planning to make a circle around the entire neighborhood, which really wasn't that large anyway. Just ahead of her, she saw a thin woman in bright yellow jogging shorts and a white T-shirt stretching out her calves. Ann mumbled a "hello" as she walked by her.

The woman straightened up, her red hair glinting in the sun's light. "Oh, hi. Sorry, didn't see you. I'm going to do a cooldown lap. Mind if I come with you?"

"Sure." When Ann saw the woman's face, a bolt of recognition shot all the way through her. "You were at the . . . I mean, you gave me some water the other night. Downtown. Car accident."

The woman nodded. "I thought you looked familiar. I'm glad to see that you're all right." From the corner of her eye, Ann could see the woman studying her face. "How is your sister?"

"She . . . didn't make it."

"I'm sorry." Something about the way she said it was comforting—not the embarrassed kind of pity, or even the overly gushy sort. Just stating the truth for what it was. "My name's Eleanor, by the way." Eleanor looked to be in her midforties, but her smooth skin and classic beauty would rival a woman half her age. And her hair was the prettiest color Ann had ever seen— not exactly red, not quite brown.

"I'm Ann."

"Nice to meet you." She fell into step beside Ann and neither of them said a word for almost five minutes.

Finally, Ann asked Eleanor, "Where do you live in the neighborhood?"

"Oh, me? I don't live in this neighborhood actually. I'm a

real estate agent and I specialize in the West Ashley area, so I come over here to jog sometimes, just to keep my eye on things. Besides, it's nice and flat. The outer loop is almost exactly a mile, so it's easy to measure and see if I'm improving my time. I keep thinking I'm going to do a few 10Ks, maybe even a half marathon. How about you, you like to run?"

"Not so much. Back home I'm more of a gym rat."

"You're not from here, then? Somehow I thought you were local."

"I grew up in this neighborhood, but I haven't lived here in a long time. My sister does . . . did. Last house before the corner."

"The one catty-corner to Tammy?"

"That's the one. You know her?"

"I don't really know her personally, but I do know Keith. He's the most amazing kid."

Ann nodded. "I've only just met him."

"Ah, but to know Keith is to love him. A lot of people seem to be especially disturbed by him, although I've never understood why. Does he make you uncomfortable?" There was no hint of judgment in her question, just curiosity.

Ann shrugged. "He talks about angels a lot; he actually *believes* he sees and hears them. It just sort of makes me feel, I don't know, weird."

"Don't you believe in angels?"

"Not really. If they were real, and if they actually spoke to Keith, why wouldn't they do more to help?"

"Maybe Keith is exactly the way God intended him to be. I'm sure that if he really does see angels, they're sent to him for a specific purpose that's beyond our understanding. And if someone else—say, you, for example—were to see or hear angels, it might be for an altogether different purpose."

Ann shivered. "Let's talk about something else, shall we?"

"Good idea." Eleanor lifted her face to the sky for just a moment, her eyes closed. "What an incredible day."

"Yeah. Not too hot—yet."

"Have you met Tammy's cousin, Ethan? That's his house, right there." Eleanor pointed at a white house with green shutters and a whale-shaped weather vane atop the chimney. It looked like the kind of place where Ethan would live.

"Yes, I've met him. Didn't know this was his house, though."

"I helped him find it. This is nowhere near the house he *could* buy, but it is absolutely the perfect place for him." She smiled in satisfaction.

"What makes it so perfect?"

"This area is considered the birthplace of Charleston, did you know that? The neighborhood may only be around sixty years old, but the first permanent settlement was here in West Ashley—Charles Towne Landing to be exact. Like Ethan, the roots here run deep. His father builds flashy new condos on the Florida coast, but Ethan has always been one to see the potential in what's already there, in something that most people would overlook. Some hard work, some tender loving care, and when he's finished, everyone will see the beauty that's been there all along."

"I gather he's good at what he does."

"His work is always featured in trade magazines, he's got a waiting list almost a year long, but he doesn't charge the rates he could, and he keeps his work crew small—says he doesn't want work and success to become his priority."

"What is his priority, then?" By now, they had reached Sarah's driveway and Ann stopped walking, waiting for the answer.

Eleanor smiled in a way that hinted at a long-held secret. "You'll have to ask him that yourself."

"You're here!" Keith's shout sounded down the driveway as he ran toward them. He came right up between the women and looked at each, as if uncertain which to hug first. Finally, he threw his arms around Ann but turned to Eleanor. "I knew you would like each other."

"Keith. Keith? Where are you?" Tammy's voice came from the backyard.

"Out front, Mama. With Ann and—"

Eleanor bent down to hug Keith. "I've got to hurry on now. I'll see you again soon, okay?" She looked toward Ann. "Nice to meet you, Ann. Let me give you my card." She reached into a zippered pocket on the leg of her shorts and retrieved a small wallet. She flipped it open, pulled out a card, and handed it to Ann.

Next to a smiling picture of Eleanor, she read:

Eleanor Light
Making Dreams Come True
843-555-5723

"Thanks. I'll be in touch."

"I'm counting on it." Eleanor jogged away.

Keith took her hand and said, "Now come with me. We need some quality time."

"Well, I don't think I can. I really need to—" Ann looked into his earnest blue eyes and saw the serious expression on his face. As much as she wanted to avoid disturbing conversations,

she just couldn't say no to that face. "That sounds really good."
And oddly enough, it kind of did.

Five Alcohol-Related Crashes in Two Days. Ann saw
the headline in the morning's paper and knew that she would
read no further. She didn't want to know details of their accident, didn't want to know the name of the man who'd hit them,
whether or not he had a family, or even a job.

She flipped to the next section of the *News and Courier*, but
the damage was already done. Her emotions started racing
faster than her brain could think. Why couldn't that monster
have controlled his drinking? Why couldn't he have had a little
more self-control? If he'd wanted to live dangerously, why did
he have to take his death wish on the streets? She flipped page
after page blindly, until she saw a headline that caught her attention with enough force to cool her ire: Stinson Son Visits
Charleston.

The story was buried back in the Life section of the paper, a
place Ann seldom bothered to even skim. She pulled the paper
closer so she could read the rest of Charlene Pemberton's social
column.

Patrick Stinson, dashing New York City developer and son of
Charleston's own Marisol Stinson, made an appearance at the
Dock Street Theatre last night. He came not only to watch the
magnificent *Flora, an Opera,* but also to be a part of the dinner
afterward honoring his mother. Marisol Stinson was recognized for her tireless work in supporting the opera, the Spoleto
Festival in general, and all the arts in the city of Charleston.

Mr. Stinson's presence set several of Charleston's most eligible belles atwitter. He was never without a beautiful companion. His young nephew, Cedric, looked pleased to have his uncle in town, although when asked, his only comment was, "His plane is broken back in New York, and they didn't get it fixed in time. He'd promised to take me flying and now he can't."

This columnist, for one, hopes that Cedric will continue to remind his uncle of his promise and perhaps coax this most charming man back to our fair city. Soon. Ooh la-la!

Plane broken back in New York City? So much for having a small carbon footprint. So much for being honest too. Perhaps Ann needed to be extra cautious in dealings—business or otherwise—with the charming Mr. Patrick Stinson.

Chapter 9

Ann had never been so glad to see the New York skyline in all her life. Here, her world made sense; she was in firm control of her destiny. Now she just needed to make certain her destiny involved landing the Stinson Towers account.

She took a taxi straight to the office, where a stack of invoices would be waiting, among other things. The elevator doors slid open at the familiar tenth floor. She walked the long hallway, pulling her suitcase past doors that led to everything from lawyers' offices to the headquarters for some sort of plastic bead manufacturer. This is what she loved most about this city: the variety.

She paused at the glass doors that led to Marston Home Staging. This is where she belonged; hopefully she could regain some sense of equilibrium here. She entered the small waiting room, which was tastefully appointed in hues of beige and taupe. It was a little too "brown" for Ann, but Margaret was into "warmth." Funny, her decorating style was the only thing about

Margaret that could be described as warm. Still, putting up with Margaret's brusqueness was worth the price if everything worked out as planned.

Jen smiled up from the reception desk. "Thank goodness you're back. It's been crazy around here."

"It's always crazy around here."

"Yeah, but it's been worse than usual today. That penthouse over on Fifth Avenue fell out of escrow this morning, and Mrs. Trumbull has been calling every five minutes to see why we don't have the place set up again yet. Sylvia's job in that loft over in Chelsea fell apart, and Ms. Simpkins decided last minute that she actually does want us to stage that three-bedroom over by Gramercy Park, but she's refused to even talk to anyone but you. She said that you had 'earned her trust.'"

Ann shook her head, partly in exasperation, partly in the glow of knowing that she was needed here. "I'll call her right now." She started toward the row of cubicles that housed her desk, then turned. "Is Margaret in?"

"She's in, but I wouldn't go back there if I were you. She's in the worst mood I think I've ever seen."

Ann glanced back toward the glass doors at the far wall and decided to brave it. "I think I'll chance it. If I'm not out of there in a few minutes, send in the SWAT team, will you?"

"Like a SWAT team could help you against that." She paused a second. "Maybe if their guns were loaded with silver bullets, or if there was an exorcist in the group or something, but even then, I have my doubts."

Ann dropped her suitcase beside her desk and shuffled quickly through the mound of paperwork waiting for her. It was going to be a long night before she could finally make it back to her little apartment. Time to get started. But first on the list, face Margaret.

She tapped against the glass as she pushed open the door and leaned in. Margaret was, as usual, sitting at her desk with the Bluetooth earpiece in her ear. She waved Ann in with one hand, held her fingers up for silence with the other. "The contract that you signed specifically states that we do not accept the burden of the responsibility for the sale of the property."

She rolled her eyes and shook her head while she listened to whatever was being said on the other end of the line. "What I said was, according to a recent article in *Newsweek*, the average staged home sells in about seven days, as compared to eighty-seven days or more for a nonstaged home. We most certainly did not guarantee your loft would sell in seven days."

Margaret moved her head from side to side, stretching out her neck. It was a joke around the office to stay away from Margaret if there was any noticeable twitching or stretching. So Jen had been right. This was not going to be the right time for decisive conversation.

Ann pointed toward the door and offered a dismissive wave, indicating to Margaret that she was going to her office and would catch up with her later, no big thing. But Margaret jumped to her feet in a defensive stance and shook her head sternly. She pointed at the chair Ann had just been sitting in.

Uh-oh.

"I'll be happy to continue this conversation with you at a later time, but right now I have a meeting. I believe if you read through your contract you will realize that further talk here is unnecessary. Good-bye." Margaret pressed a button on the phone on her desk, removed the head set, and dropped back to her seat.

"Idiot. I can't believe how many *stupid* people there are in this world. How do they make it through childhood?"

"Got me." Ann turned both hands palms up and made her best attempt at a sympathetic shrug.

Margaret shook her head again, as if to clear the whole conversation from her mind. "Welcome back."

Ann nodded. "It's good to be here. Looks like I've got a few things I need to sort through."

"Yes, but more importantly, we have a meeting with Patrick Stinson tomorrow morning at nine o'clock. I trust that you have everything together for it."

"Yes, I'm ready." It wasn't technically true. Ann had worked on it some during the last few days, but there had been more pressing matters at hand. She had many hours of fine-tuning ahead of her tonight.

Maybe it was exhaustion, or maybe it was the grief that made Ann not care about the possibility of an explosion, but she suddenly blurted, "Of course, after we secure the deal with Stinson, I'll be taking some time off in the next few months, getting my sister's estate settled. I'll stay on top of work here, though."

"Your sister?" Margaret paused for a moment, as if trying to remember whether Ann actually even had a sister. "Your sister, oh right, I was sorry to hear about that." This was about the limit of sentimentality when it came to Margaret, but Ann took it for what it was. "Of course, I'll need you in town for the immediate future, until we get the Stinson thing buttoned up tight."

"Of course. Speaking of which, I was wondering what you've told everyone, about our agreement, I mean."

"Not one word, of course. I don't want a bunch of chitchat and speculation going on that will distract them from their work. I simply told Beka that we will continue to need her while we're working toward the Stinson project, and that if it comes through, I plan to keep her on."

You've decided to keep her on? Right. Ann nodded her head. "All right then. I've got work to do; I'd better get busy." She walked out of the office and directly into Beka, who threw her arms around Ann's neck. "How you holding up?"

"I'm all right." Ann needed to change the focus if she was going to keep it together. "How is Gracie doing?"

Beka continued to look at Ann with a worried expression as she answered, "She's getting better every day. The new medication is amazing."

"That's great to hear."

Beka smiled and squeezed Ann's arm. "Thank you so much, Ann—for bringing in the Stinson account."

"What makes you think I had something to do with the Stinson account?"

"Oh, come on, I'm not stupid. I overheard Jen saying he'd called here looking for you. Even in college—which was what, a couple hundred years ago?—you were the one who scored the big breaks, not to mention caught the eye of men like Patrick Stinson. Besides, it would never have been Margaret's idea to give me a reprieve—that had to come from you."

"If I ever need a private eye, I'm giving you a call. You have got to be the most observant human on the planet."

"Yes, and by observing the tense way you're holding your shoulders, I'm guessing you need to sit yourself down and get to work. Now quit goofing off with the hired help and get busy."

"Yes, ma'am." Ann saluted.

"By the way, I want to have you over for dinner later this

week. I've got a new stir-fry recipe that will knock your socks off."

"Sounds good." Ann took a seat at her desk. She looked at the Stinson folder in her hand, willing the sudden wave of grief to stay firmly buried until she made it home tonight. Work, hard work, was the only thing that would get her through this. Maybe the Stinson account was just the thing to keep her sane. Yeah, well, she needed to get busy if she had any chance of actually succeeding.

It was almost 2:00 a.m. when Ann rode the elevator up to her studio apartment on the eighth floor. She lit a fresh-linen-scented candle and walked into the kitchen, hoping she could at least find something to eat, but the only inhabitants of her refrigerator, aside from condiments and salad dressing, were two cans of tomato juice, a Diet Coke, and a case of bottled water.

Ann pulled out a water and unscrewed the lid. She needed to go to the market, but it would have to wait until tomorrow night.

Well, at least she was home. She looked around the small place, relief washing over her. The black bed with a white duvet, the white sofa, the white countertops, her little chrome coffee table. Oh, it all felt so good to be back in this neatly ordered world, no matter how chaotic life around it was.

She slid open the door to her small balcony and looked down at the street below, still moving with activity even though it was the middle of the night. Yes, this was her world. And here in her own world, she looked forward to a good night's sleep. Without nightmares, without memories, and without waking from dreams of hearing music that wasn't there.

"As I said before, this is a very impressive portfolio, and your company has an equally impressive track record." Patrick Stinson looked at Margaret over the photos she'd placed on his desk. "I definitely think that I see the potential for a long-term partnership here."

"I absolutely agree. It just makes sense." Margaret's tone was as calm as if she'd just been told that the sky was blue, but her left pinky finger began to tap against the desk.

"And I must say, I really think Ms. Fletcher has just the type of approach that will work well with our team. I'd like to see her personally involved in this project." He looked at Ann then, a casual expression on his face, but there was a gleam in his eyes that suggested other intentions. He smiled his half-dimpled smile toward her, looking a bit too sure of himself for Ann's liking.

Jen's warning played through her mind, but she wasn't overly concerned. She'd seen plenty of his kind over the years and she'd learned how to handle them. She'd play along now, all innocent and naive, get the job contract signed, and then when Patrick Stinson started to cross the line, Ann would explain that she didn't mix business with pleasure, but thanks just the same.

Of course, Patrick Stinson was more charming than most, and many people were depending on this deal. Ann would have to take a little extra care not to offend him, at least not yet.

He picked up one of the sketches and held it up for closer examination. "Why don't we spend a little time mulling these things over and meet again after I've had a little time to talk with my team?"

Margaret was already nodding. "Perfect."

"Can I buy lunch for you ladies? We could continue to talk about the project."

The invitation held little appeal. Ann wanted to keep some space between Patrick Stinson and herself until the deal was

made—no sense asking for trouble. Besides, lunch with Margaret
was never a happy thought.

She stood and loaded her purse on her arm. "I'm sure the
two of you will want to talk over the details, so I'll leave you to
it. I've got several things to take care of at the office."

Margaret grabbed Ann's arm and hissed, "I don't think
it's anything that can't wait, Ann." She looked at Patrick. "Of
course, lunch sounds wonderful."

And so Ann spent the next two hours not getting the
work done that she needed to do, and listening to increasingly
flirtatious comments from Patrick Stinson. He *was* charming,
and Ann found herself enjoying his company. This seemed to
unnerve Margaret, which made it all the better. Somewhere in
the back of Ann's mind, she knew this was dangerous, but after
a while, she thought maybe she simply didn't care.

Chapter 10

Ann had ordered takeout Chinese for dinner, too exhausted to attempt a trip to the market. She stood at her kitchen counter eating Kung Pao chicken out of the carton while thumbing through the large stack of mail she'd retrieved on the way in.

There were the usual assortment of bills, the newest edition of *Elle Decor*, and plenty of junk mail. Then a pale blue envelope caught her eye. The return address was missing, but it was postmarked Charleston. She ripped the flap open and saw a single piece of folded white paper inside. She pulled it out, opened it, and stared down at a crayon drawing of a stick figure with long dark hair and tears dripping from her face onto the ground. On the far edge of the paper was another stick figure, shorter, with big glasses. In between the two was a large glob of golden octopus. She knew instinctively what this picture was. It was Ann, and Keith, and an angel in between them.

She'd spent the last twenty-four hours convincing herself that nothing in Charleston mattered. She had almost completely put all the people, all the events, all the music out of her mind, until one childlike drawing smacked it right back in. This was something she couldn't indulge; strength was needed at all costs. She wadded up the paper and threw it in the trash.

Leaving the remainder of the mail behind, she wandered out onto her balcony. There was something comforting about the sound of the people on the street below, the mindless hum of many voices, some laughing, some shouting, some simply talking. They all blended together into a kind of mind-numbing buzz that kept any one voice from mattering too much. That's what Ann liked. Voices that were at a safe distance. Not up close. Not giving hugs and saying how much they loved her. And definitely not talking about songs that didn't exist, sung by angels that didn't exist. Yep, a good dose of the drone of reality was all Ann needed to put her head back on straight.

She tried to refocus on her work. She'd been sketching a kitchen for Mrs. Benson this afternoon. Something about it still wasn't quite right; something seemed to be missing.

When exhaustion threatened to overtake her, she walked back inside. A quick glance toward the stack of mail, then in the direction of the trash can, triggered an idea. What Mrs. Benson's kitchen needed was more color—shocking color, much like the brightness of Keith's golden octopus. High-gloss yellow cabinetry, even a yellow ceiling. It would contrast with the Lake Placid Blue granite and turn the entire kitchen into an abstract work of art.

Before she even realized what she was doing, she walked to the trash can and uncrumpled Keith's picture. Her hands seemed to act of their own will as they smoothed out the creases and wrinkles. Then she walked to the refrigerator and hung the paper in the clip she usually reserved for her grocery list or important to-do memos.

She put her fingers to her lips, then pressed them to the picture. "I don't think much of your angels, but the color scheme is great. Thank you, Keith."

Ann dreamed of Keith that night. She saw his face ghost-white, his lips pale, and heard him gasping for breath. Behind him stood an angel—at first it was the chubby toddler version of a cherub frequently depicted in paintings. Then the sky turned gold, taking on a brilliant phosphorescent glow that continued to morph around him until it became one of Keith's yellow octopuslike creatures, breathtaking and fearsome. Music came from all around, filling the room, the building, and even the air he was breathing. Keith smiled weakly up into the glow above him. "I knew you'd come," he rasped. "I knew it."

Ann awoke with a start, the same song still flowing through her brain. Or was it here in her apartment?

She knew, in that moment, a truth she'd hoped not to face. The song, the insanity, *had* followed her to New York. Her mind would never be free from thoughts of Charleston—it wouldn't be free of the paracusias—until all ties to that place were gone.

She got dressed as quickly as possible, then took pen and paper down to the corner coffee shop. There she sipped a chai latte and composed a list of all the things she needed to do to prepare the house for listing, then ranked each in order of priority. She'd hire Ethan to work on the place. If she actually paid him, their barter agreement would be null, and she wouldn't feel guilty about not going back there and helping.

Relieved to see that it could be so easy—on paper at least—she left the shop with a renewed sense of purpose. She was going to be stressed to the limits financially, but the end results—the Stinson job, her new partnership with Margaret, and her sanity—would be worth it.

It was just a few minutes after seven when she arrived at the office. No one would be there for another hour, and it would be a good time to get a big leap on her day. Except the lights were already turned on, and the door to Margaret's office was open. This was not a good sign. Even less of a good sign was the handwritten note Ann found on her desk: *Come see me as soon as you get in.*

Ann couldn't imagine what had gone wrong since she'd seen Margaret in such high spirits yesterday. Had Ann forgotten to do something? She'd already blazed through a good portion of the paperwork on her desk, and the Stinson presentation had been well received. During the course of yesterday afternoon, she'd managed to greatly calm the über-uptight Stephanie Simpkins and promised to come by late this morning to start getting her Gramercy Park project all set up. Well, whatever Margaret's problem, best to get on with it. Ann had a full day ahead of her and needed to get to it.

"Good morning, Margaret." Ann said the words as she walked into the office.

Margaret put her hand to her heart. "Thank goodness you're here. I got a call last night from Patrick Stinson. He definitely wants to use our firm."

"That's great news." And it was, but something about the stress in Margaret's tone said something was not so good.

"Yes. Yes, it is. He's having his lawyers look over the

contracts, but apparently they are already backed up on another issue. He has asked that we go ahead and begin to get the groundwork done for the job in the meantime."

"We don't do that." The words slipped out of Ann's mouth before she thought enough to stop them.

Margaret stared back, her penciled-in left eyebrow cocked almost to her hairline. "Don't we?" Her words were cold and hard.

"That's your rule; obviously you know we don't. We've never started work on a project before the contracts were signed and sealed."

Margaret stretched her neck, tilting her head from side to side. "True. But we've never had a client with the clout of Patrick Stinson. If we can keep him happy and earn his business, the sky is the limit as far as what we'll be able to do."

Ann knew Margaret was right. She also knew that Patrick Stinson did not have the same incentive; he had no reason to make certain that Marston Home Staging was happy. Still, Margaret was the boss. If she wanted to gamble with her company, that was her prerogative—at least until Ann became a partner. For now, it helped Ann get what she wanted as well. "Okay, I'll start getting things together."

"Fine. By the way, next Thursday night the Stinson Company is having an open house at their new condo project over on Eighty-sixth Street, and Patrick Stinson wants us there."

"Why?" They hadn't been the designers on the job, and they'd already seen the pictures. It didn't make sense.

"It doesn't matter. He's our client, our *biggest* client *ever*. If he wants us to come to an event, I don't care if it's his son's bar mitzvah or his grandmother's funeral, we're going to be there."

A nighttime event made the perfect setup for line-crossing relationships—something Ann knew she should avoid for the time being. "Do we both need to go?"

"As owner of the company, of course I'm going to go, and as the designer that Patrick Stinson specifically requested on this job, of course you're going to be there."

"Obviously, I would love to be there. It's just that I was planning to leave for Charleston on Thursday night and take a long weekend." These words were out before Ann realized it. Still, she decided that perhaps, in this case, it was better to face hallucination-inducing twelve-year-olds than the alternative.

"Next weekend? You're thinking of leaving next weekend?" Margaret's voice almost screeched, revealing a rare loss of control. "That is not acceptable. You need to change your plans because we need you to be at that open house. This is not the time to offend Patrick Stinson."

Little did Margaret know, that's exactly what Ann was trying to do—keep a safe distance and avoid any potential offense. "I could change my flight to Friday morning, I suppose, then come back Tuesday morning." If Margaret knew the tickets had not yet been purchased—and in fact, the trip had not been planned—she would shut it down, and Ann couldn't allow that. At least a next-morning flight gave her an excuse to leave the reception early.

Margaret rubbed her temples. "Am I to assume this will be the last of such trips for some time to come?"

"There might be more, but I'll keep them as few as possible, and over weekends." She paused, then added, "Of course, I'll make certain to keep up with my projects here; I won't let the travel take away from that."

"This is the worst possible time for this. Couldn't you let the house sit for a month or two? What's it going to hurt?"

More than Margaret knew, but better to stay with concrete facts that she could understand. "Margaret, I believe we made a deal allowing me to buy in as partner, so I have plenty of incentive to seal the deal with Stinson. Besides, as I'm sure you recall, a few months ago I agreed to a sizable pay cut to help keep this company going without layoffs—and yet layoffs happened anyway. I'm barely making my rent and expenses right now; I can't afford the financial burden of a second home." Ann didn't mention the fact that said home was paid off, and the only financial burdens were Internet, cable, electric, and water. "I'll make certain the office can reach me at all times."

"You'd better. Or else." There was no hint of levity in her voice.

Chapter 11

As Ethan pulled into Tammy's driveway, he glanced toward the empty house next door. Just to make certain that things looked in order, that nothing appeared to be disturbed. Keeping an eye on the place, that's all. It had absolutely nothing to do with Annie, or the still urgent feeling that he was supposed to help her somehow, even though she was in New York, and in spite of—or maybe because of—her fierce independent streak that refused offers of help.

Why was it that the more she claimed *not* to need help, the more determined he became to help her? Sarah's independence never struck him that way, but with Ann, it was almost an obsession. Then, of course, there was the single freckle on her right cheekbone that he had the insane desire to touch.

No, none of that mattered. It was probably just old habit, since he'd had so many good memories over there when Sarah was alive, when he'd have lunch with Tammy, Keith, and Danielle on the patio. *Whatever you do, don't ask Tammy if she's heard from her. You make one move toward weakness and more are sure to follow.*

"Ethan, hi." Keith was climbing down the steps, waving, before Ethan even got out of the truck. "You ready to play?" He held a small football in his hand.

Ethan climbed out of the truck and held up both hands. "You bet I am. Hit me, I'm open."

Keith threw the ball, almost falling in the process. It landed several feet short. "Oh, man, I'm not very good at this. Sorry, Ethan."

"Like I've told you before, buddy, even professional athletes warm up before the big games. I should have been closer for our warm-up throws."

"Keith, didn't I tell you not to demand Ethan's attention the minute he pulled up?" Tammy was at the door now, fists on hips, looking a mixture of frustrated, amused, and exhausted.

Ethan held up his hands. "My fault. I told him I was open."

Tammy rolled her eyes and smiled. "You could at least bring in the dessert first. Especially if you did the usual stop-at-the-grocery-store-and-buy-a-gallon-of-ice-cream-on-the-way kind of dessert. It'll just sit in your truck and melt."

"Who, me?" Ethan tried to look offended but was pretty certain he wasn't pulling it off very well. "As a matter of fact, that's not at all what I did. I brought homemade brownies, thank you very much."

"You? Made brownies?"

"That's not what I said. I said I *brought* homemade brownies."

"Then who made them?"

"You know that colonial I've been remodeling? Their youngest daughter just graduated from high school, and they had a big family shindig last night. This afternoon they sent me home with a couple boxes of leftovers."

"So you're bringing recycled food?"

"I wouldn't exactly call it that. It sounds so . . . *gross*."

Tammy laughed. "Well, get me the brownies before they get all gooey."

Ethan opened the passenger door and removed the plate of plastic-wrap-covered brownies. He nodded toward Sarah's house. "This neighborhood is never going to be the same, is it?"

"No, it's not." Tammy shook her head. "I miss her so much." She wiped at her eyes. "You want to hear something weird? Keith keeps talking about 'Annie,' and about angels watching over her, and I've realized I really miss Ann too. Almost as much as Sarah, which sounds really strange. I mean, maybe it's just because Keith is sending her a new angel drawing every single day, and I'm the one mailing them, that she's on my mind so much. I just met her, but somehow I just feel like she's a part of this place. Sounds crazy, doesn't it?"

Ethan understood more than Tammy knew. "Really? I mean, she seems to be a New Yorker through and through. Do you really think she could belong here?"

"Don't you?" She asked the question point-blank. There was no mistaking her meaning.

"Well, I . . ." *No weakness. Don't you dare give an inch.*

"Hey, Ethan, you ready yet?"

One thing Ethan could say about Keith, the kid had great timing. "Yes, I am, buddy."

Ann's computer screen cast a hazy green light around her

cubicle. This place definitely needed better lighting—how was she supposed to get inspired while working in flubber-colored ambience?

"Have I told you lately how much I love you for landing the Stinson account?" Beka leaned over the partial wall that separated their work spaces. "Well, I know I told you yesterday, but have I told you today yet?"

Ann looked into the tired eyes of her friend, and in this moment, she knew that whatever it took, holding on to that account was worth it. "You can thank me if I come out on the other side still alive."

Beka laughed, having no idea how much truth was in Ann's words. "Yeah, right, Miss Cooler-than-the-Rooms-She-Designs. I'll bet you won't even break a sweat. In fact, I'm guessing you already know exactly what you're going to do for all twenty units on the ground floor. Am I right?"

It wasn't until this very moment that Ann realized just how strong of a front she actually put on. It helped to calm her, though, realizing that not even Beka knew how terrified she was. "Almost." No point in letting down her guard now. Beka needed her strength, and Ann would fake her way through it for as long as she could.

"Hey, I've got to take some things over to that penthouse by Central Park—you know, the one on Museum Mile. Would you have some time to come with me? I'm still not sure what to do with the terraces and I was hoping to get your opinion."

"Like you have ever once liked the outdoor furniture I've selected for anything." Ann grinned, knowing that Beka's traditional taste did not run toward Ann's edgy designs.

"I'm actually thinking more of landscaping. You've always had a good eye for proportion." Beka looked at her. "Please? We can go walk around the Met during our lunch hour. They have an exhibit by one of my favorite artists, and there're a couple of paintings I just can't get enough of. It's like they replenish my soul."

Ann had a pile of work to plow through, but she knew that if she didn't go, neither would Beka. If anyone needed to take some time to replenish, she did. "Sure, sounds good."

"Thanks, Ann. You're the best."

"Yeah, yeah, that's what you always say after you've talked me into something."

"That's right." Beka flashed a quick smile.

"Let me just finish what I'm doing. It'll only take a few minutes."

"By all means, take your time. As Mrs. Crawford used to say in Design Development class, 'Excellence cannot be rushed.' Besides, I'm counting on your design genius to make us all rich and famous someday."

Ann knew Beka *was* counting on her. Not for riches but for survival. She just hoped she'd be able to come through.

"Okay, come over here, check this out. Isn't it amazing?"

Ann stared, trying desperately to figure out what Beka could possibly see in this painting. "Well, uh, it's nice, I guess."

"Nice? *Nice?* Ann, look at it. Can't you just feel the emotion pulsating off the canvas?"

"Not really. Besides, it's not canvas; it's wood. See, says right here, 'Oil on wood.'"

"Will you quit being so literal and look? Tell me what you see."

"Well, I see a really pale, depressed-looking woman, holding a piece of paper in her hand."

"Use your imagination. It's a letter. Who is it from? Is it from her beloved, telling her he will return on the morrow? The look on her face is not depression; it's longing. She doesn't have what she wants right now, but it's coming so soon she can taste it. Her dreams are about to come true."

"'On the morrow'? Since when do you talk like that?"

"Not me. Her. That's what she's thinking, so that's the way I said it. Lighten up."

"I'll lighten up, all right. Right over to the next painting. This one's a little more my style. A city on fire. Yep, that must have been one big party."

"Oh, stop it."

"Look, it's even the same artist, Camille Corot. She must have let loose a little in her later years or something. Instead of waiting for her love to return *on the morrow*, she decided to party like there *was no morrow*." Ann had always loved teasing Beka, but lately, it was the only time she saw Beka smile. Ann stopped when she noticed a figure at the top of the painting. "Oh, wow, that's an angel up there throwing down all that fire, isn't it? Yikes."

"Yes, it's Sodom and Gomorrah, you doof. Now keep moving. See, here's another of *his* pictures. He's one of my favorite artists."

"Camille Corot is a guy's name?"

"His full name is Jean Batiste Camille Corot, if that tells you anything."

"More than I cared to know, thank you very much. Come on, let's go look at some modern art. My soul needs feeding too."

"Wait, the next one is my other favorite—*Hagar in the Wilderness.*"

Ann looked at the picture of a woman—a mother, probably—kneeling beside a child on the ground, who looked as though he might be dead. The mother had one hand in the air and the other on her forehead, crying in despair beside him. "What could you possibly see in that picture? It's past depressing. It's downright abysmal."

"No, you've got to look at it, to see the whole picture."

"Let me guess, you've made up a story to go with this one too."

"Didn't have to—it's in the Bible."

"Huh?"

"You know who Abraham is, right?"

"More or less."

"Well, Hagar was Abraham's servant—well, his wife Sarah's servant—and when Sarah wasn't able to have children, she had Hagar sleep with Abraham, to bear him a child. The boy lying on the ground is that son. His name was Ishmael."

"Ew. What kind of wife would do that? And what kind of servant would agree?"

"Times were different then, I guess."

"I guess so. So they didn't like the kid after he grew up, or what?"

"Sarah eventually had her own son, Isaac. Ishmael didn't treat him so well."

"Don't think I need imagination to figure that one out."

Beka laughed. "I guess not. Anyway, eventually Sarah got so angry that she insisted that Abraham send Hagar and Ishmael away. They were sent into the wilderness."

"Tell me again now, why would you want to look at a painting of that story?"

"Look in the sky. See the angel?"

Ann did see it, hovering above the trees in the background. "Yeah, what about it?"

"At the very darkest times of my life, I know that there are angels watching over me."

Ann knew that Beka's faith ran deep, even though they rarely talked about it. "Doesn't seem to be doing her any good." *Or you and Gracie any good.*

"He will. In just a second, she'll hear his voice, telling her that her son will be a great nation. She's going to find a well of water in the very next scene. That angel, he's with them, even though they don't know it yet."

A picture flashed through Ann's mind of the handful of angel pictures currently in her top dresser drawer. She couldn't quite bring herself to throw them away, as much as she really wanted to. One picture in particular showed Ann looking toward the sky, much like Hagar was doing now, with an angel in the background. "I . . . I've got to get back to the office."

Beka reached over and hugged her. "Do you have any idea how precious you are?"

"Precious? I think I'm offended."

Ann saw the red hair a second before she saw the face, but the recognition was instant. Yet—it couldn't be.

"Well, hello, Ann. What a treat to find you here." Eleanor Light approached from the left, wearing a beige pantsuit and a smile. "Checking out some Corot paintings? He's one of my favorites."

"Mine too." Beka smiled. "I'm Beka, by the way."

Eleanor extended her hand. "Eleanor." She looked at Ann. "Somehow I don't quite believe he's one of Ann's favorites."

"I like the one with the letter." No reason not to be polite.

Beka shoved her arm. "You do not. You told me you hated it."

"Ah," Eleanor said. "Perhaps that was before she saw the next ones—they can be a bit more shocking than the first." She moved forward as if to study the painting of Hagar. "Funny, I've always found that when a piece of art disturbs me, there's something in it I need to learn about myself. I wonder what this one is trying to teach us?"

"To stick with modern art." Ann tried to laugh, but it didn't work. Time to change the subject. "What brings you to New York?"

"Oh, I'm here on business for a few days. I thought it would be nice to visit the museum while I was here." Eleanor moved closer to the painting of Sodom and Gomorrah. "Interesting, isn't it, the different jobs that angels have. This one is destroying a city; this one is helping an outcast in the wilderness. A rather diverse job description." She looked at her watch. "Oh dear. I hate to be rude, but I have to run. It was awfully nice to have met you, Beka." She squeezed Ann's forearm. "See you soon, I hope." She turned and walked briskly from the room.

Beka sighed. "Wow, she has the most beautiful hair. It's the exact same hue as that burnished-copper Moroccan wedding tray I just bought for the Browns' loft. I showed it to you, right?"

"Let's get out of here."

"Eleanor was right. You *are* disturbed."

"Back to the office. Now."

Chapter 12

Through the spotless floor-to-ceiling windows, Ann watched scores of well-dressed people mill around the new lobby. As she climbed out of the cab, she questioned the wisdom of not bringing a date. She was certain that she wouldn't know anyone here, and she was not in the mood to make small talk. In fact, she wasn't in the mood to talk at all.

She wished she'd thought of calling Richard. He was always good for an evening out on the town. Somehow he could work a room at a party, taking all the pressure off Ann to do so, yet he never came across as obnoxious. He was one of her favorite dates for an event like this and was usually available for last-minute calls. But she wanted to get in and out as fast as she could, and things always got more complicated when there was another person to consider.

"Welcome. I need your name, please." A woman in a black pantsuit stood at a table near the door.

"Ann Fletcher."

The woman smiled in a knowing way. "Ms. Fletcher, right." She looked down the list of names and made a check mark. Then, gesturing toward the guests, she said, "Bars are set up on both sides of the lobby. Feel free to have a look around." She smiled. "Enjoy yourself."

"Thank you." Ann walked toward the bar, trying to decide whether having a couple of drinks to take the edge off tonight was worth feeling sluggish tomorrow. Definitely. The bartender wore a black vest and white shirt. "What's your poison?"

"Chardonnay, please."

He turned around and lifted a green bottle out of an ice bucket, the cork already removed and lightly resting on top. Before he could pour, a voice from behind Ann said, "Don't give her that. Ann is a special guest; she gets the good stuff."

The man nodded without saying a word and reached beneath the counter. Ann turned to face Patrick Stinson. "That's really not necessary."

"Of course it is. If we're going to be working together for the foreseeable future, I want to make certain that you are treated well when you are in my territory, just like you're taking good care of me in yours." His eyes were a deep shade of brown framed by dark lashes. Everything about him was . . . *perfect*.

Yes, she definitely should have brought a date. "Thanks. I'm looking forward to our upcoming projects."

"As am I." He lifted his glass in a silent toast and Ann clinked her glass against his. "I'm thinking that later on tonight—"

"Patrick, you've outdone yourself. This is the best building yet." The man in an Armani suit made just enough distraction to break the magnetic pull of Patrick Stinson.

Time to move elsewhere. She mumbled something about seeing someone across the room and made an escape while she had the chance.

"Hi, I'm Meredith. You must be the new stager."

Ann looked at the breathtaking blonde who had just stepped in front of her and wondered who she might be. "Yes, I'm Ann Fletcher. I'll be working on the Stinson Towers project."

Meredith tossed her golden curls over her bare shoulder. "What do you think of the condo setups for this place?"

"I haven't walked through yet, but I've seen pictures. To tell you the truth, I've never seen anything so amazing." Ann could have added, "I am totally unworthy to follow in these footsteps and scared out of my wits," but she didn't. She settled for, "Incredible attention to detail."

Meredith stared at Ann long and hard, as if trying to decide whether or not to believe her. Finally, she said, "I'm the one who designed them."

Ann felt the heat on her cheeks. It seemed wrong to be at the party to celebrate the job done by the person her company was replacing, but it certainly hadn't been her idea. "Well then, I'm especially glad to meet you. I think you are extremely talented."

Meredith nodded, but her eyes looked doubtful. "Maybe you can keep his attention longer than I did. I wish you the best of luck." She flung her hair over her shoulder and walked toward the bar.

Ann watched for a few seconds. Sour grapes? Or yet another legitimate warning to keep a distance between herself and Patrick Stinson?

"Ann, you're looking lovely as always." Margaret's fourth husband came to stand beside her.

"Thank you, Edward. And where is your lovely wife?"

He shrugged and tossed back most of the contents of his martini glass. "She's around here somewhere. You know Margaret."

"Yes, I do." Ann smiled, as if it were cute that Margaret avoided her husband at parties, or that she needed to because he drank to excess in social situations. She started to make an excuse to move on but saw Patrick heading their general direction. "So, Edward, do you want to take a tour with me? I've been dying to check this place out and would love some company."

"Sure. Let's make a little stop at the bar first."

Two hours and several bar stops later, Ann managed to make it out the door and flag down a taxi. As it pulled to the curb, she heard a voice behind her. "Surely you're not leaving so soon. Was my party not exciting enough for you?"

"It was perfect. I've got an early flight in the morning, so I'm sneaking out a little early."

"You're leaving town while my job is getting started?"

"I've got to get back to Charleston for a few days—estate issues."

He nodded. "You know, I've been thinking about some real estate down south. Maybe we'll have to talk project ideas after you get back."

Ann nodded. "Don't worry. I'll still be working on your project, even while I'm down there."

"Good, I wouldn't want you to forget about me while you're gone." There was no subtlety in his tone. This was going to be tricky.

Ann looked at him as if he'd just recited tomorrow's weather and said, "Enjoy the rest of your party." She climbed into the cab and waved good-bye to the handsome Patrick Stinson.

Chapter 13

Ann pulled her rolling suitcase through Charleston International Airport, stood in the line at the car rental counter, and drove to the house, all while functioning on autopilot. There were things to be done, and she was doing them by focusing on the next task ahead. It was the only way she could move forward.

She turned into the driveway of Sarah's house and let the tires follow the two narrow strips of concrete separated by grass that was overdue for mowing. She hit the brakes. Her autopilot clicked off, and reality burst through. And Ann was forced to navigate it alone. Not until this very minute, when she looked at the outside of the gray stucco house that had been her home for most of her growing-up years, did the full impact of her aloneness . . . the absolute finality of it . . . hit her. She was alone. She was always going to be alone. The only two people who had ever loved her were gone forever—Nana, who died of cancer several years ago, and Sarah just two weeks ago. Ann was a thirty-year-old woman with an entire lifetime of aloneness in her future.

Sobs exploded from her chest while she sat in the driveway, her car still running. The subconscious mind had a terrible sense of timing. Why couldn't it be when she was back in New York? In her own apartment? With other ways to cope?

"Annie, you oh-kay?" The voice was slightly muffled by the driver's-side window, but she could still tell it was Keith's. When she looked up, his face was a half inch from the glass, and both his hands were cupped above his eyes and pressed into the window.

Ann barked out, "I'm fine," without bothering to lower the window. She slowly eased off the brake, and when she was certain she wasn't going to run over Keith's foot, she rolled forward until she reached the small detached garage. She reached inside her carry-on bag to find the remote. Fumbling beneath her wallet, her iPod, and her latest design magazine, she finally grasped the plastic box and pushed the button. She watched the old wooden door rise slowly, then she eased the car inside. She turned the engine off and prepared for the next assault by Keith.

"You look sad." Sure enough, Keith had followed her, his face now plastered against the driver's-side window. His hands were planted a few inches from where they'd left smudges just seconds ago. In the weird light filtering into the garage, his face looked pale. Very pale. It brought back a flash of her dream in New York.

Ann slowly pushed the door open, careful not to hit him. She wiped her hands across her face and climbed from the car. "Hi, Keith. I'm glad to see you, but I'm really busy right now. I'll talk to you later, okay?"

She moved past him toward the front door. Once she was inside the house, she could lock the door and cry alone.

"Oh, Ann, I'm so glad to see you. We hoped you might be back sometime soon." Tammy's drawl seemed thicker than usual, maybe because Ann had just spent the week in New York, or maybe just because she was in a hurry, which made her notice the drawn-out speech.

Ann turned her face away. Keith might be easy enough to trick, but Tammy would take one look at her and know that she'd been crying. "Yeah, I'm just back here to do some work on the house. The sooner I get this place fixed up, the sooner I can get it on the market." Ann opened the screen door and put her key into the lock.

The silence that followed made her believe that Tammy must have taken the hint or had been offended enough that she'd left. She peeked over her left shoulder to confirm. Instead, she saw Tammy standing at the foot of the steps, her mouth agape. "You're going to sell the place?"

Ann turned the key. "Well, yeah, there's no one to keep it up. It's silly for me to hang on to it." Ann walked inside and tossed her purse on the kitchen table, knowing instinctively that Tammy and Keith would follow.

A musty smell had invaded the place. It had been empty for less than two weeks, and it seemed that the lack of an inhabitant was already taking its toll. She heard Tammy's footsteps behind her and had a brilliant idea for a new tactic. "I know you want to keep the neighborhood nice, and I'd hate for you to be stuck next door to a house that no one is tending. The lawn's already a mess, and see how this place smells? It's only been a little over a week since I was here."

"I guess I'd just assumed . . . just hoped . . . that maybe you would consider moving back here. I know this house has been in your family for a long time; I thought you might want to hang on to it for a while."

There were very few things about her past that Ann cared to hang on to, not the least of which was a traditional Charleston homestead. She shook her head and said simply, "I don't think so." Let Tammy make of that what she would.

"That's too bad, then." Tammy didn't say anything else, but didn't make a move to leave either. This woman took a hint slower than anyone Ann had ever met.

"Well, I'm going to bring in my suitcase now, go do some grocery shopping, that kind of thing. So I'll see you later, okay? Thanks for stopping by, bless your heart."

"Oh, of course. Of course you have things to do." Tammy turned to look at Keith, who was hovering in the doorway, smiling timidly at Ann. "Keith, let's help Ann bring in her things from the car, okay?"

"Okay." He disappeared without a further word, and she followed.

"That's really not necessary." They were wasted words; Ann knew this even as she said them. "I'm perfectly capable of getting it myself."

"Of course it's necessary; doesn't matter what you're capable of. We want to help you in any way that we can, don't we, Keith? That's what friends do, help each other. In fact, I need to go to the grocery store too. Why don't we make it a group shopping trip? Things like that are so much better when shared with a friend."

"No, really—"

"I insist. Let me just go get my list and lock up the house. Do you want me to stop by and pick you up, or do you want to just walk over?"

Ann pictured Keith hovering in her doorway and talking about angels while Tammy waited in the car outside. The picture disturbed her enough that she said, "I'll walk over. Give me a few minutes."

"All right then. Come on over when you're ready." Tammy and Keith made their way across the lawn to their house.

What had just happened here? Ann lived in New York, for crying out loud. She worked in the business world and was not afraid to play hardball with the best of them. So how was it that this woman with a bow full of badly permed hair and hovering son managed to get her to do something she absolutely did not want to do—and they managed to pull this off over and over again?

Then she remembered her dream. And she began to wonder. Was she just imagining it, or did his face really seem extra pale today?

Ann shook her head. Apparently her imagination was still having trouble staying in check while she was in Charleston. Time to take control of this. These things were not real, and by sheer determination, Ann would excise them from her mind.

Chapter 14

"We'll help you bring your groceries in." Tammy was out of the car and grabbing bags from the trunk before Ann could protest. Keith followed, carrying a twelve-pack of vitaminwater and humming softly to himself.

"Danielle will be so sorry that she missed your visit. She's out of the country, you know. Did she tell you about her photo safari?"

"Safari? Like Africa?" Ann had trouble picturing Danielle anywhere other than an air-conditioned home with all the amenities.

"Yeah. She goes on those things for a couple of months at a time. One of the benefits of never marrying, I suppose, is the freedom to retire the way you want to." Tammy looked a little wistful as she said it. "It's not just play though, she does volunteer work with WorldVision, helping rural villages find ways to capture clean drinking water. Oh, the stories she'll tell you when she gets home." She reached for her bag. "I'll help you put these things away."

"Really, I've got it. I know you've got ice cream that's melting as we speak." Tammy's smothering helpfulness was getting old. It wasn't that Ann didn't appreciate it exactly; she simply didn't need help.

"Thanks for taking me to the store; I'll see you later." This sounded a little more New York direct than she'd intended, so she followed it up with, "You've just done so much for me already, bless your heart."

Ann knew what Tammy's next move would be. She would say something like, "I bought a pot roast, which is too much for just Keith and me. Don't you want to come over for dinner?" Ann was preparing a firm but gracious "no" when Tammy said, "Okay then, all done. I'll see you tomorrow, okay?"

What? This stunned Ann enough that she couldn't think of a way to respond. She finally managed to say, "All right, sounds good." The weirdest thing about it was, after Tammy closed the door, Ann felt more than a little sting of rejection. She hadn't been *that* blunt, had she? Why didn't Tammy want her over for dinner?

Ridiculous. Absolutely ridiculous.

Ann plopped the milk carton into the refrigerator, then put a couple of John's Island tomatoes in the windowsill so they could finish ripening, just the way Nana used to do it. That little bit of nostalgia brought back the grief from earlier today, and she found herself crying again. Not with all-out sobs this time, just an overflow of sadness that kept running down her cheeks.

The doorbell rang. "Just a minute," Ann called, loud enough, she hoped, to be heard. She splashed cold water on her face and dried it with a kitchen towel, then went and opened the door.

"Hello there." Ethan McKinney stood on the doorstep, his hair slightly damp. "I heard you were back in town."

Ann didn't have to ask where he'd heard the news. She glanced toward Tammy's house, wondering if this was the reason she hadn't mentioned dinner. "Yeah, just arrived a little while ago, still getting settled."

He nodded. "Did I interrupt anything?" He was careful not to look directly in her eyes. Ann surmised that he could tell she had been crying and was choosing to ignore it. She was grateful for that.

"Oh, I'm just putting away groceries. You want to come in and have something to drink?" Now would be a good time to talk to Ethan about her new plan. She'd been meaning to call him ever since she'd figured things out at the coffee shop.

He looked doubtful. "Well, I don't want to intrude or anything. I mean I know you're just getting settled, and I know you've had a long trip, and I know that things around here—"

"No, it's fine. Really, come on in." She held the door a little wider until he walked in. "I've just got to get a couple of things into the fridge, but there's something I wanted to talk to you about anyway. Come on into the kitchen."

"All right if I help? I'm sure I'll put everything in the wrong spot, but I figure there's not really much you can mess up when you're putting veggies in the fridge, right?" He picked up a bag of produce and walked toward the refrigerator. "What'd you want to talk to me about?"

Ann unloaded the bread and some wheat crackers into a cabinet that served as a pantry. "I need to get this place ready to sell faster than I'd originally thought, and things are really busy in New York right now. I know we made a barter agreement, but I really think it would simplify things if I just hired you and let you finish up the work while I'm gone."

"I don't mind working while you're gone, but like I said, I'm not for hire in your case."

"Then I'll have to find someone who is." Ann turned and leaned against the counter, arms folded across her chest.

Ethan looked at her evenly, then finally said, "How long you in town for?"

"Tuesday."

"All right. How about tomorrow I rent a couple of sanders and we start refinishing the hardwood floors?" He nodded toward the scarred floor under the kitchen table. "They're pretty beat up. I could get here a little before noon; we could at least get the back rooms done."

"This might be my last time back here for a long time. I'm telling you I likely will not have a chance to repay my part of the bargain."

"That's my problem, isn't it?" Ethan put his palm against the wall beside the kitchen door. "You know, if we blew out this wall right here and took out this little breezeway, we could add a nice walk-in pantry. I'm sure it would help the sale price of the house a lot. Kitchens and baths are what everyone looks at." He looked at Ann then, and his face turned faintly red. "Guess I don't need to tell you that, huh? You know about that kind of stuff as much as I do, more probably, because I'm sure in New York—"

"That's not a bad idea." Exactly how many times could she interrupt one person without offending him? Somehow, with Ethan, she was more than certain she was going to get to that answer eventually.

Ann looked at the wall and considered what he'd just said. She was used to a small space, living in a New York studio, but she knew that most of today's consumers preferred a larger kitchen. "It'd be a little pricey for what I was planning to do, but do you think it would pay for itself in the end?"

"I told you. I'm working for free."

"And I told you I'm not taking charity. Besides, there would be all the dry wall, et cetera. The supplies alone will be costly. And . . . it would require more time than I was hoping to spend on this project."

"That wouldn't bother me."

Ann wasn't sure if he was talking about the supplies or the extra time. She chose to believe it was the supplies. "Let me think about it, but you might be right."

"You want to try out Magnolia's tonight? We can work on our plans while we eat."

"I don't think . . ." Ann was searching her mind for an excuse that seemed valid enough not to hurt his feelings when her cell phone rang. "Excuse me for just a minute."

"Sure." He leaned against the counter, his hands on each side of him, looking perfectly at home.

Ann walked toward the living room. Ethan would still be able to hear her there, but at least she wouldn't be talking in his face. "This is Ann."

"Yes. It is." Patrick Stinson's tone fell somewhere between silky and oil-slick. "I'm calling to make certain that you are thinking about me, just like you promised you would be."

"As promised, I'm thinking about your project. I worked on some of the sketches today during the flight—fine-tuned some of the things we've talked about, started working on a few new ideas."

"Good, that's what I like to hear. I want our partnership to keep moving forward because I think we make a great pair." He paused then, waiting—Ann supposed—for her to fawn some sort of agreement. The fact that he used the word *pair* instead of *team* was not lost on her. Instead of responding, she simply let the silence hang between them like a shield.

Finally, he cleared his throat and laughed. "I think I like your style, Ann Fletcher. You hurry back to New York." And with that, the line went dead. Ann flipped her phone shut, fighting against an uncomfortable, almost slimy, sensation that oozed through her chest. It was silly really; he hadn't done or said anything truly wrong. Maybe it was just another symptom of her overactive imagination. She shivered once, then returned to the kitchen.

There, still leaning against the counter, stood Ethan McKinney—king of the run-on sentence. Something about his presence made her feel better; it seemed to clear the ick from her mind. Maybe a dinner with a normal human being was just the thing she needed. "You know what? Magnolia's sounds great."

Ethan looked over the edge of the menu. "I noticed there were a lot of bean sprouts and stuff like that in your groceries, but whether or not you avoid eating fat, you cannot eat at Magnolia's in Charleston and not have the she-crab soup. That just wouldn't be right."

"I don't think so. I grew up in Charleston, so I shouldn't have to do all the things a tourist would do."

"That all depends. How long's it been since you were here—other than two weeks ago?"

Ann slowly removed her napkin and set it on her lap, then took a sip of water. "A few years, I guess." She continued to stare at the white linen tablecloth.

"How many's a few?"

Ann took a sip of water. "Seven." She whispered the word, as if it hurt her to say it.

He knew as much. He took a sip of his own water. "Since your grandmother's funeral."

"How did you know that?"

Sarah had often talked about trying to get Ann to come for a visit. She'd also talked about their mixed-up childhood and how Ann had fled Charleston, as if leaving here somehow removed her from the pain. Sarah's field of study had led her to psychoanalyzing most everything and everyone, but Ann's refusal to return home in particular disturbed her. "Well, I was at her funeral too, and I remember seeing you there. That was just after I got my contractor's license, and I know I've been in business over seven years now. It all adds up."

Ann toyed with her silverware, her eyes focused down. Perhaps he'd veered too far into personal territory, which always seemed to happen around her. He supposed that after living up north for a decade, she was used to people being a little more guarded. He leaned back in his chair and smiled. "Well, if it's been seven years, then you are a tourist, so yes, you do have to eat the soup. In fact, we'll also have to schedule a drive-through of some of the more historic districts, and maybe even a visit to Fort Sumter. We have to get you acclimated."

Ann looked up, clearly surprised by this change in subject. She leaned forward, elbows on the table, and gave him a half smile. "I've never been much of a history buff myself."

"You've just never had the right tour guide." *Danger, Will Robinson. Danger, danger. Stay focused; keep a clear head.* Ethan leaned toward her, pulled against his will. "I think I might know just the right person who could change your mind about that." Wow, she was beautiful. The candlelight danced in her eyes and even seemed to glow in her dark hair.

"You ready to order?" The waitress was suddenly standing beside them, looking at Ann.

"Sure. I'll have a salad, with honey mustard dressing on the side." She smiled at Ethan. "And a cup of the she-crab soup."

"That's my girl." No. She wasn't. But a guy could dream, couldn't he?

Chapter 15

The feeling of complete peace slipped away with Ann's dream, disappearing the very second she awoke, leaving a hollow place in its wake. She longed to return to the cocoon that had surrounded her—the warmth, the love. The music alone remained now, and it seemed to continue through the house long after she knew that she was fully awake. But that couldn't be.

She listened. It sounded like it was coming from somewhere near the back of the house. What was *wrong* with her? Well, she was going to hit this paracusia head-on. "You're not real," she said aloud as she threw off the blanket and walked into the short hallway between the two bedrooms. She stood motionless, not even daring to breathe. Was it coming from behind the door of her old room?

She reached for the doorknob and somehow managed to turn it, although everything inside her screamed against it. She pushed against the door, taking an involuntary step back as it swung slowly open. Then the music ceased.

Ann chanced a look inside. The room was mostly dark, her childhood curtains with the black-out lining still doing their job this many years later. She stood waiting for a few seconds, then reached inside and flipped the switch.

The old dresser lamp came to life, flickered for a moment or two, then went black. Well, changing a bulb was easy enough. She went to the linen cabinet where she'd seen spare bulbs, retrieved a seventy-five-watt compact fluorescent, and walked back to the room. Leaving the door wide open and hallway light on, she crossed the bedroom and raised the balloon shades on the windows. The morning light slanted across the room, creating a rectangle on the floor beside the dresser. She changed the bulb, repeating beneath her breath, "It wasn't real. It wasn't real."

The lamp blinked to life and Ann looked around. *See? Nothing here*. She breathed easier. The bedspread was different than when Ann had lived here. Back then it had been white and pink eyelet. Now it was a lacy floral combo in shades of purple and pink that made her think of elderly women in white gloves and hats. What had ever possessed Sarah to purchase such a busy piece of fabric?

Ann walked over and opened the closet, just to see what might be inside. A small canister vacuum, a dust mop, and a large clear plastic bag holding bed linens—one item so large it appeared to be a blanket or a comforter. Ann opened it. Sure enough, it was a dark blue cotton comforter, almost denim but not quite, and a set of white sheets. They looked almost new.

Well, here was the first order of business, changing the bedding. Not only would these bedcovers look better for future showings, but they also were something that she might actually be able to sleep under. After several nights on the couch, that was becoming a real possibility. She couldn't picture her psyche ever shutting down under that neon floral design, and she doubted a future buyer could either. Neutral colors allowed buyers to imagine themselves in the house.

The white linens smelled perfectly clean, but she didn't know how long they'd been stored. Better safe than sorry. She tossed the sheets into the washer just off the kitchen and set the comforter beside the front door. She'd have to find a Laundromat with a washing machine big enough to hold it. That would be part of her mission today.

Now she'd get busy on other ways to prepare the house. Item one on today's agenda was window measurements. She might as well get started in this room.

As she measured the double-hung windows, her thoughts drifted back to last night's dinner with Ethan. He'd seemed perfectly at ease and in control, unlike the Ethan she'd encountered before. This side of him was in charge. She had to admit it was comforting, although his bumbling side was not without its charm. Definitely refreshing after spending far too much time with the far too polished phonies she knew in New York.

It didn't matter, though. Ethan was the settle-down, raise-a-couple-of-kids, white-picket-fence type. Definitely no future in that kind of matchup. Time to quit thinking about it and measure the next set of windows. She walked to Nana's room.

Sarah's clothes still hung in the closet, and her books were piled on the dresser as if waiting for her return. Even her digital clock announced the time in its red numbers as though nothing had changed. Ann took a deep breath, willing herself to push through this. The room smelled a bit dusty, but underneath that, even after all these years, there was another scent. It smelled like . . . *Nana*. A hint of sachet, Jergen's lotion, and biscuits, all rolled into one nostalgic fragrance that was almost too much to bear. She turned and walked out, without ever measuring the windows.

The knock at the kitchen door could mean only one thing. Ann opened it to find Tammy, with Keith peering from behind her as usual. "Good morning. How'd you sleep?" Tammy was already walking inside as she asked the question.

"Not bad." It was less the sleeping and more the waking part that was a problem for Ann. She wouldn't mention that, though.

"Here, Annie, I made this for you." Keith held out a drawing of the usual Ann stickfigure, completely surrounded by golden sky. However, this time there weren't discernable octopuslike limbs, just bright light all around. "They're all around you, see?"

The picture reminded Ann of the warm sea dream. A lot. "Yes, I see. Thank you." She went to hang it on the refrigerator, while the memory of the peacefulness she'd felt washed over her.

"You know, if you're having trouble staying here by yourself, you're more than welcome to come stay at our place." Tammy was staring toward the blanket and pillow on the living room sofa. She shook her head almost imperceptibly. "I know I've told you that before, but I really do mean it. I want to make sure you understand that."

"Yes, I understand. I really am fine on my own. I'm just not ready to sleep in my old room yet. The sofa's just what I need. It's plenty soft."

"If maybe a couple of feet too short." Tammy continued to stare at the bedding on the couch, but she pulled up the large bag she was carrying in her right hand and set it on the counter. "I made something for you. I made it during your last visit, but the time just never seemed right to give it to you." Her voice broke.

"Made something?"

Tammy sniffed and nodded her head. "Yes." She reached into the bag and removed some decorative pillows, covered in the same bright fabric that currently covered the bed in her old room. "I made the bedspread in time for your visit, but I got busy on some rush projects and didn't finish the pillows in time. After the accident . . . well, I just wanted to do something special for you, so I finished these."

Ann's throat seemed to close. "You . . . made the bedspread in the guest room?"

Tammy beamed with pride. "Guilty. Sarah was always doing things to help me, I was so happy to be able to do something nice for her for a change. She mentioned that she thought the room was too dark with the navy comforter, and she was afraid you would find it depressing. So I surprised her by making something a little more colorful."

It occurred to Ann that the blue comforter in question lay piled by the front door, preparing for a trip to the laundry. She could only imagine how hurt Tammy would be if she saw it there. Ann could say she was getting rid of the comforter, but that would require a white lie—one that would be easily caught after she changed the bedding. So she instead put her arm around Tammy's shoulder to steer her away from its view. "Thanks for bringing the pillows over. I'll just go put them on the bed. You have a nice day, okay?" She pointed Tammy toward the kitchen door as she made this pronouncement.

"I'll come with you. I'd love a chance to see the whole ensemble together."

By now, this shouldn't have surprised Ann. She made a quick calculation about how she could get Tammy to and from the bedroom without giving her a clear view of the front door. "Sure. Right this way." Ann purposely positioned herself between Tammy and the door as they walked. "Let's just see how they look, shall we?"

"They'll be pretty." Keith's voice from directly behind them caught Ann off guard. She hadn't thought about what he might see, or what he might say.

Only when they were safely inside the bedroom did Ann fully relax. Mission accomplished.

Tammy arranged the pillows on the bed, then tilted her head to the side and tapped her index finger against her chin. "You know what? I think there might be a little too much pattern in here. Maybe I should have made the pillows solid purple. Or solid pink." She looked at Ann. "You're the interior decorator. What do you think?"

Ann paused before answering. If she confirmed that Tammy was correct, it would likely lead to more pillows being made and brought over. Things could only get worse from there. "I'm not really sure. It's been awhile since I did anything with florals."

"Really? What do you use, then?" Tammy sounded perfectly scandalized.

"Well, I mostly do white, black, and chrome. It's kind of my trademark."

Tammy sucked both her lips inside her mouth, and Ann knew it was only her ingrained southern manners that were keeping her from making a face. Something about this fact made Ann want to giggle. But then the lamp flickered, went dark for just a split second, and lit the room again. "Hmm. I just replaced that bulb."

Tammy said, "Must be a short in the lamp itself. That just happened to my favorite lamp—Ethan rewired it for me, though. He's such a sweetheart." Tammy was walking toward the bedroom door before Ann realized it.

She quickly caught up and positioned herself between Tammy and the front door for the walk back. This proved to be unnecessary, because Keith began to mumble behind them, sounding agitated but forming no words that Ann could understand. Tammy turned around as they walked. "What's the matter, darlin'?"

"I don't know why . . . Why would they do that?"

"Do what?" Tammy asked.

"The light blinks."

Ann supposed the blinking light must have scared him. The poor kid probably needed to get back home. She looked at Tammy. "Thanks again for bringing the pillows over. You've done so much for me it makes me feel guilty. I wish I could do something for you."

Tammy tilted her head to the side and studied Ann for a moment. "Well, if you really mean it, there is something you could do for me."

It had never occurred to Ann that Tammy might accept that offer. What had she gotten herself into now? "Of course. What can I do for you?"

Tammy's slow smile should have been the first clue for Ann to run. Fast.

But half an hour later, Ann found herself in Tammy's house, standing on a small stool, drowning in yards of blue satin jutting out from her waist in a bell shape. The bodice was several sizes too large, which made the scoop neck hang loosely around her shoulders, revealing the black T-shirt she was wearing underneath. All this she could put up with, but the thing that just about put her over the edge was the hoop skirt she was wearing beneath the dress. Tammy had failed to mention that this was part of the bargain.

Tammy chatted nonchalantly as she circled around Ann, mouth full of pins. "I can't remember if you knew that I make the garments for several of the historical plantation tours around here."

"No, you didn't tell me that." Definitely not.

Ann looked around the interior of Tammy's house. It was probably a little smaller than Sarah's, and the furniture was old and worn, but the word *dreary* could in no way be applied here. Brightly covered pillows festooned every possible stick of furniture, and the curtains were frilly and colorful. Ann thought maybe now she understood Tammy's taste, or absence of it, a little better. She obviously lacked much in the way of physical comforts, so she aimed to make it as cheery and bright as possible. Ann sort of admired her for that.

Keith sat happily at a kitchen table with a fake-wood Formica top, drawing on a piece of white paper with crayons. Ann had to admit, there was something about his simple sweetness that was beginning to grow on her. She watched his concentration, and once again thought he looked a little pale. No. She wasn't going there. Time to remain firmly planted in reality.

"There now, all done. Thank you so much." Tammy still had at least a half dozen pins in her mouth.

"Glad I could help." There was more than a little truth in those words. It felt good. "Isn't it dangerous to talk with all those pins in your mouth?"

Tammy reached up and pulled them out. "Yeah, I'm sure it is. It's just a lot more convenient, you know what I mean?"

"Yeah, I guess I do." Ann slipped the dress over her head, careful to avoid the pinned hem. "Well, I'd better get back."

"Thanks again."

"Here, Annie." Keith stayed in his seat but held up a crayon drawing as Ann walked past.

She stopped and took it from his hand. "Thanks, Keith. This is great." It looked like a table, but she couldn't be sure, and a lamp, casting a bright glow on the wall.

He pointed. "See, it's your room. Right?"

Ann nodded. "It looks just like my room. I really like the way the lamp is shining on the wall."

"It's not."

"Are you sure? It looks really bright to me."

"That's the angel." He pointed at the glow on the wall. "There, the angel's beside the lamp."

Ann smiled at his innocence. "It wasn't an angel, Keith. And that's just an old lamp. That's all."

"No! It was an angel!" Angry tears filled his eyes. "He was there. I heard him."

"What did you hear, Keith?" Tammy came and knelt beside his chair.

"Music. Angel music."

"In the lamp?" Tammy asked.

"No. In the wall. The music's in the wall. I bet Annie hears it too."

Ann hurried toward the door, picture in hand. "You know what? I'm expecting Ethan to show up any minute with floor sanders. I'd better get back to the house." She couldn't get out of there fast enough.

Chapter 16

Several hours later Ann leaned a weary arm on the electric sander. "I'm really thinking about putting tile floors in the kitchen."

Ethan shook his head and smiled. "Nothing doing. I know what you're up to, and nothing's going to get you out of sanding these floors—*all* the floors." They had spent the last few hours sanding the bedrooms, Ethan working in Ann's old room, Ann working in Nana's. "Besides, tile's too expensive for your budget, you know that, and it would take away some of the down-home integrity of the original house."

Ann felt the grit on her face, in her hair, and even between her teeth. "Well, you might be right about the trying-to-get-out-of-work part, but I'm not a big fan of the down-home integrity of this house. So if I could modern that up a little, I'd love to do it."

He put his hands over his ears. "Never let me hear such hateful words spoken near my delicate ears ever again. Modern up this beautiful old home?" Then he squatted down and put his right hand over his heart and his left hand on the floor. "Please forgive her, she knows not what she says."

Ann tried to scowl at him, but somewhere along the way, it erupted into laughter. He began to laugh too, then slowly stood and walked toward her, looking her full in the face as he did. He came to a stop when they were only inches apart. "It's good to see you laugh, even if you are covered in wood dust." His finger brushed lightly across her cheek, sending tan-colored specks floating to the ground. Ann's heart started to race, then stopped beating altogether when he took a step closer. His hand moved toward her right shoulder, and she waited for the feel of his embrace.

A deafening roar filled the room. He had reached past her and flipped the switch on the sander. "Now back to work." The smile on his face was just a little too smug.

Ann watched him walk away. It was a good thing, really, that nothing had happened. Who needed complications down here, when New York was plenty complicated? Patrick Stinson might not be a poster boy for long-term relationships, but they at least shared some of the same interests.

The next break was early afternoon. Ann fixed turkey and cheese sandwiches while Ethan changed the sandpaper on the machines from 80 grit to 150. "We're making progress now."

"On two rooms." Ann groaned the words, only half teasing. This was hard work.

"Patience, patience. Good things come to those who wait. Or, in our particular case, we could say that good floors . . . come from bad floors . . . to those who work hard for several days."

"Hmm, I never knew you were a philosopher."

"One of my many hidden talents." He picked up his sandwich and came to sit beside her at the kitchen table. "You have to admit it was a stroke of genius to get two sanders so that we can do twice the work."

"Mr. McKinney, I concede to your geniusness, and I am happy for it. I'll be glad to get this part done."

"Even after we're done sanding, we'll be far from finished. We'll have to put on stain, then three coats of polyurethane. You'll have to sleep in the living room for the rest of your stay."

Ann shrugged. "Not a problem."

"And when do you think you'll be back?"

"After you've agreed to let me hire you. I'll come back when the house is ready to list."

"Un-uh. There you go again. If you want me to do some work while you're gone, no problem, but I am not now, nor will I ever be, your employee, Miss Fletcher."

"That is so unfair. You know I'm not going to let you do all that work for free without me returning the favor in kind."

"That's too bad." He didn't sound at all sorry. "So when did you say you might be coming back?"

Ann took a bite of her sandwich, simply because she wanted the time chewing to think of an answer. Finally, she shrugged, resigned to the fact that—for now, at least—he'd won this battle. "I'm not sure. To tell you the truth, I wasn't really planning to come back this weekend, but things just kind of happened. I would like to get this finished as soon as I can, though."

After they finished lunch, Ethan stood and said, "Okay, now we change rooms. You take the one on the right; I take the one of the left."

"Why?"

"Well, sometimes it's easier to see something that someone else has missed rather than seeing your own mistakes."

"Are you saying that I've missed some places?" Ann wasn't sure whether she was teasing or offended.

"Absolutely not. I'm saying *I've* probably missed some places. I'm the worst. My mind goes on autopilot; I start to daydream, and soon enough I've messed up an entire section of floor—or whatever it is I'm working on."

"Yeah, right." Ann was pretty sure Ethan just wanted an excuse to double-check her work; he was the contractor, after all. But she wanted this work done right too, even though this trade would also mean that she would have to go back into her old room. Well, perhaps that was a good thing. In the full daylight, nothing seemed quite as ghostly as it did in the early morning, and as loud as the sanders were, there wasn't much chance of hearing music.

With all the furniture piled in a heap in the living room, her old room was an empty shell. It didn't feel as much like the place where she'd spent so much time.

Before she even started the machine, she walked around the floor, inspecting it for any patches that looked as though they'd been improperly sanded, determined to show Ethan one of his mistakes before he found one of hers. She couldn't find even a ding in the floor that remained. She heard the whirring sound from the room next door and flipped the switch on her own machine.

She started against the far wall, then moved into the closet. Suddenly, a memory poured over her with such force she felt almost as if she'd gone back in time. Her seven-year-old self was sitting in the corner of this closet, knees pulled up to chest, arms wrapped around knees, trying to hold herself together. If she let go, surely she would explode into a million tiny pieces— just like her heart already had.

How had things gone so wrong? This day had started out like any other, a typical day at school—no, better than typical—she'd finally beat Jaci Sharitz in a race across the monkey bars. Nana had come to walk her home from school that day, as usual, except something was different. Nana was practically dancing. "Guess what? Your mama's coming tonight."

"Mama? Really?" Now Ann was dancing too. Maybe her mother had finally found that job she was looking for and they could be a family again. "She's really going to be here? Tonight?" Ann twirled in a circle, watching her sundress form a mushroom of floral cotton around her. Today was the perfect day.

"Not only that, but she's bringing a very special surprise with her."

"Woo hoo! A surprise!" Ann twirled again and again, the pink flowers on her dress dancing right along with her. "What is it?"

"Can't tell. Wouldn't be a surprise then, would it?"

"I bet I'll figure it out." Visions began to dance through Ann's mind—her mother standing on the porch holding a plate of cookies she'd baked herself, maybe a sweater she'd knitted, or . . . maybe even the latest Cabbage Patch doll. She bounced up and down, trying her hardest not to squeal like a baby. She wanted Nana to tell her mother what a big girl she'd become. That goal in mind, Ann ran directly to her room as soon as she got home. She tucked a stray sock inside the dresser drawer and closed it nice and tight, straightened and re-straightened the pillows and stuffed animals on her bed, then went and found a rag and dusted every single piece of furniture at least twice. Everything needed to be just perfect when Mama arrived.

Ding dong.

Ann ran as fast as she could, but Nana had already beat her to the front door, her wide frame blocking Ann's view. Ann stood on tiptoes, searching for any glimpse of her mother's beautiful face.

Nana leaned forward, like she was reaching down to pick up a suitcase or something. "Hello there, you sweet darling. Let me pick you up. Oh. I just can't believe it." When she straightened back up, she was holding . . . a *baby*. Nana spun round and round in circles. "Look at you, precious. You are so beautiful. Growing into a big girl, aren't you?" She kissed the little baby on the forehead, on the hair, the arms.

Wait just a cockle-doodle minute. Nana's hugs belonged to *Ann*, not this *baby*. "Who's she?"

Nana turned then, sheer joy on her face. "Oh, sweetie, come meet Sarah. Isn't she beautiful? She's two years old, and she's your sister."

"My what?" Only now did Ann see her mother in the doorway, standing sort of hunched down.

Her mother smiled in that really big way grown-ups often do when they want a kid to believe something that's not true. "Hi, sweetie, I've missed you."

Ann looked from her mother, to her dancing grandmother, to the baby. "No!" She fled to her room, locking the door tight behind her, and crawled into the back corner of this closet. She hid behind the long flannel nightgown that smelled fresh from the dryer, then just sat, rocking back and forth, back and forth, trying her best to figure out what had just happened.

Her mother, who had left her here so long ago while she "looked for a job," had brought this baby here. Her sister—yeah, right. Ann might have been only seven, but she wasn't stupid.

Apparently her mother had enough money to raise this brat for a couple of years.

That's when she knew the truth. It wasn't that her mother left to get a job like they'd always told her. Truth was, she simply left to get a better daughter.

A few days later, Ann was back in this closet, curled into a ball once again. Mama had gone and taken the crybaby with her. And left Ann here. Because she wasn't special enough.

The sander suddenly stopped working, which pulled Ann from the memory. Thank goodness for timely mechanical malfunctions. She flipped the switch to the off position and went into the other room.

Ethan turned off his sander as soon as she entered the room. "Hey, what's going on? You already found a spot I missed?" His smile melted when he looked at her face. "Are you hurt?"

Was she hurt? Well, not in the way he was talking about. She looked back toward the other room, thankful for the excuse to turn away from his probing eyes. "Sander went dead. I'm not sure what happened."

"Hmm, let me see." He followed her into the other room, brought the machine out into the open, and flipped the switch. It roared to life. He smiled and turned it off. "Are you trying to fake your way out of some work?"

"No." She grabbed the handles. "I was working along, and it stopped. I flipped it off."

"Easy there, I didn't mean to cause offense." He flipped the switch on, then off again. "Works fine now. Maybe it overheated or something."

"Yeah, that must have been it." Ethan was still looking at her with a worried expression, so she pointed toward the door.

"Now get back in there and get back to work; we're on a time schedule here."

"Aren't you a taskmaster of a boss? I think I might have to ask for a raise before it's all over with." He smiled as he disappeared out the door.

Ann went back to sanding, making a point of thinking only about the here and now. She thought about the Stinson project and began to envision the model apartments she would set up. She would need a few more upscale items than usual, but there was a supplier she'd worked with a few times who carried the high-end items she wanted. And they were good about a delayed pay schedule—something she would need until the contracts were signed and the payments started coming in. First thing Monday, she would have to call them and set up an appointment.

She pictured a Baccarat light fixture in the hallway, black granite in the kitchen. As she began to envision the room, the black countertops drawing her full attention, another memory attacked out of nowhere. This time, her memories found her standing outside a black door.

Nana had loaded Ann into the car, saying nothing about where they were going, but Ann had been happy to enjoy the rare ride to Summerville and didn't push for details. She was eight years old, and after they drove for what seemed like hours, Nana pulled down a country lane. She could still remember the tiny brick house with black shutters and black door.

"Come with me, darling. I have a surprise to show you."

"Won't the people who live here be upset that we're in their driveway?"

"No, no, darling, they won't. I think you're going to like

them a whole bunch." Nana led her up to the front porch and rang the bell.

Ann needed to go to the bathroom, really bad, and she hoped that whoever lived here would answer the door, and soon. The door swung open, and there stood the crybaby—a year older than the last time. "Annie, my sissy, my sissy is here." The crybaby jumped up and down.

Ann's mother came to the door then, looked right at Ann, and said, "Welcome home, sweetie."

"Home?" Ann looked from Nana to Mama.

"Yes, darling, you're coming to live with me. We'll be together all the time." Mama looked so happy.

Her mother wanted her—really, really wanted her. She wanted her to come live here all the time. The joy of the moment exploded inside Ann with an intensity she couldn't believe.

"Ew." The crybaby covered her mouth and pointed at Ann, who hadn't, until that very second, felt the wetness running down her legs.

The sander went dead, and Ann ran from the room, not stopping until she was on the front porch, gulping huge deep breaths. What was going on here? Why the sudden onslaught of all these memories, and why so real? She put her hands on her knees and continued to gasp for air.

"Annie, you okay?" Ethan was beside her, although she hadn't heard the door open.

"Don't call me Annie. My name is Ann." She stood up straight but didn't look toward him. "And I'm fine. Just needed a little air."

"Well, okay, *Ann*, there's plenty of air out here, if that's what you need." He leaned against the door and waited.

Finally, she looked at him. "Didn't mean to snap."

"I'm just glad to see you out here. When I saw that you'd left the sander running, I thought you must have been kidnapped or something, because I knew you would never purposely leave your work." He grinned at her.

"The sander was running?"

"Yeah. I went over to check on your progress, and I could see the sander scooting its way across the floor. I flipped it off and came out here, prepared to fight off the wild beasts that must have dragged you away."

The sander was running. Ann tried to shrug it off, change the subject, and pretend like it didn't matter. But it did. Or actually, it *didn't*. She needed to prove to herself that it didn't, and she needed to prove it right now. "You know what? That wall, the one the sander is plugged into, it's the same plug that my lamp was plugged into earlier and it kept going off, even after I changed the bulb. Can we check the plug for a short?"

But it wasn't a short Ann was interested in at all. She was thinking of all the coincidences and Keith's music and Keith's drawing and her consistent hysteria about music that had never been there. She wanted to open up that wall and prove to herself that there was absolutely nothing there. No problems. No music. And no angels.

Chapter 17

"Everything looks good. Connections are tight. Voltage meter looks right." Ethan looked up from the jumble of wires now suspending the faceplate from the socket. "I don't know what the problem is, but it doesn't seem to be in this plug."

Ann took the large Maglite from Ethan's toolbox and pointed the beam into the small hole in the wall, looking for . . . what? Wings? The whole notion was ridiculous. Of course there was nothing. There had never been anything. Ever. She put the flashlight back, feeling silly. And relieved.

Ethan started to replace the plate, but he had trouble getting it lined up. He pulled it back out, put his face in close to the wall, and grabbed the flashlight. "What's this?"

"What? What are you talking about?"

"There's something in here." He drew his head back but shoved his hand inside the wall.

Ann's heart stopped beating. "Something . . . alive?"

"No. At least I sure hope not. And if it is, I sure hope it's not poisonous. You ever learned to suck venom out of a snake bite?"

"Get your hand out of there!"

"Oh, quit squealing like a girl. It's . . ." With some straining and contortions, he moved his hand deeper into the wall. "It's some kind of paper." He finally pulled his hand out, bringing with it a roll of paper secured by a rubber band.

"Isn't this mysterious?" He looked up at her and wiggled his eyebrows, but Ann was in no mood for humor.

"What is that?"

"Don't know. It's your house. Do you want to open it?" He held it out to her.

Ann kept her hands firmly planted on the floor and shook her head. "You do it."

The paper was yellowed and the rubber band holding it together split as soon as Ethan put pressure on it. He uncurled the paper and looked at the page, his brow furrowed in concentration. "It's a handwritten letter. 'To my daughters, from Lorelei.' Do you know a Lorelei?"

"Yes." Just the sound of the name made Ann want to cover her ears and run. She tried to keep a neutral expression, but it required great effort.

"A cousin?"

She looked down at her hands, suddenly tightly clasped together. "My mother." The words hurt too much to say in more than a whisper.

"Well, I guess that's my signal to stop reading because it's not any of my business. Here, I'm assuming you'll want to read this. You want me to give you some privacy?"

As he handed Ann the paper, the edges curled up again.

"You know what? I think I'll save this for later. I want to get the sanding finished before the day is over." Ann tossed the paper out into the hallway floor as nonchalantly as if it were a piece of junk mail.

Ethan watched evenly. "You sure about that?"

"Positive." Ann plugged the sander back into a different plug and began working.

It was just after five o'clock when they finally finished sanding and cleaning up the mess it left behind. Ethan was dotted head to toe with fine wood dust. His sun-bleached hair hanging from beneath his cap was saturated with little brown specks. Ann smiled at him. "You'd better get home and get yourself cleaned up. I definitely owe you dinner, and I refuse to be seen in public with any man who looks like you do right now, even if he did just put in a whole day working in my house."

"And I'm not letting any woman buy me dinner. I don't know how they do things in New York, but here in Charleston, a man is still a man, and I'm buying dinner."

"See, this is your problem. You're stuck in the old. Old houses, old floors, old ways of doing things. Take a look at what's new around you; it's so much more freeing to be able to live in the moment."

"There's where you're dead wrong. We need the old to—"

Knock. Knock.

"See, even the universe is on my side. Notice the timing of that knock?" Ann smirked as she walked toward the door. Since the knock came from the kitchen door, she didn't have to wonder who it was. She opened it and said, "Come on in, Tammy, Keith."

She knew they would anyway. At least if she issued the invitation, she could retain some semblance of control. "You're just in time to hear Ethan tell us why he's stuck a few decades back."

"Yeah. Then maybe Annie"—he shot a glance in her direction —"excuse me, *Ann*, will enlighten us with her explanation of disposable lifestyles."

"Excuse me?"

"Ethan! I didn't know you were over here." Keith knocked his glasses off in his excited bouncing. He reached down and picked them up but continued to wriggle with excitement. "Oh boy!"

"Hey, buddy, how's it going?"

"Good." Keith's smile covered his whole face. "You want to play football with me?"

"Well, I was just going home to get cleaned up so I could take Ann out for dinner. I've had her working hard all day and she's hungry."

"Annie's coming to my house for dinner. You coming too?"

Tammy laughed uncomfortably. "What Keith means is, we were coming over to see if Ann wanted to come over for dinner. I didn't know that you were still here, Ethan. I didn't see your truck outside."

"It's parked around back. We were unloading some heavy equipment, so I brought it right up to the back porch."

"Well, we're cooking burgers on the grill, and I was coming over to see if Ann wanted one. You're welcome to one too." She looked back and forth between the two of them, and Ann could practically see the matchmaker wheels spinning. "Of course, the two of you would probably rather go out somewhere."

"Please, Ethan, you come to my house?"

Ethan looked from Ann to Keith, clearly torn about what he should do. And for the first time ever, he seemed at a loss for words. The effect was charming, in spite of his pigheadedness.

"I'm conceding nothing, but for now, I suggest a cease-fire. Let's say that for tonight, Tammy's got dinner."

Ethan smiled good-naturedly. "Conceding nothing is right. We'll continue this discussion later. You'll come to see the error of your ways, I'm sure of it."

Later. Ann thought she might like the sound of that word. Uncomfortable with the thought, she turned toward Tammy. "What can I bring?"

"Not one thing. I've been listening to the sound of machinery running over here all day, and I've felt bad about how hard you're working and the fact that I haven't done enough to help you. I've already gone to the store and bought everything. I want you to come over, sit down, and relax."

Tammy continued to amaze. She had a life that most people would consider hard to the point of debilitating, yet she continued to go out of her way to help Ann—someone she hardly knew. Sure, maybe Tammy and Sarah had been close, but Tammy's selflessness went beyond that. Ann found herself wondering what made her tick.

Ethan said, "Do I have time to run home and take a shower?"

"Believe me, honey, we'll make time." Tammy shook her head, looking from Ann to Ethan, then back again. "Now, both of you get cleaned up and back over to my place ASAP. Time for some good food and good fellowship."

"Bye, Annie, see you soon." Keith smiled tentatively at her, then looked at Ethan. "I'll have my football ready."

"Honey, Ethan's been working all day. He's too tired to want to play ball tonight."

"There you go, Tammy, thinking like a girl again—which, I guess, is fine since you are one. Personally, I'm a guy, and I'm never too tired for a little football. Especially with my man Keith."

Tammy looked at him, and Ann thought she could see the sheen of tears in her eyes. Tammy mouthed the words *thank you* silently, then turned to her son. "Come on, Keith, let's go set the table for four."

"Woo hoo." Keith hugged his mother. "Party time!"

The two of them walked out the door and Ethan followed. He turned to look over his shoulder as he reached the bottom of the steps. "See you in a bit."

Ann nodded. "Sounds good." And it really did.

Ann walked back into the empty house, surprised by how much she was looking forward to the evening ahead. It was almost like having an extended family.

That thought caused her to look at the rolled-up paper— a letter written by the mother she'd hardly known—currently sitting on the kitchen counter. Part of her wanted to read it; another part wanted to burn it. What good could possibly come out of this? If it offered explanations, Ann didn't want to hear them. What reason could possibly justify taking your kids for a "weekend visit to Nana's" and then sneaking off in the middle of the night with nothing more than a note saying, "I'm leaving?" How many times had her mother offered what seemed like love, or acceptance, only to run out on them again? And if the letter asked for forgiveness . . .

The house suddenly felt stuffy. Well, she hadn't checked the mail today, and there were likely bills that needed to be paid. She walked outside, purposefully avoiding a glance at the letter as she went, and took her time making her way to the mailbox. She paused to pick up stray leaves that had fallen onto the concrete and veered off the path to pick the occasional weed.

"You look like someone who's trying to avoid something."

Ann looked up, surprised to see Eleanor squatting at the end of the driveway, lacing her running shoe. "Hi, Eleanor. And what would make you say that?"

Her hair, pulled tightly back, still glinted in the sunlight as she stood. "Well, I don't know that I've ever seen anybody walk quite that slow, and you've found more excuses to stop than I would have imagined possible."

Ann laughed. "Busted." She noticed Eleanor's face looked flushed. "Just finishing your run?"

"Yep, I beat my best time by twenty seconds today."

"Good for you."

"Yep." She reached behind and grabbed her right foot with both hands, stretching out her quads. "A lot of times I feel like avoiding my evening run, but you know what I've always found to be true?"

"What?"

"If there's something you don't want to face, the sooner you get to it, the better." She dropped the right foot and grabbed the left. "And if it looks to be too big to handle, I break it up into smaller pieces. On the days I don't think I can make two miles, I aim for one. Or even a half. But I don't let myself avoid the goal altogether."

"You're probably right."

"You know what I think your first goal should be?"

"What?"

"A shower. Looks like you've got a pound of sawdust currently roosting in your hair."

"Ha. You'll appreciate that part, though, when it comes time to sell the house."

"I'm sure I will. You have a good evening now, okay?" Eleanor jogged off down the street, her ponytail swinging in the air.

Maybe Ann should face the letter. But now, thanks to her stroll, she didn't have time. She'd have to hurry if she was going to make it to Tammy's before Ethan did.

Chapter 18

Tammy smiled. Ann was watching Ethan and Keith through the open kitchen window. Even though Ann was still going through the motions of chopping vegetables, her attention was definitely elsewhere. *Oh, the possibilities!*

Ann turned her direction for a split second and saw Tammy watching her. She motioned with her knife. "Ethan's really great with Keith."

Tammy nodded, although she doubted Annie noticed. "I don't know what I'd do without him." Ethan was running with his left arm in the air and shouting, "I'm going for the bomb; give it all you've got!"

Keith threw the ball, which turned end over end instead of spiraling like a professional football player's ball would. It obviously wasn't going to get as far away as Ethan was, so Ethan corrected course, ran forward, and made a diving catch. He held the ball up in the air, as if to show the referee that he'd caught it, then yelled, "Touchdown!"

"Woo, woo, woo!" Keith pumped his elbow in victory. "Yeah!"

Ethan threw the ball back to Keith. It hit his hands, bounced off, and hit him on the face. "Ow." Keith put his hands over his nose.

Just then a black truck came speeding down the street, loud music booming through the open windows. A teenage boy leaned out the window. "What's the matter, retard? Can't you catch the itty-bitty ball?" The tires squealed as the truck sped away, the sound of the boys' laughter echoing through the neighborhood.

Tammy felt her fingers closing tighter around the handle of the vegetable peeler. She wished she could take those boys out of their charmed lives—full of black trucks, sports teams, and Saturday night dates—and just for one day put them in Keith's place. Let them see how it felt to walk into a room full of strangers, expecting to be welcomed because he always welcomed, only to find himself ignored, cut off from the group, or even laughed at. Yet Keith survived this over and over and over. If only everyone could see, they would realize that the one they thought weak was actually the strongest one among them.

"How do you stand that?" Ann slammed the end of a cucumber into the trash can. "Don't you want to chase those boys down and beat some manners into them?"

Tammy moved her head from side to side, trying to make her voice calmer than she was. "Sometimes. A lot of times, actually." She sliced the tomato in front of her. "I just wish they could all slow down long enough to really see him. To know how truly wonderful he is."

Ann noticeably stiffened, her knife freezing halfway through the cucumber. "I'm glad I got the chance."

"Lyle—that's my ex-husband—left me not long after Keith was born. He was upset enough when we found out Keith had Down's, then Keith had terrible colic and started screaming before the sun went down. I guess the thought of a lifetime spent with a handicapped son just scared him right out of here."

"When you were pregnant with Keith, did you know that he was . . . that something was . . . ?"

Tammy placed the sliced tomatoes in a fan shape on the plate, then went to tearing slices of lettuce. "Not for most of the time. I was an older mom, you know, so I had the tests done, including an amnio. It came back normal, so we were making plans for a healthy baby. But two weeks before Keith was born, we got a call from the doctor's office. There had been a mix-up. They'd sent my results to some other woman, and sent me hers."

Ann's knife slipped and caught her by the finger. "Ouch." She stuck her finger under the kitchen faucet and looked up at Tammy. "You're kidding. The other woman, she'd thought that her baby . . ."

Tammy nodded. "Yep, she'd spent the last half of her pregnancy thinking her baby had Down syndrome. I'd spent the last half of mine thinking my baby was perfectly healthy."

Tammy remembered locking herself in the bedroom and crying for three days straight after the call came. She had refused to speak to anyone, had hardly eaten. At the time, she thought her life was ruined. "Looking back on it, I see God's hands all over it. The other woman was still pregnant when they figured out their mistake, so she'd obviously planned to keep her child, was prepared to deal with all the issues. I . . . well, I mean, to tell the absolute truth, I wouldn't have done the same."

She went back to arranging the lettuce on the plate, the

shame burning her face. "It's not something I'm proud of, but it's the truth." She stared out the window toward Keith, who was now sitting beneath the shade of his favorite oak, rolling the football around in his hands while he talked to Ethan. "I'd never believed in God until Keith was born. I realize now that God knew all along that I needed Keith, and that Keith had a special place in this world. I am so grateful that it happened the way it did." It was absolutely true, in spite of how hard her life often was.

"Do you really believe, you know, that Keith sees angels?"

"Yeah, I do. I think maybe he is less distracted with the things that distract most of us, so he's able to see the things we all miss."

Ann rubbed her temples with both hands, as if this thought gave her a headache. "If there are angels with him, why don't they at least him help catch a football when there are jerk-boys driving by? I mean, what's the point if all they do is go around haunting people?"

"Haunting?" Tammy looked at Ann. "That's an interesting choice of words."

Ann shrugged. "What else would you call it? A bunch of spirits flying around making random appearances but not doing much else."

"That's where you're wrong." Tammy looked outside where Ethan was demonstrating some sort of football grip and Keith was smiling, but his head was leaned back against the tree. "There's a verse in the Bible about angels that says, 'Are not all angels ministering spirits sent to serve those who will inherit salvation?' I think they serve him in the way he needs to be served—not with physical strength, but spiritual. Keith has a heart problem, which often leads to lung problems. He gets ill for long periods of time. The angels may not make him well— only God can do that—but he always emerges on the other side stronger, and with more peace, than before he got sick."

"He and Ethan sure have a great time together. Keith already looks worn out from the fun." Ann's voice took on that extra-cheery tone people always use to redirect a hard conversation.

"Yeah, Keith doesn't have a lot of stamina. He'll be asleep before we eat if we don't get this stuff to the table." Tammy leaned forward and called out the window, "Hey, Ethan, will you get the burgers off the grill for me? Everything else is almost ready."

Ethan hopped to his feet. "You got it." A few minutes later Ethan walked in the door with a plate full of burgers.

Ann moaned. "I'm not much of a meat eater—in fact, I can't remember the last time I had a burger—but I've got to tell you, the smell of the charcoal and smoke makes me glad I decided to lay aside my healthier tendencies for the day."

"I knew we'd win you over eventually. You'll be eating fried chicken in no time." Ethan set the plate on the table.

Tammy recognized the gleam in his eyes. He was falling for Annie; there was no doubt about it. She started to insert a comment of her own but didn't want to interrupt any chemistry that might be happening.

"Oh yeah?" Ann laughed. "Don't count on it. I'm thinking you're due a visit to a sushi place."

"Yuck. Don't count on it." He made the motion of sticking his finger down his throat, complete with gagging sound.

"That's it, the gauntlet's been thrown. My new goal in life is to see you eat sushi."

"Sushi? I love sushi. Can I come with you?" Keith blinked up at Ann with a crooked smile on his face.

"Honey, you've never had sushi." Tammy kissed him on the forehead. "Now go wash your hands."

Keith walked over to the kitchen sink and did as he was told while saying, "Doesn't matter, I still like it."

"And how would you know that?"

"If Annie likes it, then so do I."

Ann walked over and hugged him. "Then you should definitely come with us. Right, Ethan?" She looked over her shoulder, a dare in her eyes.

Ethan picked up a ketchup bottle from the kitchen counter and carried it to the table. "Hey, buddy, she doesn't like to be called Annie. Call her *Ann*, okay?"

"Really?" Tammy looked at Ann, hoping for an argument. "We've been calling you Annie this whole time. Why haven't you said anything? I feel terrible."

Ann shrugged. "That's what everyone called me when I was kid—when I lived here. When I moved to New York, I thought it was time to grow up a little. I've been Ann ever since. Of course, to Sarah, I was always Annie." Ann returned to her seat. "However, I don't believe we were talking about my name. I think we were talking about sushi, and how Keith wanted to come with us."

Keith was bouncing up and down saying, "Sushi, sushi."

Ethan looked toward him, then shook his head. "Looks like I'm outnumbered."

Tammy swatted him with the dish towel. "I'd say it was more like *outsmarted*. Either way, you lose."

"Seems like cheating to me." Ethan sat down in his seat, but the look on his face made Tammy think that maybe he'd been the winner after all.

Chapter 19

Ethan stood beside Ann at the sink. He rinsed the dishes, then handed them to her so she could load them into the dishwasher. She was so close, so very close, and every time she turned her head, a nice fruity fragrance filled the air. He wanted to lean closer and breathe it in. Instead, he scrubbed at the remnants of ketchup, mustard, and baked beans with a little extra vigor.

"I can't remember the last time I've felt so completely stuffed. It's been years since I last had a hamburger." Ann put one hand on her stomach and groaned.

"Admit it, though. When you took that first bite, you were wondering what ever possessed you to give them up."

Her shoulder brushed against his. "Okay, I'll admit it. But right about now, I remember exactly why I gave them up. Blah."

"I'll bet in New York you eat at fancy restaurants all the time."

"Not all that often." She loaded a plate in the dishwasher, her face thoughtful. "But sometimes."

Ethan wondered who took Ann to nice dinners in New York. He could almost picture the guy—wearing an expensive suit and speaking with a European accent. "Charleston has some nice places too, you know. I should have told Tammy we were going out tonight."

"I'm the one who told her we would come over, if you recall. And to be perfectly honest, I can't remember when I've had such a nice dinner." She toyed with the trio of forks in her hand, then put them in the tray. "It's funny, as much as I've avoided coming here for all these years, somehow at dinner tonight, I felt almost as though I'd come . . . home." She straightened up.

Ethan's hand seemed to move of its own accord. It would not stop until it touched her hair; he knew this, yet he didn't seem to be in control of it. Her dark brown hair was simple—long and straight—and it looked so soft, so amazingly soft. He'd wanted to touch it ever since he first saw her. His fingers were an inch away when he heard the sound of Keith's door closing in the hallway behind them. His hand dropped to his side, goal thwarted. At least for now.

"He's sound asleep," Tammy said as she moved back in to join them. "Thanks to both of you for coming over tonight. You have no idea how much it means to him, and to me, to have company."

"Thanks for having us over," Ethan and Ann said at the exact same time. All three of them laughed.

"Well, I guess I'd better walk Ann home." Ethan hoped his voice sounded sufficiently casual to be cool, although he was pretty certain it sounded more like the desperate dork he was.

"What, do you think I might get mugged between here

and there?" Ann looked at him, her eyes shining with . . . either flirtation or irritation. How was a guy supposed to know the difference?

"Well, usually I'd say no, this is a plenty safe neighborhood. But I've heard a rumor that some crazy New Yorker has been seen in the area recently. You know how those Yankees are. There's no telling what they might do. I think we need to set up a neighborhood watch, and, well, I just don't want to send you out into the night alone to face that kind of danger."

Her laughter fed the hope that it had been flirtation. "Don't tell me a southern gentleman would let a little bitty girl from up north scare him."

"First off, I didn't say *I* was scared; I said I'd better stick around to protect *you*. Second off, don't ever confuse me with a gentleman."

"My mistake." Ann reached over and hugged Tammy, which seemed to surprise both of them. "Well, good night. I'm sure I'll see you tomorrow." The way she said it, it sounded like she was looking forward to it. A very good sign.

"Count on it." Tammy hugged Ethan, then went to hold the door open for them. "Good night."

Ethan and Ann walked slowly across the lawn toward the house. They were close enough that Ethan could easily reach out and take her hand; his fingers twitched at the thought. But he didn't want to do anything dumb at this point, and how was he supposed to know how she would react?

By now, they were at the kitchen door. Ethan mustered what was left of his courage, reached out, and touched her hand. "Hey, do you want to go to church with me in the morning? It starts at nine, and Tammy and Keith will be there too."

"Church? Um . . ." Ann looked him in the face, and her voice came out firm, almost hard. "I don't do church."

"Really?" Ethan knew his voice did not hide his surprise. "I . . . well, living in New York I would think there would be lots of churches to choose from, but maybe in a city that size it's hard to find one with just the right mix of people, huh? I think you'd like the one here. Sarah went there and lots of her friends. Tammy goes there, and Keith—I already said that, didn't I?"

"Ethan, when I say I don't do church, what I mean is, I don't do the God thing."

What? How had he been so oblivious that he'd never picked up on that? He pulled his hand back to his side, the finality of it burning through his veins. She was off-limits. As a non-believer, Ann was off-limits for anything more than friendship. And he certainly was feeling more than friendship toward her.

She was still looking at him, a dare in her eyes, waiting for a response, but the shock made it difficult for him to think of anything coherent to say. "Really? I just assumed, I mean, you're Sarah's sister, and your grandmother . . . well, she was . . . you know . . . and I guess I just figured that with that kind of family, you would—"

"Yeah, that kind of a family. Just look at where it got them."

"What do you mean?"

"Well, my grandmother suffered terribly for months before the cancer finally took her. Sarah was killed two days before she graduated with her master's in social work. And even Tammy. She believes, and she has a handicapped son—who means the world to her, I'll grant you that—but her life is just plain hard. If there was a God, why wouldn't He take better care of the people who actually believe in Him?"

Ethan leaned against the door frame and looked at her. More than any other time he'd been around her, he wished he could think of the right thing to say. Speaking about his faith came so naturally down at The Washout. His words just seemed to flow there, in the midst of testosterone-fueled—or some other substance-fueled-adrenaline junkies trying to catch a wave. Here, away from the surf and on the same porch he'd stood on a thousand times, he could say nothing. The right words always seemed to elude him around her, even now when it really mattered. *God, help. She's got a well of hurt that she's afraid is going to drown her if she lets it out. Help me show her that she's not facing it alone.* "Well, I'm not sure that I can understand God, and I certainly won't try to explain Him. But I do know that He loves your grandmother, and your sister, and Tammy, and even you, more than you could ever imagine."

"If believing that works for you, then fine, but it doesn't work for me." She crossed her arms across her chest.

This was not going well. It was not *going* to go well. Ethan didn't think he was the right person to have this conversation with Ann, and he needed to get out of here before he made things worse. "I guess I'll just . . ." He couldn't bring himself to finish the sentence. *Stay with it Ethan—she's worth it.* "It's just that . . ."

Something flickered beneath the hard glint of her eyes, and in that moment, Ethan understood. She was a scared little girl hiding behind words that she thought would keep her safe.

"I wish you'd open your heart, Ann. You need to deal with your past instead of trying to pretend the pain doesn't exist."

"And how would you know that?"

"It's as plain as the wall you build around yourself. You need to learn to believe in something again."

Ann looked hard at him, and just a hint of moisture gathered in her eyes. "I . . ." She blinked twice and looked away. "I don't know how." Then she opened the door, walked inside, and shut it behind her without looking back.

He'd said the wrong thing again. All he wanted to do was help her, but all he kept doing was messing things up.

Chapter 20

When Ann finally settled down on the sofa with her blanket that night, she couldn't begin to relax and fall asleep. The tiny space prevented her from tossing and turning as she might have in bed, so she finally got up and paced—as best she could around the furniture piled up everywhere.

She saw the old letter they'd found in the wall on top of Sarah's nightstand and thought about what Eleanor had said. Better to face these things right away. And a little at a time. Yeah, maybe she could just read the first paragraph or something. She carried the paper, still rolled, back to the couch and sat.

For a few minutes, she simply held it in her hand, trying to decide what she was going to do. It was silly, her aversion to opening this. How bad could it be? It was just a letter from her mother written who knows how many years ago? Likely it didn't have anything to do with anything. Still, there was something about this whole situation that set off all sorts of warning bells. Finally, she unrolled it.

April 3, 1988

Ann looked at the date and dropped the paper. This had been written the day before her mother left them for the last time. How was it that she'd found the time to write this letter, but she hadn't been able to work in even one little word of good-bye to her family? *Coward.* Anger surged through Ann, making her feel suddenly stronger, less vulnerable. *All right, Mama, let's see how you tried to explain yourself away. Don't expect me to buy in, I'll tell you that right now.* She unrolled the paper again.

> My Darling Girls,
>
> I don't have the guts to begin to tell you everything, so I'm acting like the coward I am and writing it all down in a letter for you. Doesn't much matter, I know I'll be too chicken to even leave it where you can find it because I'm afraid of what you'll think. I'll hide it in the same place I always hid my marijuana from Mama. How is that for lame?
>
> I'm hoping that we're reading this together. It will mean I've finally got my act together and I've come back to get you. That seems like such a distant dream for me now, but how I do hope it will someday come to be. If something should go wrong, if I never make it back, then no one will ever even know how much I tried. This letter will go down with my house someday and I suppose that would be a fitting end. It will mean I've crashed and burned; my letter should probably do the same. There's no way you will find it otherwise—unless God Almighty Himself should intervene, and I haven't exactly seen a lot of that in my life lately.

Ann tossed the paper onto the floor. She'd had more than enough reading for one night.

You were right about one thing, Mother. You were too far gone to turn yourself around. Unfortunately, you were wrong about this letter going down with the house, because here I sit. Ann looked at the roll on the floor.

The words she'd read kept repeating in her mind. *If something should go wrong, if I never make it back, then no one will ever even know how much I tried. This letter will go down with my house someday and I suppose that would be a fitting end.* Even her crazy, mixed-up mother had known that this letter would never be found. After all, that wall had been the perfect hiding place for her pot all those years. And now—ironically—someone did find this letter, thanks to Ann waking up and thinking she heard music coming from this room, and to Keith's insisting there was an angel and music in the wall, and to the electrical appliances that turned on and off in spite of the fact that Ethan said nothing was wrong with the wiring.

The letter had been in that wall. It was almost as if someone—or something—wanted to make certain it was found. *Unless God Almighty Himself should intervene, and I haven't exactly seen a lot of that in my life lately.*

Ann walked back to Sarah's nightstand and opened the top drawer. As she had somehow known there would be, a Bible lay inside. Ann pulled it out and flipped through it mindlessly for a few minutes. Then she turned to the back for an index. She'd wanted to see just what that Bible had to say about angels and their songs and blinking lights, and why they let all the good people die and let other people—who were all clearly less deserving—succeed.

She found what was labeled a "concordance" in the back, which seemed to be basically an index. Under the word *angel* was a long list of references, which Ann scanned blindly—until she saw the word *Hagar*. That was the lady from the painting, wasn't it? The one with the angel that didn't seem all that helpful?

That whole story didn't make sense. Why would God have allowed the bad to happen in the first place? Where was He when all of that was going on?

The story, the painting, it all haunted her. Before she even realized she was doing it, Ann went to the computer and pulled up the Metropolitan Museum of Art's home page. After some searching, she found Beka's painting again and printed it out. Then, for whatever reason, she googled "Hagar" and "painting." It turned out, a lot of artists had done that story. She became intrigued with a couple more and printed out copies.

One was *Abraham Casting Out Hagar and Ishmael* by Guercino. On the left was Sarah, with her back to the scene, and the side of her face in shadow. In the middle, Abraham's face looked troubled as he pointed Hagar and Ishmael toward the highway. And then there was Hagar, looking toward Sarah while holding a crying Ishmael against her. The whole image was so cold.

That poor woman. Sent out into the desert, along with her son, probably to die, by the man who had fathered her son and by the woman who had insisted on her having this child in the first place. There was no one who cared. She was all alone.

Ann wondered if her own mother had had that same hard look, just like the biblical Sarah, when she packed up her car and left here that last time. She'd done it in the middle of the night, so who knew? In their version of the story, Nana had been the one who held on to the crying Sarah, like Hagar held Ishmael. But Ann hadn't cried, not that time. For the few months she'd lived in her mother's home, she'd lived in dread, knowing it wouldn't last this time either. When her mother finally disappeared, it was almost a relief to get it done with. Better yet, this time she'd left Sarah too. Finally, Ann wasn't the only one who didn't measure up.

She fell asleep, dreaming about the unloved and unwanted Hagar. She could hear her wailing in despair, crying out through the empty wilderness. Somewhere during the night, the song from the chapel infused the dream. Not long after, Hagar's moans were quieted.

Ann woke up in a sweat. The night of dreams filled with Hagar, angels, and haunting music was over, but there were more to come. She knew it. "Why? Why?" she screamed through the empty house. Why was she the one left alone, left to dream and hear strange music? The man who had caused all this lay perfectly at peace somewhere in a graveyard. Why couldn't *he* be the one to deal with the grief . . . to wonder if his mind was slipping? It was so unfair.

She sat up and rubbed her eyes, then stumbled to the kitchen for a glass of water. Every muscle in her body ached. She sat down at the kitchen table, rested her forehead against her left hand, and wondered how much longer she could take all this before she simply snapped. Maybe she needed to find a counselor when she got back to New York; maybe there was some sort of medication she could take. For now, she'd just have to stay too busy to think.

Today the plan was to put stain on the bedroom floors, then buff them, then start applying the polyurethane. She began to plan for the day, but her mind wandered to Ethan, and Tammy, and Keith. She thought about how at home she'd felt at Tammy's last night, so much a part of the group. In the clarity of the morning, though, she knew it had all been some big illusion she'd built up—illusions about caring for people. About caring for people who cared for her. Well, and for angels. And a God who would care enough to send one. Yep, she needed to hurry up and get out of here before she completely lost all grasp on reason.

She ate a banana for breakfast, then hurried to start her work. She dressed in old clothes and prepped the materials, then began with the far corner of her old bedroom. It was better to do this room first because she reasoned that first thing in the morning, she would be less vulnerable to the imaginations that seemed to haunt her later in the day.

She spread the stain in a circular motion in four-foot-square areas, trying to focus on what she was doing. As always happens with work this repetitive, though, her mind would not listen, and soon she was thinking about yesterday, last night, everything.

Her back and arms were aching by the time she finished the room. She washed her hands in the bathroom sink and went into the kitchen for a glass of water, then dropped onto the couch for a quick break.

Try as she might to look the other way, the rolled-up letter seemed to stare up at her from where she'd dropped it on the floor. "You have no power over me!" Even as she said the words, Ann returned to the kitchen and refilled her glass. She was the one in charge of her life, she was the one who would determine when, and *if*, she would ever look at that thing again. She was certainly under no obligation to her mother, that much was certain.

A duo of joggers ran down the street past her driveway. They looked to be teenagers and were running hard. Training for the track team maybe? They reminded Ann of Eleanor. What was it she'd said? *"Better to face these things as soon as possible."*

Maybe she was right. Maybe if Ann just finished the stupid thing, she could forget about it and get on with her life. She scooped up the paper.

Annie, my sweet darling, even though I was just a teenager at the time, from the very second the EPT showed positive I was thrilled. It was like I'd finally found a reason for my life. I'd dropped out of school and been out of the house for a while by then. I thought it would be great, being on my own, no one to tell me what I could and couldn't do. The worst times were when the kids I knew from school came in the Pizza Hut on dates, after ball games, whatever. They'd sit in their booths and laugh and joke, and talk about football games and proms, and I was working full-time, trying to pay the rent. Barely made enough for that. Rent and booze are about all I could afford. And men—well, that comfort at least came for free. I wish I could tell you who your father is, but I really have no idea. I probably shouldn't tell you things so shocking, but like I said, if you're reading this, I've changed.

Her mother didn't even know who her father was? Ann thought of all the times she'd dreamed about her father and pictured what he must be like. She would fantasize about him coming to Charleston, because, of course, he must have moved out of the city or he would have been with her. He'd take one look at her and say, "This darling child has to be my daughter. Why did Lorelei not tell me she was pregnant? I would never have left if I'd known." Then he would sweep Ann up in his arms

and they would drive out of town in his fancy car to live happily
together for the rest of their lives.

"Or not." Ann carried the paper into the kitchen and dropped
it into the trash can. "That's enough of that." The words sounded
brave when spoken, but then something inside her disintegrated
and she fell apart.

Chapter 21

Ethan turned into the parking lot of the church and pulled his truck into the usual area, but he couldn't make himself turn off the engine. Everything inside him was screaming to get out of here and go to Ann's. But that couldn't be right. It had to be wrong.

What would that say about his commitment if he missed church to go spend time with a woman—especially after what she'd said last night? The Bible was very clear that a believer should not marry a nonbeliever, and although they were a long way from matrimony, the "unequally yoked" principle was something he'd learned the hard way a long time ago. That was a line he wouldn't cross. Yet . . . why this compulsion to go see her?

He finally turned off the ignition and forced himself out of the truck, whispering a quick prayer. *God, will You please clear my mind so I can focus on You?* He walked across the pavement toward some friends. As he smiled and waved, every cell in his body screamed for him to turn around. *Okay, God, if for some reason this compulsion to turn around is coming from You, if there is some reason I'm supposed to go to Ann's right now, then I need to get that message loud and clear. Otherwise, please give me strength to overcome this temptation.* He pressed himself forward as if pushing against hurricane-force winds.

"Ethan, hi." Stephanie Jones waved as he approached. "Ed was just looking for you."

"Hi, Mr. Ethan." Four-year-old Samantha looked up at him with big brown eyes.

"Hi there, Samantha. And how are you today?"

"Fine. I'm teaching Sunday school to the little kids today." She said the words *little kids* in several syllables for added emphasis.

"Oh really? All by yourself?"

"Well, Mommy's helping me—you know how two-year-olds are; you gots to have lots of help with them. But I'm helping her tell the story. You wanna hear it?"

"Sure. Lay it on me."

"It's about good Sam Martin. He helped this guy who was hurt and needed his help."

Ethan looked over Samantha's shoulder at her mother. Stephanie smiled. "I think you mean the Good Samaritan."

"Right. That's what I said. All the religious people passed him by, they were too busy going to church and stuff to even talk to him. But not Sam Martin. He saw that the man was hurt and so he stopped and helped him a whole bunch. That's how we're supposed to be."

The kid could have whacked Ethan on the head with a baseball bat and the message would have been less subtle. "You know what, Samantha? You're exactly right." He looked at Stephanie. "Tell Ed I'll give him a call later. I just remembered something I need to do."

"Sure thing." Stephanie took Samantha by the hand. "Come on, sweetie. We teachers have to be on time."

Ethan turned and fled back to his truck. *God, that had to be You, right? I'm supposed to go help Ann for some reason, right?*

He got into his truck and drove toward her house, hoping that it truly was God's intervention and not just his own thoughts twisting things to their advantage. What seemed like seconds later, he was letting himself through the gate, across the patio, and to the front door. Before he could allow his better thoughts to stop him, he rang the doorbell.

Nothing.

He walked around to the garage, peeked through the window, and saw the rental car. Maybe she was out for a walk? Or at Tammy's? No, Tammy was at church. He was certain he'd seen her car there.

He walked back up to the porch and rang again. Still nothing, but he thought he heard the muffled sound of crying coming from inside. His instinct was to leave her with her privacy, but this had to be the reason he was here. He knocked this time. Loud. "Ann, are you all right?" He knocked again. "Ann?"

This time he heard the shuffling of approaching footsteps. She flung open the door, her eyes red and swollen, her cheeks wet with tears. "Take a good look. This is just how messed up I am."

"Uh . . ." The shock stopped him for the space of a nanosecond, and then he realized he didn't care what she thought of him, whether or not he irritated her, whether or not he was perfect enough to help in this situation. The fact was, he was going to dive in headfirst and give it everything he had. Sink or swim. A step of . . . faith. He walked inside without asking her permission, closed the door behind him, and asked, "What's happened?"

Ann shook her head. "Nothing's happened. This is just me. My messed-up, broken life."

Out of pure instinct, he put his arm around her shoulder and led her to the sofa. "Sit down and tell me about it. Please."

They sat, side by side, but she didn't speak. After a few minutes of decreased sniffling, she looked toward the clock. "It's nine thirty. Aren't you supposed to be in church?"

He shrugged. "Well, it is time for church, and usually that's where I am at this time on a Sunday. But today, I don't know, somehow I just felt as though you needed me here more than I needed to be at church. Looking at your face right now, I'd say that I must have been right about that."

"Yeah, well, there's nothing you can do for me, so you may as well get back to where you belong. Go hang out with people like you and Tammy, the ones who have it all together—not some mixed-up piece of work like I am."

"People who've got it all together? Is that what you think about us?"

Ann nodded. "Isn't that what church is all about? It's a meeting of people who aren't as messed up as the rest of us."

He laughed outright at that. "Not even close—you've been around me long enough. I'm sure you know better. But . . . I want to hear about you. What's wrong?"

"Like I said, this is just me."

He watched her quietly, just waiting. Normally he would launch into nervous conversation right about now, but this time he planned to wait her out. Apparently she planned the same, because the silence became unbearable. He noticed some papers lying on the floor by the sofa, so he leaned forward and picked them up. They were images of paintings. He flipped through them, trying to see what about them appealed to Ann—maybe she was just into art, for all he knew, but they were way too traditional. He wasn't going to ask, because he was going to win this silent contest if it took all day. So he just kept feigning interest in the paintings while silently praying for guidance.

Finally, Ann leaned forward and pointed. "See this woman with the child crying against her, while the other woman has her back turned? That's Hagar." She seemed to choke on the word. "Do you know who that is?"

He nodded. "Sure. She was Sarah's maid and Ishmael's mother."

"And nobody gave a rip about whether or not she died. See, that's the father of her child sending her away. It's the woman who insisted she sleep with him in the first place who's making him do it while she stands there with her back turned."

Ethan flipped to the next picture, thankful now that he'd looked through them. "Here's the picture that proves you wrong. Maybe the people in her life didn't care, but God did. See, look here, He's sent an angel to help." He pointed to the painting of a child and woman in the desert, with an angel flying over the trees toward them.

"I saw this painting in New York with a friend of mine. I thought it was a horrid image of a child dying and his poor mother crying beside him. My friend said the same thing you're saying, but I disagree. Angel or not, there's no comfort for her. Look at her face."

"That's because she doesn't know he's there yet. We can clearly see that he's watching over her, even though she feels completely alone. Every person who should have taken care of her may have let her down—more than that, they sent her out to die—but she was not unseen. At this point she feels alone, unloved, but that was never true. God had been there all the time, even when she didn't feel Him or see Him. The same is true for us. We are never alone."

He flipped to the next picture. It was labeled *An Angel Appears to Hagar and Ishmael in the Desert* by Salvator Rosa. Hagar stood beneath a tree, the entire landscape was wild, windswept, and Ishmael was lying on a rock. It was difficult to distinguish the angel from the clouds in the background.

"I like this one," he said. "See how the angel is almost one with the backdrop? He would be easy to miss, wouldn't he? And yet he *is* there and Hagar notices him. That's how God is, Ann. Even when we don't see Him or feel Him, He is there, trying to get our attention. He knows what we need."

"Then why doesn't He give it to us? Why didn't He carry Hagar to someplace safe instead of letting her reach this point? Why didn't He protect my sister from that drunk driver?"

"I don't know. But I do believe that He loved Sarah, was with her, and offered comfort right up to the end. Have you ever considered that?"

"No." She sounded more defensive than truthful.

"What about you finding that letter from your mother? What are the odds? If it's been in the wall for who knows how many years, and we 'just happened'"—he made air quotes around the words—"to find it while you were here, after your sister died, then there's obviously something in that letter that you need to know."

Ann stood, walked over to the trash can, and reached in.

She pulled out the rolled paper, which she then tapped into the air with each point as she made it. "Yeah, like the fact that my mother didn't even know who my father was, or that she left some sort of confession letter to ease her conscience when she dumped us here." She tossed the paper aside and dropped back onto the couch beside the printouts.

Ann flipped back to the first picture, the one of Hagar getting kicked out, Sarah's back to her, and said, "Maybe that's why I feel so strongly about this story. That was my mother with her back turned as she left me here." She touched Abraham's finger as it pointed Hagar away. "I didn't get sent away—I got to stay with my grandmother who loved me and took care of me as best she could—but abandonment still feels like abandonment." Ann started crying again.

Ethan turned and put his arms around her. He wasn't sure which of them was more surprised, but she stayed there and cried on his shoulder. He rocked her back and forth, stroked her hair, and said absolutely nothing while she dumped buckets of sorrow. Finally, she seemed to have cried herself out. She pulled back and looked up at him, wiping her hands across her eyes. "I'm so sorry about that."

He reached out to wipe her wet cheek. "Don't be. I'm glad I could be here for you. You've had a rough time of it, and with Sarah's accident, I'm surprised you've held up as well as you have."

"I have to. There's no one else to do it for me."

"You and I have more in common than you might think. In my version of that painting, it would have been my father with his back turned. It was hard for me, nothing like your situation, but as you said, abandonment still feels like abandonment.

It was during that time that I came to understand the love of God, of the One who will never leave." He put both hands on her shoulders and put his face at eye level. "Ann Fletcher, you are not alone." Every ounce of his being wanted to lean forward and kiss her. Comfort her. She was so close, so very close. But he couldn't . . . no, he *wouldn't* do it.

She stared hard at him, as if she were trying to see something buried deep inside of him. After a minute, she took a deep breath, turned away, and shrugged a bit too casually. "Well, as long as you're here, do you want to help me with the floors? I stained the smaller bedroom already. You want to help me with the bigger one?"

"Tell you what, I'll help you get those done, but you've got to promise me that you'll take a break midday and let me take you for a special lunch. It's time for your next tourist adventure."

"I've already done my Charleston she-crab soup thing. What else is there?"

"Oh, the lunch this time won't be so special, but the place I'm taking you will make up for it."

"As long as it's something laid-back."

"This place is as laid-back as they come."

Ann nodded. "All right then."

Ethan stood to his feet and held out his hand to help her up. "Let's get to work." And, boy, did he need something to keep himself busy. Now that he'd allowed himself to hold her, even if it had been under duress, it would be that much harder to keep his distance.

Chapter 22

"You know, you should probably give me a set of keys to your place."

Ann put her hands on her hips in mock offense. "Excuse me? Just what kind of girl do you think I am?"

Ethan's face burned a deep red. "I didn't mean . . . really, I . . ."

It was just after one o'clock, and they had finished with the stain in Nana's room and put the first coat of polyurethane on the floor in Ann's old room. She knew what he meant, but seeing Ethan speechless was so completely amusing, she wasn't ready to let him off the hook just yet. "Then what exactly *did* you mean?"

"I was thinking I could come over here when you're back in New York, set the furniture back up, maybe start the sanding in the living room and kitchen. You know, just help out around here. You *did* say you wanted to get this place done soon."

"*Sure* that's what you meant. I get that from the men in New

186

York all the time. 'Give me the keys to your place, baby, and I'll come over and sand the floors and move furniture.' Can't you at least come up with something original?"

"Really, I . . ."

She looked at him and burst out laughing. "Oh, come on, Ethan, lighten up. I know you didn't mean it that way."

He grinned, his cheeks still a bit pink. "Whew. I thought you were really mad there for a minute."

"Trust me on this one, if I'm mad at you, you will not have to wonder about it. It will be crystal clear."

"Yeah, I guess so. Well then, before I get myself into any more trouble, I'd better get out of here. I need to run back over to my house and change out of my church clothes before our lunch outing. Seems to me this might be a good time to make my exit. I'll be back in about half an hour. Okay?"

"Better make it forty-five minutes. You know how long it takes us Southern belles to get ready!"

"Forty-five minutes, then." As he walked out the door, Ann could hear him mumbling something. It sounded like "Didn't mean it that way," but she wasn't certain. Whatever it was, it made her smile.

She went to her suitcase, suddenly wishing she'd brought something a little cuter than the T-shirt and shorts she had with her. Oh well, there was absolutely no reason to want to look cute for Ethan. Her future was in New York, her dreams were in New York, and the means to fulfilling her promise to Sarah and Nana were in New York. Patrick Stinson might be a bit dangerous, but there were endless possibilities there.

Ann took a quick shower, then settled for a black, fitted tee and denim shorts. She ran a brush through her hair and dabbed

SHEILA WALSH & KATHRYN CUSHMAN

a little bit of color on her lips and cheeks, then added a light coating of mascara.

"*Ann Fletcher, you are not alone.*" Ethan's words ran over and over in her mind. She couldn't shake them. What exactly did he mean? Who did he mean was with her? Him . . . or God? Or angels and their unseen watchings and ethereal music? Which of these would be more terrifying? She didn't currently possess an answer to that question, so she made herself busy cleaning the kitchen sink.

When Ethan arrived at the front door, he was wearing an Atlanta Braves baseball cap, blue T-shirt, and long khaki shorts. "You ready?"

"I guess so." Ann started to walk outside, but Ethan stopped her with an extended hand. "You got sunglasses with you?"

"Yeah, in my purse."

"Good, you're going to need them." It was the last thing either of them said for almost twenty minutes. He started down Highway 17, which ran north-south along the coast. Ann remembered it well from her childhood. She recognized they were going in the general direction of Savannah, and her curiosity was piqued. But she was determined not to ask. Finally, he pulled off at a little shopping center, climbed out of the truck, and came around to open the door for her.

"I'm confused."

He smiled and pointed toward a Subway sandwich shop. "I told you I was buying you lunch, didn't I?"

"Not to seem ungrateful, but I'm quite certain there's a Subway much closer to my house than this one, and I certainly don't see anything touristy about this little strip mall."

"Well, we're not eating here. We're just getting the food and moving on."

"Like a picnic?"

He smiled but didn't answer. "Not telling." A few minutes later he turned off of Highway 17 onto Main Road, a two-lane thoroughfare that, if her memory was correct, would lead them to the beach.

"Wait a second. This is the road to Johns Island. You're trying to sneak me into Folly Beach from the back way, aren't you? What's that surf spot out there all you surfers like so much? The Washout, right?"

He sat in silence for a second, then said, "I'm still not telling you where we are going, but I will tell you I have enough common sense not to take you to The Washout."

"Oh really? You mind telling me why not?"

"Are you kidding? The surf's been up lately. The place will be packed with guys looking for big waves and beautiful women. Right now, you're Charleston's best-kept secret. I'm not taking you down to The Washout and letting them all get a look at you. I'd end up beaten to a pulp trying to defend your honor."

"Right." Ann started to tell him that it didn't matter, because surfers in general had always annoyed her. But when she looked at Ethan and felt the thrill of the compliment running through her veins, she began to wonder if maybe that wasn't quite as true as it used to be.

They finally pulled into a parking lot. As Ethan unloaded the food and drink, Ann found herself staring at the most incredible tree she'd ever seen. It was an oak, or at least that's what she thought it was, but its branches were thicker than most oak *trunks*. Several of the heavy, lower limbs had to be held up by some kind of human-rigged support system. The canopy

probably reached sixty feet high, and it cascaded in all directions, like an abstract work of art.

"She's beautiful, isn't she?" he said. "Hurricane Hugo beat
her up pretty good, but she dug in her roots and refused to give
in. Did you know that this tree is thought to be about fifteen
hundred years old? Just think about it. This tree was here for
one thousand two hundred fifty years before the United States
ever became a country."

"This is perfect," Ann breathed. She walked over and touched
a piece of the bark, just to make sure it was real. "I know this
place. Nana used to bring us here."

"Yup, Angel Oak." He set out lunch on one of the picnic tables.
"Your pictures this morning got me thinking about it. That one of
the angel up in the tree that looked almost like clouds. They used
to say that this tree got its name because it looked like an angel."

"Don't know that I see it." Ann looked up through the
maze of limbs. "I suppose it does remind me a little of some of
Keith's drawings of angels. I used to feel safe here."

"Truth is, it was named after the people who used to own
the place. Their last name was Angel." He took a bite of his
sandwich, then looked at her. "That may be the true story, but
to be perfectly honest, I like the other story better."

Ann looked up into the massive limbs over her head. She
could see wispy clouds in the sky above. A gust of wind picked
up a napkin, flipped it over, then fluttered it across the ground.
In a movement born purely of instinct, Ann stamped it down
with her foot, holding it in place. The leaves above them flapped
in the breeze, doing a spontaneous kind of dance. The smaller,
uppermost limbs swayed in time with the rushing sound of the
wind. It sounded like music.

Almost.

"I like the other story better too," she said in a quiet voice.

Later that afternoon Ethan and Ann walked up the driveway toward her old house. A slight breeze had cooled the air just enough to temper the warm sun shining through the wispy clouds. *Almost perfect.*

"You want to come in for a while?" She walked a little closer, close enough that their arms brushed. Just that morning, those arms had felt so good wrapped around her as she'd cried, so secure. How long had it been since she'd felt so utterly safe? She craved that peace again.

"I . . ." He stopped walking and turned to face her. He put his left hand against her cheek and moved a loose lock of her hair. "I really . . ."

He closed his eyes tight. For the space of a few seconds, he didn't move. He hardly seemed to breathe. Then his eyes opened.

"I can't." He backed up three steps. "I've got some things I've got to do."

"Okay."

"And tomorrow's a really busy day at work. I probably won't make it by. I'll come move the furniture back later in the week, though, okay? I'll try to get it all set back up and everything, so it will be ready next time you come back, whenever that is. I'll have things together then." He started walking quickly back toward his truck. "I'll see you next time. Have a good trip." He sort of waved as he jumped back into his truck.

"Alrighty then." Ann chuckled under her breath, but a stinging pain burned in her chest. Ethan had returned to run-on sentences and gone into all-out escape mode. Was it nerves? Or rejection?

Chapter 23

"Help. Annie. Please."

Ann ran toward Sarah, her arms outstretched. "Sarah, I'm right here. I'll help you."

"You can't go back there." The bouncer-nurse blocked Ann's way. When Ann looked over her shoulder, she saw Sarah's gurney being pulled away from her. One of the nurses looked up at her and smiled—the face was so serene that it almost glowed.

That's when Ann heard the music.

She jerked awake, gulping for breath, but the music was still there. She shook her head to wake herself up, even though she knew she was awake. "You are not real; this is not real!" She pulled her pillow over her head. "I refuse to give in to this. You are nothing—nothing but my imagination." Slowly, one note at a time, the music faded into the background until it disappeared altogether.

Wow. Maybe she could control this after all. Yes, of course she could. Time and determination were the only things needed here.

It was a good thing that today was Monday and Ethan had a

full day of work. Every time he came around, she seemed to lose her focus on what she needed to do, and it was becoming painfully obvious that what she needed to do was to get out of here. And stay out. After his hasty departure yesterday, she wondered if maybe he thought so too.

Ann put on her work clothes and added the final coat of polyurethane to each bedroom's floor. The manufacturer recommended that furniture not be replaced for several days, and the rugs for a full week. Well, that wasn't a problem. She didn't plan to be back anytime soon. She needed to return to New York and get her career back on the fast track. She was even looking forward to seeing Patrick Stinson. So what if he played the field a lot? She could still go out with him and enjoy herself, right? There was something freeing about that kind of a no-strings-attached, living-for-the-moment lifestyle. It was fun. It was exciting. Why even bother looking for something different?

By lunchtime, she was inside a wholesale window treatment store that specialized in modern. That's what the house needed, some modernizing. In fact, Ann had also decided to find a place where she could rent some furniture for the open house, after she sold most of what was currently in there. Now was the time to get rid of the old and fill up that space with something new.

After she got back to the house, she was unloading the boxes of blinds from her car just as Tammy and Keith came walking across the lawn. Those two had the uncanny ability of showing up at the most inconvenient times. "Hey, Ann, I was wondering if you could find it in your heart to be my mannequin again sometime today. I know you're really busy, but I've got one more little hem to finish up and it's such a blessing to have a live model."

"I don't have—"

"And while you're there, I'll show you my new elephant. She's beautiful." Keith grinned at her.

In spite of her best intentions to send them away quickly, Ann couldn't help but ask Tammy the question. "His elephant?"

"He got a postcard from Danielle today. She's somewhere in Kenya, I think."

Ann tried to reconcile the Danielle she'd seen—setting tables, serving muffins and Krispy Kremes, and bossing everyone around—with a person who could spend months in Africa. Somehow she couldn't quite do it.

"I'll draw a picture for you too." Keith had come beside her, smiling like it was Christmas morning.

Ann took one look at Keith's innocent face, thought of all he lived with on a daily basis, and the excuse died somewhere in her throat. She turned toward Tammy and pretended to fan herself while batting her eyes. "Li'l ol' me? Be a model for you? Why, I never heard anything so darlin'."

Tammy burst out laughing. "Sarah was right about you—you are a riot." She looked at the boxes in Ann's hand. "Let us help you carry these things in."

"That's okay, I've got it."

"I'll help you, Annie." Keith had picked up a long carton and was hauling it toward the door before Ann could stop him.

"Really, it's okay, I can get it."

Tammy reached into the trunk. "Of course you can, but so can we. Remember, Keith, we're supposed to call her Ann."

"Right. Sorry, Annie, I forgot."

"It's okay."

Tammy lifted a couple of boxes and started toward the house. "What's in here?"

"Some blinds for the windows."

"Blinds? Oh, Ann, I wish I would have known you were thinking about doing this. I would have been happy to make some curtains for you."

A picture flashed through Ann's mind of petunias and paisley, and varying shades of pink, yellow, and purple. "Oh, you can't do everything for me, Tammy. Besides, I wanted to add a little of my own touch to the place."

"Your own touch, really? Are you thinking about staying, then?" There was no mistaking the hope in her voice.

"No, Manhattan is my home. I'm just trying to spruce things up a little bit so the place will be ready when the time comes to list it."

By then, they had entered the house. Since the bedroom furniture was squashed into the living room, there was very little open floor space. "Just set the boxes anywhere you can find a spot. I think I'll go ahead and try this one over the kitchen sink, just to get an idea of how it will look."

"Oh good, I'd love to see what you picked out, but aren't you going to repaint in here? Shouldn't you wait until after that?"

"Yeah, I'm not actually going to hang it, just hold it up and make certain I like it."

When she removed the semi-sheer, white, tone-on-tone roller shade from the box, she heard Tammy gasp. She didn't turn but went ahead and held it up to the window. She pulled the shade down and admired the nice, clean lines against the window. Much better than all that lacy stuff. "What do you think?"

"They're . . . nice." Tammy's face belied the truth, but she wouldn't say anything. Ann knew she wouldn't. "Well, are you ready to come be my southern belle for a few minutes?"

Why had she let Keith's sweetness guilt her into agreeing to this? Best to get it over with. "Sure, let's go."

Keith was sitting at the kitchen table, his chin in his hand. After a big yawn, he said, "They look real pretty, Annie. I like 'em."

That's why. How could anyone stand against that? Before she could think better of it, she bent down and hugged him. "It sure is good to have you around here, Keith. I don't know how I would have carried those things in by myself."

He smiled and hugged her back. "I love you, Annie."

In spite of every instinct inside her, she kissed him on the top of the head. "Me too." It was as close as she could come to saying the words.

Tammy tried to keep a straight face when she looked up at Annie wearing the cream-colored, lace-lined creation. For the most part, she had to keep her focus on the hem to accomplish this. If she looked up for very long, she started to get tickled.

"Who uses all these dresses?" The tone of Annie's voice was as funny as her expression.

"These are actually going to be sold at an auction they're having downtown to raise money for the historic foundation."

"It's Wiggle time. You like the Wiggles, Annie?" Keith was standing by the television, where he'd just inserted a tape into the VCR, pointing excitedly at the four men in black pants and brightly colored shirts.

"Uh . . . I . . ." Ann looked at Tammy.

"They're the Fab Four of the preschool set." She nodded toward Keith. "And Keith."

Keith had extended both pointer fingers and was moving his

hands in rapid circles. "It's Wiggle time," he said again, bouncing in dysrhythmic time with the music. "You like them, right, Annie?"

Ann nodded. "Now that I know who they are, I sure do." She giggled as she turned her attention back to Tammy and whispered, "Guess I know what I'm adding to my iPod next."

"Sure you are. Now hold still."

"So people pay money for one of these dresses. Why? It's not like you can wear them anywhere."

"Oh, there are the occasional historic balls, and of course Halloween."

"Somehow I'm having trouble seeing myself at a Halloween party in Manhattan dressed like this. Unless, of course, I was supposed to be Scarlett O'Hara. I could probably do that. I've always kind of admired her."

"You *admire* Scarlett? I hope you're kidding."

"I most certainly am not. I suppose it's because she's such a strong woman. Life dealt her a few bad hands, and she picked herself up and kept going. Saved the family plantation in the process. A woman who knew how to get things done—she would make it big in New York."

"I'm glad I don't live in New York, then." Tammy pushed the next pin into place before continuing. "Think of how many people she hurt along the way."

Ann shrugged, which pulled the hem from Tammy's hand. "Most of them would have hurt her in the long run; she just beat them to the punch."

Wow. How to respond to that? *God, give me some right words here. This poor doll is all broken up inside, but I don't know how to help her without offending her.*

"How much do these sell for?"

"Depends on what kind of mood the bidders are in, I guess. They usually go for a few hundred dollars, give or take. The highest one I know of fetched just over a thousand."

"You've got to do the monkey." Keith's singing was loud and off key. "Do the monkey."

"Darling, you're being just a little loud. Didn't you promise to color a picture for Ann?"

"Oh right. Sorry." He sat back down and started coloring but continued to sing a little lower than before.

"A thousand dollars?" Annie whistled. "Who'd have thought? You know, I don't get why people like to dress up like the old days anyway. It's like they're trying to be something they're not."

"You're one to talk." The words slipped out, and Tammy immediately wished she could take them back. Her mouth was full of pins, and Keith was still singing; maybe Ann didn't hear it. She continued her work without even looking up.

"What do you mean?"

Well, the words were out there now—may as well spit the rest of them out, she supposed. She took the pins from her mouth and laid them on the table. "Ann, you know I love you to pieces, but the truth is, you're trying harder than anyone I know to pretend you're not who you are. You're running from yourself as fast as you can, but it's still catching up with you." She spoke in a pleading voice, begging Annie to see the truth for what it was.

"I have no idea what you're talking about."

"Really? Take those blinds, for instance. They might look just right in a high-rise New York apartment complex, but in your grandmother's old house, they look like you're trying to pretend it's something that it's not. It doesn't work for the house, and it doesn't work for people either."

"You have no idea what you are talking about." Ann's voice was loud enough to cause Keith to look up from his coloring.

"When it comes to the decorating, I suppose you might be right." Tammy gestured around the living room and smiled. "In fact, I'm sure of it. But when it comes to you, I don't think so."

"Well, you're wrong."

"Honey, I wish you'd slow down. Quit running long enough to acknowledge that you've got some pretty big hurts, and give God the chance to take care of them for you."

Keith stood up and walked over to them. "The angels will help. Like they do me."

"Do your angels make you feel better, Keith?" Ann looked annoyed, but she seemed relieved for the change in conversation.

"Not on the outside, but on the inside. Like when you fall down and scrape your knee and your mommy holds you real close and kisses you. Your knee still hurts, but you feel better just the same. When they sing to me, I feel all happy inside."

"Kind of like the Wiggles?"

Keith shook his head. "The Wiggles are just pretend. They're actors, that's all. The angels, they're real."

Ann's face went pale. "Tammy, are you about done? I've really got to get back and put on the last coat of polyurethane, and I've got an early flight tomorrow."

A few moments later Ann scampered out the door and back to her house like she was running from a stalker. Tammy knew the name of that stalker.

Truth.

Chapter 24

The sun's heat reflected on the windows twenty stories up. It beat down on the sidewalks and poured itself over dozens of people emerging from the subway tunnel. The air smelled of perfume and sweat, designer coffee and grime, all mixing with the energy of adrenaline and despair. The contradictions that were New York in the summer never failed to thrill Ann. The place where anything was possible.

By the time Ann rolled her suitcase through the doors of Marston Staging, she felt energized. "Hi, Jen."

"Margaret wants to see you in her office the moment you arrive." The grim expression on Jen's face told Ann more than she wanted to know about Margaret's current mood.

"Alrighty then." Ann dropped her suitcase in the cubicle, then walked into Margaret's office. "You wanted to see me?"

She stood. "Yes, I do. Patrick Stinson has called me a couple of times today. He said you aren't answering his phone calls."

"Margaret, I've been on an airplane. There are rules about having your cell phone turned off. Remember?"

"Well, you should have checked your messages as soon as you landed and he should have been the first call you made."

"I did check messages; he didn't leave one." Ann looked down at her phone again to confirm. "No, no messages."

"I should think it would be enough to see his number on the missed calls to know that you needed to call him back."

Again, Ann looked at her phone. "I've got four missed calls, all of the caller IDs are marked private. What, do you want me to start calling Patrick Stinson every time I get an unidentified call on my cell phone? I'm sure that would go over well."

Margaret sat in her chair, then leaned forward on her elbows, not one hint of defeat showing on her face. "One way or the other, I want you to call him at his office right now."

"Of course I will." Ann stood to walk back to her cubicle.

"Ann, a lot of people's jobs are depending on this contract. You understand that, right?"

"Yes, I got it. Loud and clear."

"Good."

Ann returned to her desk but took a minute for deep breathing before picking up the phone. Calm, clear thinking was mandatory right now.

She punched in his number. Two secretaries and three minutes later, she heard, "Ann, you're back. I trust your time in Charleston was fruitful."

"Yes, it was. I found a new supplier of artwork that I thought we might want to use for a couple of your units. I've got samples I could e-mail over."

"I've never been one who liked to work by computer. I'm

more of an old-fashioned kind of guy. I like to do my work hands-on. Know what I mean?" There was just a hint of innu- endo in the question.

"Of course. Would you like me to put a copy in the mail then?"

"How about in person? Over dinner tonight?"

Everything Ann wanted was right here, wrapped up in the package that was Patrick Stinson. All she had to do was take the gift that life was offering her. So why wasn't she answering him? Why couldn't she make even a sound in response?

"I'll pick you up. Seven thirty."

"No." Wow. Patrick Stinson had done the job for her, and still she fought it. What was wrong with her? "I mean, I couldn't let you go to all that trouble. I have several errands to run in the city; I'll meet you at the restaurant. Where did you have in mind?"

She could hear the sound of a computer keyboard in the background, so she knew he was still on the phone. He just wasn't responding. Finally, he said, "Well, it goes against my old-fashioned nature," he said, his voice smooth as silk, "but if you insist, meet me at La Maison at eight."

"All right."

"I'm looking forward to it." He paused, and this was where Ann knew she was supposed to express how much she was looking forward to it too. She couldn't bring herself to say it but did finally manage, "Yes, it's always exciting to talk about new design ideas."

He chuckled into the phone. "Tonight." The line went dead.

It was almost seven when Ann arrived at her apartment building. Before she went upstairs, she stopped at her mailbox, something she normally wouldn't do when she was in a hurry. It was stupid now, she knew that, but she'd grown fond of Keith's almost-daily drawings. But she'd left Charleston only twelve hours ago, so this was obviously a waste of time. Even if he'd mailed one today, it wouldn't be here. She turned the key in the lock and pulled the door open to find a stack of bills and a couple of flyers. Of course there was nothing.

She rode the elevator to the eighth floor, and as she walked down the hall toward her apartment, she could see a letter leaning against her door. On a yellow sticky note attached to a blue envelope, she read:

> Ann, this was in my box by mistake. Welcome home.
>   Christine

She let herself inside as she tore open the envelope. She pulled out a drawing that showed Ann with her hand extended toward a yellow blob beside her. It looked like she was holding a flat letter *m*. Behind what Ann knew to be the angel of the drawing, there was something that looked like a cylinder.

Well, this one was a little harder to decipher than most. She put it on the refrigerator, thinking maybe she'd have to take this one back to Charleston next time and have Keith explain it to her. Something inside of her ached at the thought. Well, she didn't have time to think about that right now.

Despite the fact that she was going to be late if she didn't move fast, Ann took extra care choosing her clothes. She wanted to look nice, but not overly appealing. She would play along with Patrick Stinson's little game, enjoy it even, but she wanted contracts signed before this relationship took any sort of a personal turn. Black slacks and a white, quarter-sleeve, silk button-up seemed to fit the bill: professional, attractive, and traditional enough that it was neither trendy nor out of fashion.

She rushed out the door, hailed a taxi, and arrived at the restaurant at three minutes before eight. La Maison was a quaint café, candlelit tables, a pianist at a grand piano playing classical music. Patrick Stinson had not yet arrived, but the maitre d' escorted Ann back to the table. A waiter immediately came to take her drink order. She wouldn't drink anything that might impair her judgment tonight. "Just water, thanks."

A few moments later Patrick Stinson arrived. "Ann, I'm terribly sorry I kept you waiting. I got a last-minute call from one of the developers on our team, and well, you know, crisis averted, but not without making me late to meet my beautiful dinner companion. I do apologize."

"Apology accepted."

He wore a black turtleneck under an expensive gray jacket. Something about the slight curl to his hair, combined with his left-sided dimple, gave him a boyish charm. That, coupled with his confidence, born of power, was so inviting. "I could hardly wait for you to get back into town."

"Yes, let me show you some of the art I've found. Also we've recently acquired a couple of really nice pieces of furniture that I think will work well with your overall plan." Ann pulled her portfolio out from underneath her seat.

He took it from her, his hand brushing hers in the process. "Let's see what you've got here." He flipped it open and began turning pages. "Looks good. Yes, it all looks great." Then he looked up at her and set the portfolio aside. "I knew I was going to enjoy working with you."

"We at Marston Home Staging work as a strongly cohesive team. It's not just me; there are many people working on this project behind the scenes." Even Ann knew the words sounded forced and stilted, but she needed to slow things down. She needed time to think.

"Yes. Well, I appreciate all those people working behind the scenes, but I'm really interested in your work, in the front scene, where I can enjoy not only your skill but your company."

Ann watched the flame of the small candle at the center of the table. Every time the door to the café opened, it flickered and danced, totally at the mercy of outside forces. That's what she was. A flame that simply danced at the whim of things she couldn't control. She didn't like the feeling. "Why don't we talk about the office space? What do you have in mind there?"

"Let's just say, for imagination's sake, that we were going to put *your* office there. What would you want?"

There was a new undertone to his words that alarmed Ann. Still, she tried to pretend it wasn't there. "Well, I think for your clientele, a nice Moura Starr Century desk—solid white with a white leather top. Absolutely stunning. A couple of white leather chairs with black trim to go with it, and I might consider adding a tango desk for conferencing—stainless steel and glass. It would be sleek, modern, and sophisticated. Add a couple of well-placed art pieces, and it would be perfect. I brought some pictures."

"That's not what I asked. I asked what *you* would want if it were *your* office."

"But I'm not your client, so my ideal, and the ideal of someone who could actually afford to lease that office space, are not the same thing."

"If it were your office, your dream office, what would you do?"

Ann shrugged. At least they were staying on the topic of work. "Well, I'd start with this amazing desk I spotted a few weeks ago. It has a scratched glass top, frosted cross-hatch pattern until the border, which is clear. It's more like a piece of art than a desk, but what a thrill it would be to work on it. Then there would be glass shelves hung at uneven intervals, chrome accents, some carefully placed black articles just for some contrast, and perhaps a rug in a shocking bright shade just to spice it all up." Ann could see the whole picture in her mind. It sounded wonderful.

"What if I said that office could be yours?"

"What are you talking about?"

"I've been toying with the idea of starting my own staging company. It would save us money in the long term, because we spend a lot of money hiring out our staging. It would also give us another avenue of income, and when we staged for other developers, it would help us stay abreast of what the competition is doing."

"I suppose that makes sense."

"Yes, I think it makes a lot of sense. Now, back to that office of yours. Can you see your name on the door?" He leaned toward her across the table.

Ann looked into his eyes—deep brown and oh so sincere. Was he offering what it sounded like he was? "Well, I guess that depends. Would I be in charge of this beautiful office, or in a cubicle in the back?"

"Based on what I've seen so far, I find it impossible to imagine anyone but you heading it up."

And there it was. Just like that. Even more than Ann had dared to imagine, right here within her grasp. "It sounds like a dream."

He reached across the table and took her hand. "Dreams do come true sometimes, don't they?" He rubbed his thumb across the back of her hand. "You could start right now, you know, let the first job be the Stinson Towers project."

"Well, I . . ." Ann looked at his hand on hers and knew there was a price involved. "I'd really prefer not to rush things, and I have a couple of coworkers that need their jobs at Marston. Why don't we proceed a little more slowly?" She reached for her glass, wanting an excuse to remove her hand from his, and took more than a sip of water.

"Loyalty. I like that in a woman." He polished off his scotch in a single swallow, then held it up as a sign to the waiter that he'd like another. "I'll grant you there's no reason to rush, but I've never been known for my patience either." He grinned. "How about we start laying the groundwork now, and when we're ready for the next project, we'll be all set to go? Those coworkers of yours, they could be part of the deal too, you know. You'll need a staff—bring them along."

"Sounds perfect." And it did. Almost. This job offer, or promise of a job offer, came with strings attached. Looking across the table, she saw a man with whom most women would kill to make a connection—string or otherwise. If this thing panned out, she could hire Beka and Jen, and they could all be free from the tyrant that was Margaret. She wouldn't need to buy in either. The sale of the house would give her financial freedom like she'd never dreamed of. She would be crazy to hesitate. And yet . . .

Keep your head, Ann. Think this through. Ann tried to concentrate on her surroundings, to just clear her head for a moment.

A woman stood talking to the piano player, her back to Ann. The pianist nodded at her and smiled as she dropped a folded bill into the tip jar and walked away. She didn't return to her seat, however; she walked toward the exit where the outdoor lights lit up her auburn hair.

"You've fallen quiet. I can see that once again I've managed to bore a dinner companion with too much business talk, one of my shortcomings, I'm afraid. Let's talk about you, Ann Fletcher. Tell me all about you."

"There's nothing interesting to talk about there. Let's hear some of your stories."

The music changed keys, and for the space of five heartbeats, Ann heard the song she never wanted to hear again. "It can't be, not that song." She said the words aloud before she realized she was doing it.

"Mozart's Piano Sonata No. 16, I believe." Patrick Stinson nodded toward the piano player, who was now quite clearly not playing what Ann had thought she heard. "Did you know that although this is likely his most famous work, it was not published until sometime after his death?" He took a generous sip of scotch before continuing. "One of the things I find most interesting is that the opening bars were really made famous because Looney Tunes associated them with Granny in the Sylvester and Tweety cartoons. Ironic, isn't it? A work that was never published by one of the most gifted composers to have ever lived became famous only after it made its way into cartoons."

"I didn't realize you were so into music." Ann couldn't have cared less, but maybe if she kept talking, she could forestall the inevitable mental freak-out she knew was coming.

"I'm not really. In college, I wrote a paper about the serendipity of success, citing this piece of music as a major example."

Ann looked around the room again, the uncomfortable

sensation of being watched prickling against the back of her neck. Were angels watching her right now, or was this hallucination starting to develop into full-blown schizophrenia? *Hold it together, don't fall apart. Not here. Not now.* "You think success is more luck than hard work?"

"I think it's both. Look at us, for instance. What are the odds we'd just happen to be on the same plane the day after I'd told my previous staging company that I didn't plan to use them for the next project? Then I just happen to be close enough to see what you were sketching. And now, here we are, talking about a new business venture together. If you weren't a hard worker, *and* if fate hadn't intervened, then we wouldn't be here right now."

The food arrived and Ann managed to force down a few bites, but mostly moved the food around on her plate. She searched for some semblance of normal. "What made you decide to switch designers, if you don't mind my asking?"

He shrugged. "They did some nice work for us, but it was just time to move on to something new and fresh."

Ann wondered if he meant design-wise, or just a different woman. "I see."

"Did you meet Meredith at the open house—Meredith Radke?"

"Yes, I met her." Ann could still remember the perfection of both her designs and her beauty.

"Perhaps it was also serendipitous for her that our joint projects ended, because I understand that she has left her former company and gone out on her own now."

Ann suspected it was less a "left the company" and more a "fired for losing the Stinson account." "Started her own company? Really? She's very brave to do that in these economic times."

"True. But I've heard a rumor that she's doing very well and, in fact, has landed a couple of my competitors' accounts already. So see . . . once again, lady luck has worked her magic."

"Yes, magic." The restaurant grew hot and stuffy, making it difficult to take a deep breath. After the waiter cleared their plates, he brought back Ann's leftover slices of roasted duck, wrapped in aluminum foil twisted to be shaped like a swan.

Patrick Stinson walked her outside and waited while the bellman hailed a cab. "Did you not enjoy the food? Next time I'll have to let you pick the restaurant."

"No, it was lovely. It's just that after traveling all day, I'm never particularly hungry. Airplanes seem to do that to me."

"Forgive me, I should not have insisted that we do this tonight; it's just that I'm very excited about this project."

"No, it was great, really. I look forward to seeing this project through to completion." Ann extended her hand for him to shake, but instead he took it and kissed it.

"I think there are many happy projects ahead of us."

The cab pulled up to the curb, and Ann had never been so happy to make an escape in all her life. Oddly enough, she found herself wishing the cab was taking her back to the house in Charleston, away from Patrick Stinson.

When the cab stopped in front of her building, Ann climbed out onto the sidewalk and stood for a moment. She looked to her right and saw a homeless man digging through trash cans, his hair unkempt, his jacket torn in several places. Suddenly, her feet were moving by themselves, and she found herself standing next to him. He shrank back when he noticed her approach. She tried to smile so he wouldn't be frightened, but the fact was, *she* was frightened, so it didn't work so well. "Hi, I'm Ann. I just went to dinner and couldn't finish my meal. They wrapped up the leftovers for me, but I know it won't be nearly as good tomorrow as it is tonight. Would you like this?"

He looked up at her, surprise in his eyes. His hair was long, gray, and scraggly, and he had a jagged scar across his left cheek. "I've seen you here lots of times, and you've never offered me nothing before."

Ann shrugged. "Maybe I've changed."

"Good to hear." He reached out carefully, watching her the entire time as if he expected her to retract her offer. When he finally grasped the swan, he nodded. "Thanks." He turned and walked slowly away, the foil making metallic sounds as it was ripped open.

"You're welcome." Ann went to the door of her building and was punching in the combination on the keypad when she heard whistling. The door latch clicked open, and she found herself humming along as she started inside—at least until reality set in. The tune—the one the homeless man was whistling . . . the one she was humming—it was . . .

"Hey, what's that—?" She let go of the door and whirled around.

He was gone.

Chapter 25

Beka's studio apartment always smelled like warm rolls and Christmas spices. Tonight was no exception, in spite of the fact that dinner had consisted of brown rice and stir-fry chicken. It was as if the teriyaki understood that its fragrance was not homey enough for the traditional décor and chose not to intrude. Ann couldn't help but admire her friend's ability to so completely capture her own essence in her home, down to every last tiny detail.

"Mama, I think Ann needs therapy."

Ann was too stunned to say anything at first, but finally managed, "Huh?" She looked across the small kitchen table, her focus shifting from Gracie to Beka—who had burst out laughing.

Beka laughed for a solid minute before she put her hand on her daughter's shoulder. "Oh, sweetie, you've got to watch how you word those things."

"Why? What's funny about it?" Seven-year-old Gracie looked up at her mother with gigantic brown eyes. "You like to do therapy, don't you, Mama? Wouldn't Ann like it too?"

Beka stood, picked up her daughter, and swung her in a circle, then stopped and hugged her tightly to her chest. She looked at Ann, a mischievous smile on her face. "Now that I think about it, Ann needs some therapy worse than just about anyone I've ever known."

"Great. I'll get the stuff." Gracie wriggled down from her mother's embrace and skipped toward the refrigerator.

Ann folded her arms and looked at Beka. "I think I'm supposed to be offended right about now?"

Beka started giggling again, which erupted into another all-out laughing fit. Ann couldn't remember the last time she'd seen her friend like this, so lighthearted. After years of being married to an emotionally abusive hothead who finally—and mercifully as far as Ann was concerned—left her for another woman, and the past year of Gracie's medical problems, well . . . it had been a long, hard journey for Beka.

"Here we go." Gracie handed her mother a large silver mixing bowl covered in aluminum foil, then turned to rummage in the cabinets.

Beka removed the foil, revealing a large blob of white dough. She looked at Ann then. "Occupational therapy. She's supposed to be keeping her fingers exercised so the arthritis doesn't cause them to stiffen up and lose flexibility. One of the ways she can do that is with play dough. We've just discovered it's a lot more fun to do it with cookie dough. So . . . most nights after dinner, we spend some time working our dough into a fun shape; then we bake it up and eat it for dessert. Our therapy."

Ann tussled Gracie's hair. "Well, I feel a lot better now. And I'm downright thrilled that I'm getting some therapy tonight. Cookie making is exactly what I needed."

"That's what I thought." Gracie's voice was very serious. "You have to go wash your hands first. That's the rule."

"Let's get washing, then. I'm ready for my cookie."

A few minutes later Beka put a cloud, a dog, and a pony into the oven. She looked at Ann. "Before she started on Enbrel, she could never have done any of this. That drug has been life changing for us. I don't know what I would have done if I'd lost my job and couldn't afford to get it for her anymore. I just don't know."

Ann started to say something like, "You could let her father find a way to pay for it," but she didn't. It took great restraint, but she tried not to bad-mouth Richard in front of Gracie. Besides, she knew he had lost his job on Wall Street over a year ago and he and the new wife were rumored to have filed for bankruptcy. "Well, I . . ." Ann debated about whether to come clean about how precarious the deal was. When she looked at Beka's smile, though, she decided right then she would not add one more burden to her friend's shoulders. She reached over and hugged her tight. "Keep your head up. I can't give you details just yet, but I think things are about to get even better. There's an opportunity on the horizon that can change both our lives." Why had Ann ever doubted whether she wanted to work for Patrick Stinson? "It's far from certain yet, but I will tell you that it doesn't include Margaret."

"Say no more. I'm on board." Beka laughed as she opened the oven door. "Mmm, everything looks perfect."

Ann sure hoped so.

On Friday, Margaret and Ann met Patrick Stinson at the Marston warehouse. A lot of home staging companies rented furniture from specialty companies, and the Marston Company did some of that, but Margaret had decided long ago it was better to own as much of it as possible. Then, not only could she earn the rent money, but she controlled who got it, when, and for how long.

The threesome walked the rows, which in better times were all but empty. In this current housing market, the aisles were filled to capacity. People were trying to sell for less, no one could afford to buy, and paying for a stager sounded extravagant, regardless of the statistics Ann knew by heart. She wondered if Patrick would see the large inventory for the sign of trouble that it was.

Yes, of course he would. Undoubtedly he would smell in that trouble a way to talk down prices.

Ann touched a particularly high-end Danish sofa, one of their nicest pieces. "What do you think of this?"

He paused and put his fist under his chin, looking at the furniture as if pondering. "That is a nice piece. This would be fine for one of the smaller units, but for our deluxe models, I want all custom furniture."

Margaret's face remained calm, but her pinky was tapping on the clipboard she carried. "We can do that. Of course."

"I particularly like the pieces at Blazes."

Ann held her breath. As a designer, she had to admire his taste. Blazes carried the most exquisite pieces of modern furniture she'd ever seen. In fact, their inventory was more like pieces of art that you could sit on, if you chose to do so. But since they were all one of a kind, the prices were outrageous.

Margaret continued to write without looking up. Ann knew that she was thinking through her options. If they were really low on capital, where would they find the funds to buy these pieces? Finally, she looked at him and said, "I've been meaning to purchase some stock pieces from Blazes anyway. Thank you for giving me the excuse that I needed."

"Good," he said, more to confirm their agreement than to offer a compliment. "Now, I'm considering doing something a little different in a few of the kitchens. Keeping it modern, because I think we all agree that there can never be too much sleek and beautiful"—he quirked his eyebrow slightly as he looked at Ann—"but I'd also like to warm it up a bit. Do you have any suggestions?"

"My suggestion"—Ann stopped herself from the retort she really wanted to give—"is to combine Swiss pear cabinetry with anodized aluminum. The horizontal lines of the long-grain forms could work well. Natural quartz countertops would make a nice juxtaposition."

He smiled broadly, then turned to Margaret. "I'm not one to lead from a distance. I like looking at all these things and keeping my fingers in the pie, so to speak. But . . . I think with Ann here, I might be able to relax a little. She's been simply amazing so far."

Margaret nodded. "I told you she wouldn't disappoint you."

"I sure hope she doesn't." He winked at Ann, then pulled a piece of paper out of his coat pocket and handed it to Margaret. "I took the liberty of writing down some of the model numbers of the pieces at Blazes I particularly like. Would you do me a favor and call them up, make certain that those pieces will be available? I like to know exactly what I'm getting into when I sign with a new partner."

"Of course. I'll give them a call this afternoon."

"I really hate to ask, but would you mind calling now? Just so we know?" He looked from Margaret to Ann and back to Margaret, his expression so painstakingly embarrassed that Ann knew it was an act. "In fact, I'd really like it if we could go ahead and get some of the major pieces in stock. I'm a visual person. I like to see what I've got to work with."

He nodded toward Ann and smiled. "Don't worry about leaving me alone to make the call; with Ann here I'm sure I'll be in the best of hands." Once again Ann reminded herself that she needed to proceed with extreme caution where he was concerned. Proceed, definitely—but with both eyes open.

"Of course. I'll call right now." Margaret pulled her phone from her purse and walked to the far end of the aisle.

Patrick put his hand on Ann's elbow to lead her forward. "So, I'm thinking maybe next week we might take in a show and some dinner? Maybe a weekend in the Hamptons in the near future? You've been working so hard lately, and I don't want you to burn out and quit on me. I want to see you get out and have some fun."

"Oh, I have plenty of fun; don't you worry. I am looking forward to spending more time with you; it's just that I'm leaving the last part of next week and heading back to Charleston for the weekend." Another surprise Charleston trip planned spur of the moment, thanks to Patrick Stinson.

"With all these trips to Charleston, I'm starting to feel a little neglected."

Ann shrugged. "Taking care of business."

"What if I meet you down there for the weekend? I think the Spoleto Festival is still going; we could take in a concert. Even though my mother retired there a couple decades ago, I've never really spent much time there. You could show me around like a real native, hmm?"

Ann could picture the scene if Patrick Stinson showed up

when Tammy and Keith were around. The thought made her want to laugh and cry at the same time. "I'm doing a lot of manual labor while I'm there. I really don't have time for fun, and I wouldn't make a very good tour guide because I haven't done much around Charleston for a long time." Except for Angel Oak, and she wouldn't take him there. It was special.

"If I didn't know better, I'd say you were trying to avoid me, Ann Fletcher. It's a good thing I know better, because I don't like to work with people who avoid me."

Proceed, but with caution. She smiled up at him. "I must say, Mr. Stinson, I am surprised by just how sensitive your feelings are. Who would have guessed as much, underneath that tough business exterior?" She said it in what she knew was, quite frankly, a flirtatious tone.

He smiled and took a step closer to her. "I think you're bringing out a whole new side in me."

"Well, I'll just have to try and see if I can avoid that in the future, now, won't I?" She kept her tone light and teasing, although it didn't quite feel that way.

"Okay, I'm back. I talked to the manager, and he assures me we can have all the pieces by the end of next week." Margaret walked up between the two of them, oblivious to the undertones of the encounter. Or . . . perhaps not.

"I'm so happy to be working with a company that knows how to come through. So you submitted the order?"

"Yes, I did." Margaret's fingers were twitching against the clipboard. "Have I shown you our light fixtures yet? They're right this way."

"I can't wait to see them." The expression on his face was a bit too smug to just be about getting the furniture he wanted.

His iPhone vibrated in his pocket. He looked at the caller ID. "Excuse me. I need to take this one."

As soon as he was at a safe distance and engrossed in his call, Ann whispered to Margaret, "How much?"

"Two hundred twenty thousand. Nonrefundable."

"Two hundred twenty thousand?" Ann tried not to screech but wasn't certain she succeeded. "Is there any possible way we can afford that?"

Margaret looked at her face, hard. "Just make certain you don't do anything to mess up this contract. If you do . . . well, Beka will see lots of familiar faces in the unemployment line, because each and every one of us will be joining her."

That furniture would never pay for itself. Especially if Ann went to work for Patrick Stinson, effectively taking away their most high-end client. "Margaret—"

"Shh. Here he comes."

Patrick Stinson sashayed up beside them, smiling broadly. "Now, ladies, where were we? Lunch maybe?"

Chapter 26

The aisles of the market were crowded with exhausted, overwhelmed, and downright cranky people. People like Ann.

"Watch your kid," a heavyset, balding man snapped as a toddler ran in front of him.

The mother, thin, pale, and sickly looking, didn't acknowledge the comment at all. She grabbed her son's chubby hand a split second before he reached the bag of M&M's he'd been aiming for. "Jonah, stay with Mama."

It seemed to have been a long and hard day for everyone. Ann selected only the things that were absolutely necessary to get her through the week. She wanted to get out of here as soon as possible.

When she got to the aisle that displayed the peanut butter jars, she thought about the homeless man. Why it made her think of him, she wasn't sure. Perhaps it was because she'd heard once that peanut butter or granola bars made good things to give to the homeless, something about high protein and portability.

On impulse, she bought a couple of small jars of creamy, a box of honey-oat granola bars, and a pack of brown paper lunch sacks.

After she'd paid, and before she made her way out of the store, she stopped to load up one of the lunch sacks. She put in one jar of peanut butter and two granola bars, then placed it at the top of her grocery bag, just in case she saw him on the way home. And she was planning to be on the lookout. She wanted some answers, some logical answers. Maybe if she could find out the name of that song, prove that it was just an ordinary song, then she could forget about all this craziness. Surely a man who was homeless on the streets of New York would not spout nonsense about angels.

As she approached her building, she could see a figure in the shadows, leaning against the wall. She couldn't tell if it was him or not, but she took a deep breath and moved forward. She could feel her heart starting to pound as she got close enough to see him clearly. Except . . . it wasn't him. In fact, it wasn't even a man; it was a disheveled woman, a brown bag in her hand wrapped around a bottle of some sort. "What do you want?" she asked.

"I . . . Sorry, I thought you were someone else."

"Baby, I'm sure you did." The woman sort of laughed as she took a sip from the bottle.

A thought flashed through Ann's mind of her mother, always needing the next drink in spite of what it cost her. For the first time in a long time, the picture stirred a hint of compassion. "I just went to the store. Would you like something to eat?"

The woman looked at the sack in Ann's hand, then reached forward and snatched it. "Thanks." She peered inside. "How'm I s'posed to eat that peanut butter? With my hands?"

Now Ann remembered why she didn't do things like this very often. "You'll just have to figure that out by yourself . . . And by the way, *you're welcome*."

The woman laughed. "You got a 'tude, don't you?" She put the bag under her arm and pulled her body to an upright position. "He was right about you. You are changing," she said as she began to shuffle away.

"Who was right?" Ann said, her anger dissolving.

"Uri," the woman said over her shoulder.

"Who's Uri?"

The woman kept walking.

"Who's Uri?" Several people on the street turned toward Ann after she'd shouted the question, but the woman just kept walking. Ann shook her head in frustration. It was stupid really. What exactly had she been hoping to find out? How much more ridiculous was she going to become before she simply let this go?

She walked into the lobby, ready to escape to the sanctuary of her apartment. Just before the door closed behind her, she thought she heard a familiar male voice say, "Yep, you sure are changing." She jerked around and stuck her head outside the door, looking for him.

He was nowhere in sight.

Chapter 27

Everything about Sarah's house felt wrong. The beige counter-top stood stark and empty—not overflowing with the usual fruit and flowers, textbooks and cookie crumbs. The sound of laughter had been replaced by the hollow ringing of the hammer.

It also just felt strange to Tammy, being in Sarah's house—Annie's house—while neither of them was home. But Ethan seemed so at home here, and Keith had insisted that they come over and help. So she ignored the uneasiness and went back to work with the broom. "You sure do know how to make a mess."

Ethan laughed. "Tearing out the old, icky stuff is hard, it's messy—ouch!" He dropped the hammer from his right hand and shook his left. "Ouch!" He danced around for a minute before regaining his composure, picking up the hammer and nail again, then looked at her straight-faced. "And at times it's downright painful. But you've got to be willing to go through the process if you really want to see a true change. Anything less is just a cover-up."

"You talking building now, or theology?"

He shrugged and grinned. "Both, I guess. I was thinking about Ann, really, like I do all the time. She's got so much hurt bottled up inside her. I wish she'd deal with it, instead of just pretending it doesn't exist."

"I know what you mean."

"Me too." Keith looked up from his current drawing. "Ray Meal knows too."

"Who?" Tammy and Ethan asked the question at the same time.

"He's an angel. He wants to help her."

Tammy looked at Ethan and motioned toward the outside with her head. "Hey, Ethan, you want to help me carry some of this stuff out to the trash can?"

"Sure."

They both picked up enough trash bags to look believable, then walked outside and far enough from the house so they could whisper without being overheard. "Ethan, I'm scared. You know he's always talked about seeing angels, but lately he's getting more and more insistent about them, talking about them all the time. You heard him—he just called one by some name. I'm afraid his mind is starting to slip."

Ethan shook his head. "Nope. That kid has always been so much more spiritually aware than the rest of us. I've always believed that. It just seems logical to me that right now, with the heartbreak of losing Sarah, they would be that much more a part of his life."

"I guess you're right."

"I always am." He kissed her lightly on the forehead.

"Yeah, right." Tammy put her arm around his waist and

walked back inside. Keith was drawing intently on his paper, but his eyes looked tired. "Come on, Keith, we've got to get you to bed, young man."

"Okay. Bye, Ethan."

"Bye, buddy, see you tomorrow."

Later that night, with Keith tucked securely in bed, Tammy went to the sewing room and picked up the smallest of six identical blue strapless gowns. A bunch of giggling bridesmaids would be in tomorrow morning, each expecting her dress to fit perfectly. So much to do before then. Why had she let Keith talk her into going over to help Ethan instead of staying home and working on these? This was going to take hours, and all she wanted to do was collapse into bed.

The phone jangled from atop the workbench. "Hello."

"It's Ethan. Hey, I was thinking about what Keith said, and what you said, and what I said, and I just couldn't quit thinking about it, so I did a little checking. Guess what I found?"

"What?"

"The name Ray Meal, that Keith called his angel? It sounds a lot like Rahmiel. Right?"

"Yeah."

"And I was thinking about the names of angels we know from the Bible. There's Michael and Gabriel. The name Rahmiel sounds similar, doesn't it?"

"Yeah, I guess so." She tried to stifle a yawn.

"Do you know what 'Rahmiel' means?"

"No, but I'm sure you're about to tell me."

"'Course I am. That's why I called. I looked it up. It's

Hebrew, and in English it means 'God is love and mercy.' Now, doesn't that just sound like the kind of angel God would be sending around to both Keith and Ann right now? I can't think of anything better. Can you?"

"No. No, I can't." So this was why she needed to go help Ethan tonight. God had known that she needed to hear this. Tammy hung up the phone with tears in her eyes and with that indefinable feeling of being completely loved pumping through her heart. "Thank You, Father."

Chapter 28

As the sun retracted the last blush of evening, the Charleston suburbs took on their own glow. The humidity in the air was so thick that a slight haze hovered around the streetlamps and floated outside the well-lit windows. As Ann pulled into Sarah's driveway, she cast a glance toward Tammy's house.

The lights were on in the living room and the kitchen, but the rest of the house was dark. Then, somehow, Ann was walking across the lawn, pulled toward the kitchen door by a force she couldn't seem to control. She knocked on the back door softly, not sure whether she hoped someone would hear her or not.

The curtains at the back door fluttered for a split second; then the door jerked open. "Oh, Ann, it's so good to see you." Tammy threw her arms around Ann and hugged tight. "Things just aren't the same around here when you're gone."

Ann pulled away as soon as she thought it wouldn't hurt Tammy's feelings. "Well, I just thought I'd say hello to you and Keith."

"He'll be so excited when he wakes up in the morning and finds out you're here. You have no idea how much he misses you when you're gone." She smiled then. "Well, I guess you have some idea, given the volume of mail you receive from him on a weekly basis."

Ann thought about the stack of papers in her bedside table drawer. "He's in bed already? Must have had a big day."

"Every day is a big day for Keith. He doesn't do the other kind." Tammy sighed as she said it, but they both laughed.

"Okay, well, I just wanted to let you know I'm back. I didn't want you to see lights on over there and wonder if there was a burglar about or anything." Ann was already backing off the porch by the time she finished the sentence.

"There've been lights on over there most nights anyway. Ethan's been about working himself to death, I think."

Ann stopped walking. "Ethan?"

"Yeah, he brought his whole crew over a couple days, and let me tell you, there was some carrying on then. You know, the day when they were knocking that wall out. Keith, of course, thought it was the greatest thing ever."

Ann glanced toward her house. How had she not noticed a moved wall at the side door when she pulled into the driveway? It was getting dark outside, but it wasn't *that* dark. "They what?"

"You know, the wall in the kitchen. He said y'all had talked about it."

Yeah, they'd talked about it. Once. Several weeks ago. But Ann certainly never expected him to take it upon himself to do this, and without even bothering to talk to her about it. Still, she didn't want to drag Tammy into the middle of it, so she said, "Oh yeah, I'd forgotten he was going to do that while I was gone."

"He sure is a sweetheart. That's all I got to say about him."

If Ann hadn't been so angry, she might have agreed. "Well, I'm going to get settled now. I'll see you tomorrow, okay?"

She walked directly toward the new kitchen door—or rather, it was the same kitchen door, but it no longer resided inside a three-foot walkway. Now it was flush against the rest of the house, a couple of new sidelight windows on each side—these had obviously been added to make the door fit with the wall. They were an absolutely perfect match for the style of the house. Ann was overcome with the urge to break them both. How dare he do all this? He knew she didn't have the money to pay for these kinds of things.

She went inside and found that the kitchen now had a small walk-in pantry. It, too, was perfect. The shelves, everything. Each piece of bedroom furniture had been returned to its original location, and Ann could walk freely through the living room again, on floors that had been redone since she was last here. There were several paint swatches propped up against various walls. Ann picked up a couple. One showed different shades of light sage green, another pale creams advancing up to taupe. All warm colors. All colors that Ann never used.

The doorbell rang and her fury reached a new peak. Tammy had already called him? This was starting to feel like an invasion of privacy the way the two of them worked. Ann walked over and slung the door open.

He stood there wearing a ripped T-shirt, old jeans that had paint flecks all over them, and a baseball cap that might have once been blue, but now was a faded gray. He was glancing back toward his truck, looking as though he might turn and run at any second. "I didn't expect to see you here. Why don't you ever warn us when you're coming back to town?"

Ann folded her arms across her chest. "And what exactly would you have done if you had known I was coming? Re-decorated the entire house?"

The smile melted off his face. "Well, no, decorating's your bit. I'm just trying to get my part finished up for you."

The hurt expression on his face and the undeniable sincerity of his words brought an anger-cooling guilt to Ann. She shook her head. "I didn't mean to snap. It's just that I didn't expect that you would move those walls. I know we kind of talked about it, but we never decided for sure, and those sidelights have got to be expensive."

"Actually, they're not—that's why I decided I'd surprise you with them. They were scrap from another job I'm doing downtown, and they were just too nice to let go to waste. I started wondering about what I could do with them, and then I remembered us talking about moving that wall, and . . . well, it just seemed like the perfect fit. And it is. I mean, at least, I think so. If you don't—"

"If you didn't know I was back in town, then what are you doing here?"

"I came over to do some caulking in the bathroom. The tile's in pretty good shape, but we need to seal up a few edges a little better. I was already on the front porch when I noticed the lights on and realized you were here, so I guess I'll do that some other time, but it just didn't seem right to leave without even saying hello, so I rang the doorbell and—"

"I heard that you've been coming over here nights, after you get off work."

His cheeks turned almost pink. "Not every night." He put his hand on the door frame and ran his finger against the length of it. "I like coming here."

"Why?"

He looked at her and tilted his head slightly to the left. "Well, I . . ." He looked into the house and said, "Did you like any of the paint-color cards I picked up? The walls need painting, and even I know that yellowish color is kind of out of style right now. I had no idea what you like, so I picked up a little of everything I've noticed people using around here lately. That green color has been really big for the last year or so, but I didn't know if you would consider it too trendy, so I brought some of the more neutral colors too. Like I said, I don't really know what you like, so I was just kind of trying to think of everything."

He'd changed the subject without answering the question, but since that was a specialty Ann also possessed, she decided not to call him on it. "I haven't really looked at them yet. Why don't you come in?"

He followed her inside, looking down at his T-shirt. "Guess I look a little rough. Like I said, I didn't expect to see anyone here tonight."

"I like the rugged craftsman look." She was laughing as she said it, but at this moment there was more than a little truth to the words. She picked up the card with the sage green shades. "You know, I've always decorated in black and white. I'm not sure that color on the walls works for me."

"Surely you wouldn't use those colors in this house?"

Ann wouldn't, because she understood the market enough

to know that the people who liked modern furnishings also liked modern houses—not craftsman bungalows. Still, she wasn't going to admit defeat quite that easily. "I haven't ruled out the possibility." She stared him straight in the eye, practically daring him to argue.

He looked back, and it seemed as though he was trying to see inside her mind. Finally, he looked away and rubbed his palms together. "Well, I guess that doesn't surprise me."

Ann wasn't sure why, but somehow his statement offended her. "And just why is that?"

"Well, it sort of fits your personality. If there's something going on that you don't like or can't handle, you cover it up with something else, hoping no one will notice. You can pretend this house isn't the traditional building that it is by changing the trappings, but it's still a traditional house." He picked up a paint sample card with various shades of beige, held it at arm's length, and cocked his head to the side. "You can pretend like you've got everything under control and don't need anyone, but that doesn't change the fact that your heart's broken and you're scared to death of letting anyone get close to you. The outer appearance doesn't change anything about what's inside." He let the card fall to the ground.

"You don't know a thing about me."

He put one hand on each of her shoulders and lowered his face directly in front of hers. "Don't I?" He didn't move, just continued to look at her.

Half of her wanted to shove him away, to tell him to get himself and his analyzing nonsense out of her house. The other half wanted to throw herself into his arms, cry on his shoulder, and beg him to help her not to be afraid anymore. Instead, she pulled away and changed the subject. "I'll be here for four days this time. How about tomorrow I take a look at a couple of the places that you think need a little staging help. If I do some painting around here and change out the window treatments, I'll be way ahead of my schedule. I guess I won't be sanding floors like I planned. Thank you for that."

"You're welcome." He looked as though he was uncertain about how thankful she was. "And I won't hold you to that staging help thing. I know you've got a lot of things going on right now."

"Of course I'm going to carry my part of our bargain."

He shook his head slightly and fiddled with the bill of his baseball cap. "I'm not sure that's—"

"Knock it off. A deal's a deal. I want to get started tomorrow."

"If that's what you want." He pulled his cap off his head, rubbed his other hand through his hair, then replaced the cap. "Well, I'll let you get settled. How about I pick you up tomorrow afternoon around three? I'll take you over to see one of the places that's been on the market for a while."

"Sounds good. I'll see you then."

She walked him to the door. Long after he'd driven away, she thought about what he'd said about not needing her help. Then she thought about the amount of work he'd accomplished while she was away. Then the realization slowly crept in. He was trying to avoid her.

Chapter 29

Ann moved directly toward the selections of whites. Antique white, dogwood white, alabaster. She pictured each on the walls of the house, and then pictured a black leather sofa sitting there . . . The thought broke off, and suddenly she was still seeing the recovered burgundy-and-tan-striped sofa, feeling the warmth of the palette, its rightness—in that house at least. Not in New York, and surely not somewhere that she would ever live. But yes, perhaps a warmer shade for the walls. It would probably make the house sell faster, and as Ethan had said, it's what went with the house. Let's see, there was canvas tan, pewter tankard—which had kind of a nice gray cast that she liked—and a pewter green, which also was nice.

She went up to the man at the counter. "Can I buy just a quart of canvas tan and pewter tankard? I want to go try them and see which one I like better."

"Sure. I'll mix 'em up." While he squirted the appropriate cocktail of color into the base paint, Ann walked around the store, picking up brushes, rollers, and some drop cloths. This would be a nice place for a home stager to shop for supplies. With the wide selection they had here, it would be easy to help a client put her best foot forward. It lacked the frenetic pace of the places she used in New York, and it was so close to downtown Charleston, just over the Ashley River, close to Nana's house. She hoped the Charleston designers appreciated what they had here, although somehow she doubted they recognized this treasure for what it was.

When she got back to the house, she couldn't wait to get her paint opened. She painted two pieces of Gatorfoam with each color, then leaned them against opposite walls. The canvas tan was too dark for such small rooms; it felt dark and drab. The pewter tankard, however, was just the right amount of light and warmth. Besides, it had enough gray in it that she wasn't totally giving up all her principles. Yes, she could live in a house painted that color.

There it was. That thought again. She shook her head to clear the cobwebs. *Keep your guard up, Ann. Stay in control. You're not going to live in this house, no matter what color it's painted.*

Time to get to work. She returned to the paint store and bought several gallons of pewter tankard, trying to keep her mind on the business ahead. She wasn't planning to live here; she was just making it nice for whoever bought the place.

She spent the morning getting the walls prepped for painting—sanding, puttying, taping. She rolled the first of the pewter tankard up the walls of Nana's room. With each stroke of the roller, she liked the color choice a little more. A nice shade. Perfect, really. With Harry Connick Jr. music playing on her iPod, and the walls taking shape so nicely, she found herself relaxed and almost . . . happy. Bringing the iPod with her on this trip had been a brilliant idea. By listening to her own choice of music, she could shut out memories of other melodies she preferred not to think about. Why hadn't she thought about it sooner? There were obviously no supernatural beings in this house, and good music would be a way to remember that. Yep, nothing supernatural around her at all, no hallucinations, just a stress-induced dream. That's what she kept telling herself— until something grabbed her by the shoulder.

Ann jerked around, paint roller in hand, ready to face whatever force was doing this to her. By the time she realized what was happening, she'd already clocked Ethan on the head with a roller full of pewter tankard. She jerked her hand back, looking at the line of damage she'd caused to his Atlanta Braves baseball cap, and yanked the earbuds out of her ears. "Oh no! I am *so* sorry." The hysteria of relief washed over her. She burst out laughing. "I didn't hear you come in and you startled me. Oh, Ethan, I really am so sorry." As mortified as she was, she couldn't quite stop laughing.

Ethan simply stood and watched, then pulled off his cap and turned it around so he could assess the damage. "I hear what you're saying, about being sorry and all. It's just that I'm not exactly sure I believe it all that much. Call me crazy, but you don't seem overly remorseful to me. In fact, I'd say you're almost giddy about it."

Ann lost it completely. At least she had the peace of mind to drop the paint roller into the tray, but she doubled over onto the floor laughing. Her eyes brimmed with tears and her stomach ached before she finally gained some semblance of control.

Ethan had squatted down in front of her, just watching the scene unfold, a half smile on his face. Ann wiped her eyes and said, "Truly, I am sorry. I really would never have done that on purpose. For some reason, it just strikes me especially funny. I don't know why."

He was still holding the cap in his hand, his eyes squinted in concentration. "Hmm. Really?" He leaned forward and put it on her head, then cocked his head to the side and nodded. "Yeah, it is funnier when it's on someone else." His voice was serious, but his eyes were dancing. "I'm thinking you owe me a new cap, Miss Fletcher."

"At the very least." Ann pushed herself back up to standing. "I really am sorry."

"Sure you are."

Then it occurred to Ann why he was here. "Is it three already? I'm so sorry. I meant to be ready when you got here. I just got busy and forgot the time."

"You didn't forget that much time. It's only a little after one. I was running a couple of errands during lunch and I thought I'd stop by and check on your progress." He looked around the room. "I found this by the kitchen door on my way in." He held out a folded piece of paper.

"What is it?"

"Now how would I know that? I certainly didn't open it. It wasn't on *my* porch, after all. What do you think I am, some kind of snoop?"

Ann unfolded the white piece of paper to find a crayon drawing. This one showed the dark-haired Ann and an especially large yellow blob. It seemed to close her in on all sides, like it was protecting her, or hugging her. "A drawing from Keith." She walked out of the room without looking back. "I'll just go put it on the refrigerator."

Ethan followed her into the kitchen. "Yeah, since you showed up, I don't get nearly as much artwork as I used to. I'm thinking you're trying to take over my territory."

Ann used one of Sarah's sunflower-shaped magnets to put the picture on the white refrigerator door. Just like Nana used to hang up their prized works of art when they were young. "Does Keith draw angel pictures for you too?"

"Angels? Nope. Football mostly, and an occasional baseball. I've never known him to draw angel pictures for anyone other than himself. Until you came along, that is. I wonder why you get special treatment."

Ann didn't want to wonder. She didn't want to think about it at all. In fact, as soon as Ethan left, she planned to stick the drawing in a drawer somewhere she couldn't see it. She turned back toward the living room. "The painting is coming along nicely."

"Yeah, I like the color you chose. It suits both you and this place."

"Thanks." The word almost choked her. Why did she feel a flush of pleasure at Ethan's comment? It reminded her of the way she used to feel when Nana praised a good report card or put a class project on the refrigerator. But that was a long time ago, and Ethan's approval shouldn't matter to her. Neither should anyone else's, for that matter. The only approval she needed was the one that kept her paycheck coming.

"So I came by to tell you that you really don't have to do this—help me stage those houses, I mean. Like I said, I enjoyed my work here. Let's just call it a gift; what do ya say?"

What was it about this thick-skulled carpenter that made

it so hard for him to accept someone's help? "Have you eaten lunch? Are you hungry? I don't have much, but I could scare us up some sandwiches."

He looked out the window for a moment, his jaw twitching. "You didn't answer me."

"Well, you haven't answered me."

"I always eat my lunch while driving around running errands. Not exactly high class, but it gets a lot more accomplished."

"And I'm not taking charity. So I'll get back to my work so I can be ready when you get here at three."

He shook his head slowly, then sighed. "Okay, I'll see you at three. You are one stubborn woman."

"Thank you."

"I didn't mean it as a compliment." He pulled at the bill of the cap so that it almost covered Ann's eyes. "You know, it is definitely funnier when it's on you. Cuter at least." He winked at her as he turned and walked out of the room.

Long after he'd gone Ann kept finding herself looking toward the door. Almost . . . what? Wishing?

Chapter 30

Ethan's plans had failed. Miserably.

The past few weeks spent trying to get Ann's house finished, or his part of it at least, before she returned hadn't quite panned out. And he should have known she would be too stubborn to accept that he wasn't going to use her half of the barter deal. How was he supposed to keep his distance now that she was back?

As he led Ann through the house, he grew more and more nervous about what she might think. "This house has been on the market for almost a year. The kitchen was original and in terrible shape, but it took the real estate agent several months to convince the family they needed to have some work done before they had a prayer of selling it—which is when I came in. I've known the couple who owns this place for a long time. They're in their seventies, and they've already moved to Tennessee to be near their daughter. In fact, they're living with her, her husband, and their five kids right now, and will be until this place sells. I'm hearing enough rumblings from that direction to know that they need to get their own place as soon as possible. The tension's getting a little thick. Know what I mean?"

Ann laughed. "Got it." She walked through the small-ish three-bedroom house, touching countertops, sliding open drawers, staring at ceilings. "The bathrooms have obviously been updated within the last decade. They aren't cutting edge, but they aren't bad."

When she walked into the kitchen, Ethan could feel his heart speed.

"This kitchen is amazing. Is this maple?"

"Yep."

"Nice choice of granite too." She ran her hand over the countertops, then began to open and close the cabinets. When she pulled out the built-in spice rack, she said, "Is all this custom?"

"Yeah." He pretended to be looking out the window.

"You're very talented."

He turned to thank her, but she'd already walked into the dining room. "The carpet's new, right? And the walls look like they've been freshly painted."

"Yeah, they did all that when they first put the house on the market."

"This place would show better if it were a little less cluttered. If they would rent a storage unit for a month, take out about half of this furniture and most of the trinkets, this space would appear much larger and cleaner."

It made sense. "If I can talk them into that, and I can't see why I couldn't, would you help me pick which pieces should stay and which should go?"

"Of course." Ann walked around the dining room and put

her hand on one of the old oak chairs. "This table and chairs are not my style, but they suit the place nicely. However"—she pivoted to put her hand on the oversized buffet against the wall—"this piece, and the china cabinet on that side of the room, crowd this space and make it appear smaller than it is. I think the room would show better with nothing but the table and chairs."

Ethan looked at the furniture and tried to picture the big pieces gone. It probably would make the place look bigger. "Sounds good. What else?"

They walked around the house and talked about the pieces that should stay and the pieces that should go. "Well now, I'm glad I conned you into helping me with this. The Krutenats are good people. I'd like to help them out if I can."

"Conned me? Hah. I've had you doing manual labor over at my place for a month now, and I spend one hour over here and you think *you've* conned *me*."

He leaned against the doorjamb and looked at her. It took every ounce of his willpower to keep his hands at his sides, because everything inside him ached to reach out and touch her. "Ah, but I did con you. I was never doing all that work so that you would help me. I was conning you there too."

"Then why were you doing it?"

In spite of his best efforts at restraint, he reached out and brushed a wisp of dark hair from her face, his fingers lingering on her cheek. So beautiful. So incredibly soft. *Buddy, you'd better get out of here before you do something stupid. Really stupid.* Somehow he managed to pull his hand back, then turned and walked to the front door. "You'll just have to see if you can figure that one out for yourself." He opened the door and held it. "Shall we?"

She smiled and ducked under his arm. "Yes, I think we shall."

"This is not the way back to the house."

"Nope, it sure isn't."

"Well, where are we going then? To look at another one of your houses?"

"Nope."

Ann couldn't have cared less about the answer. She was just . . . happy? Seemed strange, but there wasn't any other word for it. Whether or not she cared about the answer, there was still the lure of pulling the information from an unwilling informant. "Come on. I spent *my whole afternoon*"—she said these words in as dramatic a fashion as possible—"helping you with your project. Surely you'd be willing to at least give me a hint."

"That's fighting dirty. I'm not telling, but okay, I'll give you a hint. We're back on our tourist rounds. Today we are going to see a couple of Charlestons."

"There's more than one?"

He simply shrugged and smiled. "Yep, one for me and one for you."

He pulled into a parking spot, and soon they were walking down East Bay Street. It took only a moment before Ann realized where they were going. "Rainbow Row? You brought me all the way down here to see Rainbow Row? While I admire the choice, it shows a shocking lack of imagination. Every tourist who's ever come to Charleston hits Rainbow Row. We could have stopped in a drugstore and bought a postcard for a lot less effort."

"I'm trying hard not to be wounded by that assumption. No, I did not drive you all the way down here just to see Rainbow Row, although walking past it was certainly the plan when I chose the parking place. I would think someone who is into architecture and design would appreciate this place more than most."

"I didn't say I didn't appreciate it; I said the choice wasn't very imaginative."

An ocean breeze stirred the tops of palm trees as they walked. They neared the two blocks of original Charleston-style houses that faced the harbor. Standing shoulder to shoulder in a row of pastels—blue, salmon, olive, yellow, pink—these homes had been built a couple of centuries ago and had withstood wars and hurricanes and even an earthquake. Ann felt the nostalgia begin to sneak up on her. She tried to shrug nonchalantly, but she knew Ethan wasn't buying it. "Okay, as much as I prefer a more subdued palate, I have to admit there is a certain amount of charm here."

"Ann, if there's one thing you've got, it's the gift of understatement."

Ann laughed and stopped in front of the arched doorway of a yellow-stucco house. She craned her neck to see the top windows. "Okay, I give. They are charming. And in spite of my earlier statement, a postcard does not do this place justice. It's definitely much better in person."

"That's more like it."

"Is this my Charleston or yours?"

"This is actually no-man's-land—Switzerland, you might say. That's what this little preview was all about. I'm simply softening you up for the real deal."

As Ann walked beside Ethan toward the end of the peninsula, she tried to guess the rest of their venture. "I'm a little rusty on my Charleston geography, but are we going to White Point Gardens?"

"Well, that's where we're headed, but of course I'm going to dazzle you with some fun facts as we go."

"Such as?" By now they were on Battery Row, a line of mansions from Charleston's glorious past. As much as it wasn't really her style, Ann couldn't help but be just as overwhelmed as a first-time tourist would be.

They stopped in front of a three-story brick with green shutters and two-story white columns. Ethan pointed toward it and said, "This is the Roper House."

"Greek Revival, nineteenth century maybe?"

Ethan rubbed his chin. "Not bad for a city girl. But this has to be one of the most interesting houses in the city—especially for us men—but nonetheless intriguing for you ladies, for another reason."

"Nice of you gents to include us. So I'm guessing this is *your* Charleston?"

"Yep."

"And why is that? Because it's old and irrelevant?"

"When are you going to realize the past is not irrelevant? Case in point is the story I'm about to tell you."

"Then by all means, let's hear it."

"When the Confederates had to abandon the city, most of their cannons were right over there at the Battery, right?" He pointed toward the seawall.

"Yeah, I suppose they were."

"Well, the last thing they wanted was to give the Yankees more weapons once they got here, so they started destroying everything that they couldn't take with them. They blew up a thirty-eight-ton Blakely cannon that, unfortunately for the Roper family, left a part of itself in the attic of their house. It's still lodged up there to this day—they say the thing could weigh five hundred pounds or more."

Ann looked up at the white railing framing the roof and tried to picture part of a cannon crashing into such an elegant structure. "I suppose it would make for interesting party conversations."

"You can say that again."

"Interesting story notwithstanding, you said you were going to prove relevance. What, exactly, is relevant about that?"

"Well, if you owned the house, or if you were a contractor working on the house, wouldn't you think that knowing such a heavy piece of metal was stuck in the roof could make a big difference in what you might or might not do today? If you don't know it's there, a little remodel might turn into a big demolition. Know what I mean?"

"Ah, yes. Point well made."

"Thank you." He took a few more steps.

"Yes, in one in a couple million cases—those cases with part of a cannon in the attic—the past can be important. I will concede to that."

"You're just being difficult, you know. How about previous flood damage? Wouldn't you want to know that? Or past earthquakes that might have damaged the foundation? Just because I happened to give you the most interesting scenario doesn't mean there aren't plenty more valid ones."

"Hmm. I guess so." They walked through White Point Gardens, strolling under the shade of oaks and moss, past a white gazebo and various Civil War monuments and artillery, then straight through to the Battery promenade on the far side. Ann looked over the rail at the surging water far below them. "This is beautiful."

"Yeah. It's where the Ashley River meets the Cooper River to form the Atlantic Ocean . . . in case you forget."

Ann laughed. "You're talking like a Charleston snob now. Are you going to start telling me about when your family first settled here? As much as I hate all that 'old Charleston family' kind of talk, I'll just tell you now, I'm sixth generation. Low class maybe, but sixth generation nonetheless."

"I can't top that. My mom and I moved here in 1996. I'll always just be an outsider." He said this in a mock wistful tone that made Ann want to give him a hug.

She decided to change the subject. "Just your mom?"

He shrugged. "Mom and Dad separated for a couple of years. Dad was working hard toward big success and he turned his back on everything that slowed him down—that included my mother and me. Mom wanted a clean start, so we moved here, away from anyone or anything she knew. The one thing she couldn't give up was the ocean, so we left the Florida panhandle and moved to Charleston."

"You said they *were* separated; does that mean they reconciled?"

"Yeah, it only took my father a few months to realize what a good thing he'd had and that he wanted it back. It took my mother a couple of years to be convinced to come back, but he eventually won her over."

"But you stayed in Charleston."

"Yeah, by then I'd discovered a passion for historic home restoration and a distaste for the frenetic lifestyle that caused my parents to break up in the first place. I'd also found a sense of purpose, down at The Washout."

"You find purpose in surfing?" Ann still had trouble reconciling Ethan as a surfer. He definitely wasn't the stereotypical type. "Couldn't you do that in Florida too?"

"Yes, I could surf in Florida too, although my father had never allowed it. He was the nose-to-the-grindstone sort and always saw surfing as the antithesis to everything he stood for. That's the main reason I took it up when we moved here. It was sort of my act of rebellion to get back at him for breaking up the family." He stared out into the distance. "Then I started to get to know some of the guys on the beach, and I found out there's a lot of hurting people down there, just looking for some peace, some hope. Sharing my faith, watching their lives change, well, it's one of the times I feel most alive."

Ann could think of many more questions she wanted to ask, but she didn't want to cross the line into anything too religious, so she changed the subject. "Your father's a developer, right? Have the two of you ever worked together?"

"No-oo." Ethan laughed. "Dad builds vacation condos, and he wants them built fast. He doesn't expend time or money to find the treasure in the old. To him everything needs to be new and disposable." He looked out over the water. "I think that's why I love Charleston so much. This city understands the value of the past."

Ann looked across the water at Fort Sumter. "It is amazing to think that people stood at this very spot and watched the beginning of the Civil War."

"Yeah, they did. They had no idea at the time that life as they knew it was about to change forever." He shook his head and turned around, leaning against the wall. "Now it's time to get you something to eat before we continue on."

"Sushi?"

"Not a chance. We told Keith we'd bring him with us when we ate sushi, and there's no way I'm doing it twice. So . . . as I was saying, after our non-sushi dinner, we're going to *your* Charleston."

Ann was already starting to feel like she belonged. That thought frightened her more than anything she'd yet faced.

Ethan had considered taking Ann to Café Lisa. At one point, he'd thought he would take her there if he ever got the courage to ask for a date. But now . . . well, it was probably better not to do anything that might be construed as romantic.

Tonight, it would be Hominy Grill. A diner atmosphere, well lit, lots of noise. Perfect for what he needed. When he opened the door, the cowbell on the inside handle announced their entrance.

Ann walked in, turned the bell over in her palm, and looked up at him. "Nice touch."

"What can I say? 'Nothing but the best' is my motto."

She laughed. "Alrighty then." She turned and started walking toward an empty booth near the back. Not good.

"Hey, wait." Ethan reached out and grabbed her elbow. "You want to sit at the counter? It captures more of the essence of the place."

"I think there's plenty of essence a few more yards away from the grease-splattering, order-calling, coffee-pouring action." Ann continued in her original direction and slid into the booth. "Besides, if we sit here, we have our own personal mini jukebox.

How much more atmosphere can you get than that?" She flipped over the song list as Ethan sat down across from her. "Lots of Elvis to choose from."

"Great, just great." Ethan locked his hands behind his neck and tried to stretch out some tension. When he looked up, Ann was staring at him.

"So, you mind telling me what's going on?"

"What do you mean?"

"Come on, Ethan, you've been acting all weird ever since I've been back. Did I do something to make you angry? Are you regretting that you offered to help? What exactly is it?"

Ethan unwrapped his silverware from the paper napkin. "You don't miss much, do you?"

"You're changing the subject."

Yeah, he'd tried anyway. "It's nothing really." This was going to be embarrassing. "I, well, it's just that I'd been thinking about asking you out, and I really, really wanted to, and then, just about the time I got up my nerve, I found out that you're not a believer. And, well, now that changes everything."

"What, so I'm like a leper or something?"

"No, you're not like a leper. You're amazing. But . . . we're heading in different directions. We don't share the same future."

"So, wait, I guess I misunderstood. I thought you were talking about a *date*. I didn't realize we were planning the future."

Oh, she was getting worked up now. This was going to get ugly fast. "Several years ago I was dating someone. I knew she didn't share my beliefs, but I figured that in time, she'd come to love God too. I suppose she must have been thinking the same thing. Things started getting serious between us, but there was a wall separating us at the very core of who we were. Long story short, it ended badly. My past experience alone would be enough to scare me off." He tried to look at her, but his gaze stopped at her Diet Coke and would go no higher.

She sat quietly for a few minutes, her fingers toying with the bend in her straw. "You know, I've got issues back in New York too. Neither of us needs the complication of this becoming anything more than it is, but I really do enjoy our . . . well, our friendship, I guess." She took a sip of her soda and said, "How about this? Can't we work together—even have some fun together—if I promise to keep my hands to myself?" She held up her hands in mock surrender.

The tension melted right out of him. "Well . . ." He paused a few seconds for effect. "I'm just not sure you're strong enough—my good looks and charm alone are enough to make me irresistible. Add the fancy places I take you for dinner"—he gestured around the room—"I know how you New York women really go for that kind of stuff, and I'm just not sure you can control yourself." They both laughed then. Ethan extended his hand. "Friends?"

Ann clasped it across the table. "Friends."

"Okay, from this point on, you've got to keep your eyes closed. No peeking."

"Come on." Ann tried to sound grumpy but seriously doubted she was pulling it off. "How long will this phase last?"

"Not telling." They had just climbed into Ethan's truck, and he'd made her close her eyes before he pulled out of the parking lot.

"Please tell me it doesn't involve tour guides dressed in hoop skirts. Blah." Ann shuddered at the thought.

"Not telling."

They drove for several more minutes; then Ethan said, "We're here. Eyes shut tight now. I mean it."

Ann could feel the truck turn sharply; then it stopped and the engine went quiet. It took every bit of self-control not to sneak a through-the-lashes kind of peek.

"Stay put and don't even think about cheating. I'm coming around to get you."

Ann heard her door open; then Ethan's hand was on hers as he pulled her from the truck. He put his arm around her shoulder to guide her, and she couldn't help but lean a little closer.

"Walk forward, good girl, nice and steady. Now step up. A couple more steps." He stopped walking. "Okay, you can open them."

Ann opened her eyes to find herself staring at the two diamond-shaped towers of the Arthur Ravenel Bridge. Suspension lines fanned down from the top of each tower, creating two triangles of webbing that reminded Ann of a sailboat. Light washed over the scene, both from the setting sun and from man-made floodlights shining from beneath. It was breathtaking. "Wow."

"I thought this might be a bit more to your liking. I know you're not a big historical girl, and things just don't get much more modern than this beauty—even if it's not black, white, and chrome."

Ann laughed. "Maybe they should have consulted me about that part." She craned her neck to look up. "It reminds me of the skyscrapers back in New York."

"Yeah. I saw on some documentary that these towers reach to 575 feet, so it can hold its own in height against a few New York City buildings. The Waldorf Astoria Hotel is about 625 feet high. So not that different at all—just a lot less crowded."

"You know how tall the Waldorf Astoria is?"

Ethan shrugged. "Just read an article about it this week. That building is a historic landmark, you know. I must admit, there are some buildings with character in your part of the world." He paused for a minute, looking at the bridge. "Did you know that it's the longest cable-stayed bridge in the country? Built to withstand hurricanes, earthquakes, and the occasional ship collision. She's a beauty, isn't she?"

"Yes, she is." Ann had seen pictures of the bridge on the news and in print, but she hadn't seen the real thing, never having been to this side of Charleston since the bridge was built a few years ago. "It's funny that I haven't even thought about going into Mount Pleasant since I've been here. I think it's because my subconscious still recoils from the thought of driving the old bridge."

"I always found it kind of thrilling myself—fear and fascination rolled into one. Sort of like riding a roller coaster."

"Except that with most roller coasters you have the reasonable expectation of finishing alive. Something about those narrow lanes and the way they shook when you drove over them, well . . . no thank you." Ann shuddered at the memory. "This one's amazing, though. Truly beautiful."

"I think that's particularly true right about now. Just as the sun is starting to fade. You want to walk across it? There's a nice walking-biking path on the harbor side."

"I think I'd love it."

The two of them walked across, in no hurry, simply enjoying the view, the sunset, and each other. When they got to the first of the towers, Ann stopped and put her hands on one of the massive beams. "I can't believe I haven't driven out here to look at it before."

"See, there's more to Charleston than just the past. There's the future too."

"Perhaps, but I think this bridge proves *my* point, that the old is best demolished and forgotten."

"Wrong again. If the engineers had tried to ignore past bridges rather than learn from their mistakes, well . . . we'd be standing on another narrow, bumpy bridge, now, wouldn't we?"

"Do you always have an argument for everything?"

"Not always, only when I'm right—which, of course, I am most of the time. Someday you'll come to appreciate my genius."

"I wouldn't count on that if I were you." Even as she said it, Ann realized it was becoming less true with every passing minute.

Chapter 31

Sunday morning Ann found herself moping around the house. Ethan, her "friend," had promised to come over after church, which was hours from now.

Well, there were plenty of things to be done around here. She knew she needed to sort through Sarah's things, but she just wasn't ready to do that yet. So she decided to spend the morning cleaning out the kitchen cabinets as a warm-up. There would be traces of her sister, but nothing too personal. She grabbed Ethan's baseball cap—complete with pewter tankard stripe— and stuck it on her head. It would keep her hair out of her face while she worked.

Billy Joel sang on her iPod while she reorganized the silverware drawer and refolded the kitchen towels. Then, she sprinkled Comet in the kitchen sink, watched the porcelain turn a brighter shade of white as she scrubbed, and noted that the bleachy smell made her think of fresh starts. As she rinsed the last of the white paste down the drain, she looked out the kitchen window.

Odd. Tammy's car was still in the driveway. Why wasn't she at church?

Ann took a sip of water. A dark ache entered her core as she looked across the lawn. Something was wrong; she could sense it.

When she reached the door, she knocked softly. No response. She knocked harder. Then harder. Then an all-out pounding. "Tammy, Keith, Tammy—"

Tammy answered the door, still wearing a pale blue nightgown. There were dark circles under her eyes. "Hi, Ann."

"Tammy, what's wrong?"

She shrugged. "Keith's not feeling very well. He was up a lot last night coughing and wheezing—he gets that way from time to time. Today I'm just letting him sleep in."

"Oh, and you were resting too. I'm sorry. I didn't mean to wake you. It's just that I saw your car in the driveway and knew that something must be wrong."

"No, it's okay. I was up."

"Do you need me to drive you to the doctor or anything? Go pick up some groceries?"

"You're every bit as sweet as your sister." She reached over and squeezed Ann's hand. "We really don't need anything." She smiled so warmly that Ann felt tears forming behind her eyes. "I talked to the doctor. He said he'll see us in his office first thing in the morning if Keith isn't feeling better."

Ann nodded. "Isn't there anything I can do to help you?"

"Let me go see if he's awake. I know he'll want to see you if he is." She returned a moment later. "He's asleep, and the poor thing needs his rest. I'll let him know you were here."

Ann nodded and turned to leave. "Are you sure there's nothing I can do?"

"Honey, you've done it already, just by being here."

Ann walked out, thinking that she was completely unworthy of whatever it was that Tammy and Keith thought they saw in her.

Back at the house, Ann puzzled over the overwhelming sense of belonging she'd felt during this visit. The way these people all seemed to love her, in spite of the fact she knew she didn't deserve any of it. It made her . . . *homesick*.

Her cell phone jangled from inside her purse. Maybe Ethan had decided to skip church and was calling to say he was on his way. She was smiling as she answered. "This is Ann."

"Yes. It is. And aren't I glad about that?" He paused just long enough for the reality to set in. "Since you've run out on me again, I thought I'd better call and make certain you're still thinking of me." Patrick Stinson's voice sounded hard, threatening almost.

"Oh, you'll just have to keep wondering about that." She kept her tone light. "I will say that I have your project well under control. In fact, I've spent the last couple of days checking out paint samples." Ann looked at the new colors on her wall. "Definitely making progress."

"Good, I was hoping I wasn't far from your mind. I like to know that your priorities are in the right place."

The flatness of his tone, the undercurrent of threat—they were so far removed from the warmth she'd experienced at Tammy's house just moments ago. Still, warm fuzzies did nothing to move her toward her goal, toward fulfilling her promise to Sarah and Nana. "I'd say my priorities are exactly where they should be."

"Perfect. I've been thinking about us and our future partnership, and it seems to me that with all your recent travels, we have not properly cemented our relationship."

"That's right. We still haven't signed a contract, have we? That is something we definitely need to do." She'd deliberately misunderstood him, hoping to buy herself some more time and to remove from the table the threat of losing this job altogether.

He paused just a second. "No. I was thinking more about our personal relationship. It's important to me to have a strong bond before I start doing business with someone. Your frequent absences seem to have prevented us from connecting the way I'd like for us to."

Ann was not naive enough to have any doubt about his meaning. This was an ultimatum—not even stated in a false romantic light. Still, if she remained vague in her answers, she might be able to keep her options open. "It won't be much longer. My house is almost ready to go on the market."

"That's great news. When are you coming back to New York?"

"Tomorrow afternoon."

"How about this, then? Tomorrow night we'll have dinner, go to a show, maybe even a little dancing. You like to dance, don't you, Ann? After a nice evening of celebrating our partnership, we'll all meet at the office on Tuesday morning and sign the contracts."

"Doesn't the celebration usually happen after the contracts are signed?"

"I prefer to mix things up a little." He said the words with humor in his voice, but Ann didn't miss the implications. If she was going to work with him, there would no longer be the option of playing coy.

How high of a price was she willing to pay for her dream job? She knew that she couldn't stay at Marston *without* his contract. She thought of Margaret's order for $220,000 worth of furniture, of Beka and Gracie's hope in a very expensive medication, and of the layoffs that had been in the works even before the company had been affected by a slow real estate market. Now there was nothing between unemployment for the entire staff and Patrick Stinson.

She thought about Ethan and Tammy and Keith and the unrestrained way that they loved her . . . No, not *her*. Just like Lorelei, they loved *Sarah*, not Ann. Tammy seemed to think Ann was like Sarah, but she wasn't . . . Ethan had assumed she had the same faith as Nana and Sarah, but she didn't . . .

In truth, it all was an illusion. There was nothing here for her. All that she had was her life in New York. It was the only thing that mattered because it was the only thing that was real.

Ann took a deep breath and said, "I'll see you tomorrow night, then."

"Perfect. I look forward to it."

Less than an hour later, a deliveryman brought a large bouquet of flowers to her door. The card said simply, "Anticipating." It wasn't signed. It didn't have to be. Ann picked up her cell and began the process of bringing this part of her life to an end.

"Are you sure you want to put this up now? We can wait a few weeks, until you've got the place ready to show." Eleanor's red curls danced in the light breeze.

Ann nodded. "Don't show it yet. Don't advertise or put it on multiple listings until we're ready, but I need this here right now. It's my declaration of intent, I guess you might say."

"This all seems a little sudden to me. I wish you'd slow down, think this through, make certain you're not acting on impulse."

"My decision is made."

"All right." Eleanor Light reached out to shake Ann's hand. "Whatever makes you happy. I can see you've got some company, so I'll get moving. I'll be in touch next week."

Ann turned around to see Ethan's truck pulling into the driveway. Eleanor waved at him as she walked the length of the drive and climbed into the blue Mazda parked on the curb.

Ethan climbed slowly out of his truck and walked toward Ann, an accusation in every step he took. He put his hand on the sign and asked calmly, "What is this?"

Ann shrugged in what she hoped was a nonchalant way. "It's a For Sale sign. What does it look like?"

"I thought that . . . well, I guess I hoped that . . ."

"You hoped that what, Ethan? I would stay here and pretend to be some southern belle who cares about what her neighbors are having for dinner or likes to live in old houses with floral curtains? That I would want to stay in this crummy old city because you've got a shiny new bridge? Well, I can tell you right now that's not going to happen. I've got to finish up this work and get out of here. I've wanted out of here for as long as I can remember, which is why I live in New York now. That's my home; it's where I belong."

He nodded, and Ann could see him swallow hard. The anger in her voice obviously hurt him, but that's what she'd intended it to do. She needed to hurt him enough that he wouldn't try to persuade her to change her mind. She needed to chase him off for good. "All right then. I'm sorry. I guess I didn't realize how strongly you felt about it."

"Well, now you do. You said yourself it was easier for you with some distance between us. Guess what? New York's a long way away."

He nodded. "Well, I said I'd come over and help this afternoon, so let's get started." The pain in his voice almost brought her to her knees, but she held on.

"You know what, I think I've got it from here. Thanks for all you've done, but I don't want to waste any more of your time."

She turned around and walked into the house without looking back. After she closed the door, she leaned against it, then slid to a sitting position. But she did not allow herself to cry. After she heard the roar of his truck pulling away, she took a deep breath, squared her shoulders, and stood up. She had work to do. The first order of business was to return to the paint store and buy several gallons of white paint. There would be no warmth here. Not while Ann had anything to do with it.

Chapter 32

After Ann left, Tammy had eaten a quick breakfast then grabbed another hour or so of sleep. Now she stood at the sink, washing dishes from yesterday and today. Keith hadn't wakened yet. She prayed that his day would be better after such a trying night.

"Annie, Annie!"

Tammy dropped the dish back into the sink and ran toward Keith's room, following the sound of his shrieking. "Keith? What's wrong?"

He was thrashing in the sheets: legs, arms, head, all moving in the asymmetrical dance of panic. "Annie!"

"Keith, Keith, wake up." Tammy gently reached down and shook her son's shoulders. "Wake up, darlin'. It's only a dream. Only a bad, bad dream."

Keith's body went still and his head fell back onto the pillow. When his eyes finally opened, they were wide with fright. "Where's Annie?"

"She's at her house. Everything is fine."

"Something's wrong, Mama. Something's real wrong."

"Did you have a bad dream about Annie?"

"No. It wasn't a dream. Something's wrong." His arms struggled up from beneath the sheets, and he grabbed her hand. "Something's wrong with Annie."

"What makes you think so?"

"I feel it."

"Sweetie, I'm sure she's fine. She came over to see you just a couple of hours ago. You were asleep, but maybe you heard her voice, hmm? That's what happened. You heard her and somehow your sleeping mind thought that something was wrong with her."

"No." His face began to turn red. "No!" He started coughing.

"You've got to calm down." She put another pillow beneath his shoulders and handed him a glass of water.

"Annie needs me." He took a sip of the water, but the coughs didn't altogether subside.

"Sweetie, you need to stay in bed right now and rest. Doctor said so." She looked at her son and knew she had to think of something to calm him down. "Do you want me to see if she can come over for a minute? Would that make you feel better?"

"Yes." His voice calmed and the redness began to drain from his face. "Get her, please."

Tammy looked out the window toward Annie's house. She didn't want to leave Keith alone, but she knew that if Annie was painting, she would have her earbuds in and wouldn't hear the phone.

"Sorry, Mama. Didn't mean to yell."

Tammy rubbed his forehead. "It's okay. I'll get Annie, but you stay real still, okay?"

"Okay."

Tammy rushed across the lawn, not wanting to leave him alone for too long. He was sufficiently calmed now, but what if something else happened? She was almost to Ann's kitchen door when she saw the For Sale sign. She simply looked at it, not moving, not breathing, not even able to think. Finally, she stumbled numbly forward and knocked at the door.

Ann jerked it open, her face set hard. "I'm painting. What do you need?" Everything about Ann seemed different from just a few hours ago. Her voice sounded so hollow; her eyes were flat.

"I . . . Keith wants to see you. He woke from a bad dream, and he just won't be comforted until he sees that you're okay."

Ann rubbed her cheek with her shoulder. "Tell him I'm just fine, but that I'm right in the middle of a wall and I really need to get it finished. Tell him maybe I'll see him later."

Tammy nodded toward the sign. "You're leaving?"

"Of course. That's been the plan all along, right? I've got to sell this place and get on with my life." Ann sounded so angry. Something must have happened, something terrible. Keith had been right.

"Annie, are you all right?"

"My name is Ann, and I'm fine."

"Okay." Tammy turned and took a step toward her house, but she couldn't stand the thought of facing her son alone. "Please, Ann, would you at least come talk to Keith? He's so upset and worried about you."

"I'm really busy trying to get things buttoned up before I leave. I just can't spare the time right now. Will you tell him that I'm all right, and will you tell him good-bye for me?"

Tammy looked at her, uncertain if she should force her way inside and find out what had happened, or if she should just walk away. "If you're sure that's what you want."

"I'm sure." Ann closed the door in Tammy's face. Tammy stood still, unable to even breathe. What had happened since she'd seen Annie only a couple of hours ago? Worse yet, how was Keith going to make it through yet another major blow? This would rip him apart.

She rushed back home, scared of what kind of state she might find him in. Once inside, she heard only the *tat tat tat* of the cuckoo clock in the hallway. She tiptoed into Keith's room, hoping he was asleep. He wasn't.

He simply looked up and said, "Where's Annie?"

Tammy swallowed hard. "She's really busy right now, honey. She's in the middle of painting, and it just wasn't a good time for her to come over. She told me to tell you hello." The word substitution in place of *good-bye* was one Tammy could live with.

"She's leaving, isn't she?" He said it in such a calm, resigned voice, it surprised Tammy.

"Yes, darlin', I think she is."

He nodded his head and closed his eyes. Quiet tears began to run down his cheeks. "It's not right. She's supposed to be here."

Sometime later, after Tammy had comforted him and fixed him a bite to eat, he fell asleep. Only then did Tammy's tears begin to fall.

By Monday morning, Ann had had very little sleep, but the walls were now a stark shade of snowy white. She walked through the house and gathered every single floral pillow and stuffed them inside a black, thirty-gallon trash bag. The sides bulged in places, stretching the plastic into a shade of gray. Next on the agenda—the photos under the glass on the coffee table.

She pulled an empty shoe box out of Sarah's closet and stood in front of the table. She carefully lifted the glass and leaned it against the sofa, then removed the pictures, careful not to look at any of them. When the last one dropped into the box, Ann closed the lid and sealed it with two rows of duct tape. She tucked the box under her arm and tossed the bag over the other shoulder, then schlepped it all out to the detached garage.

As she walked back to the house, she couldn't help but look at the white sign planted in her front yard—her public and irrevocable declaration that she was leaving this place for good. She never did belong here, and anyone who thought otherwise needed to see the hard truth for what it was.

Ann cast a guilty glance toward Tammy's house. She knew she'd hurt her and Ethan and Keith. They had come to mean so much to her, but she didn't deserve them. It was better to just end this whole charade of happiness and love right now. Ethan deserved a *good* girl, and Tammy and Keith deserved a friend with a heart. Ann loaded her suitcase in the trunk of the rental car and looked at her watch. The lateness surprised her; she was going to have to rush to make it to the airport in time.

She put the key in the ignition, feeling the finality of her departure. Sure, she would be back, but after this time, everything that had once drawn her here would be gone. Her eyes began to sting, and she turned the key.

Nothing happened. Not a sputter, not even a clicking sound. The engine simply didn't respond. "Great, just great."

She yanked her cell phone out of her purse and dug through

the glove compartment for the rental agreement. She knew they had roadside assistance, and they had better make it quick. She located the number, then waited through four rings before someone finally answered. "If you'd like to continue in English, press one."

Urg! Ann pressed one, her blood pressure climbing with each second. "If you'd like to reserve a car, press one. If you'd like to cancel a reservation, press two. If you'd like to hear a list of rental locations, press three."

It was all Ann could do not to slam down the phone, but she knew that would only mean she'd have to start the whole process again. Finally, she heard, "If you currently have a rental car and need assistance, press eight."

Ann smashed her finger into the number eight so hard that it hurt, then put her phone to her ear. "My car won't start, I need—"

"If you'd like to return your car to another location than in your original agreement, press one. If you'd like to extend your reservation, press two. If you need roadside assistance, press three."

Ann pressed the number three. "All lines are currently busy. Please stay on the line and the first available customer representative will be with you shortly."

Ann slammed her palm against the steering wheel in frustration. She didn't have time for this. She turned the key again and again while she waited. Absolutely nothing.

"Customer assistance. This is Debbie speaking. How may I help you?" She had a slow southern drawl, which particularly unnerved Ann when she was in a hurry.

"Yes, my car won't start and I need to leave for the airport right now. I need someone here as soon as possible."

"I'm so sorry to hear that you're having trouble. I know this is an inconvenience and I do apologize." The woman sounded sympathetic, but Ann didn't want her sympathy. She wanted results. Immediate results.

"So how fast can you get someone here?"

"Let me put you on hold for just a moment while I talk to the crew."

Orchestra music suddenly came through the earpiece, signaling to Ann that she was indeed on hold. It went on and on, its monotonous melody doing nothing to calm her nerves. Then she heard a beep. "Oh good, you're back—" But the orchestra music was still playing. That's when she realized what the beep was. It was her cell phone, letting her know that the battery was low. Wasn't that rich?

"Ms. Fletcher? I just spoke with our roadside assistance crew. They're finishing up a job near you and will be there within a half hour."

"I need someone here now." Even as she said the words, Ann knew they weren't logical. Even if mechanics showed up right now, the chances of her making the plane were slim to none.

"I'll let them know you are in a hurry."

"Thanks." Ann hung up the phone in defeat. She supposed she might as well call the airline and see if she could switch to a later flight.

She went back inside the house. No reason to sit outside in this sweltering heat to make the calls. Then she thought about her phone battery being almost dead. Sarah didn't have a landline at her house.

But Tammy did.

How could she possibly go over to that house and ask for a favor? Tammy would probably welcome her like always, but Ann didn't want to face her again.

Unfortunately, she had no other choice.

She walked across the lawn and knocked, rehearsing what she'd say. Something like, "I know I was really rude yesterday, but do you think I could make a toll-free call?" Yeah, that sounded about right.

When Tammy opened the door, a broad smile across her face, everything Ann had rehearsed fled from her mind. "Hi."

"Oh, Ann, I was hoping you'd come over and say good-bye before you left today. I just hoped you would. You've been on my mind all morning, and I've been worried that something was wrong."

"Well, if you consider the fact that my car won't start and I'm going to miss my plane as something wrong, then I'd say you're exactly right."

"Oh, do you need a ride to the airport? I could"—she glanced back toward Keith's room—"take you."

And Ann knew that she would. She knew that Tammy would go wake him up, load him into the car, and make sure Ann got to the airport. Keith would even be happy about it. But she couldn't let them do that. "No, that's okay. I've got to wait for the car rental people anyway. I was wondering, though, if I could borrow your phone? My cell's about to die, and I need to call the airlines and see if I can get a later flight."

"Oh, of course you can. It's right here."

She handed Ann a portable handset and said, "I'll just be in the sewing room. You come get me if you need anything."

"Thanks." Ann couldn't help but wonder what Tammy was

working on today—a southern belle gown? Frilly curtains? The ache she felt surprised her yet again.

She needed to focus on her life in New York, on getting back in town tonight in time for her dinner with Patrick Stinson. Too many people were depending on her.

Five minutes later she was off the phone, having managed quite easily to switch to a flight that left two hours after her original, although the $150 change fee hurt. Ann peeked around the door and saw that Tammy was sewing a black square of cloth. "Thank you, Tammy."

Tammy started at the sound of Ann's voice, then quickly stood in front of the sewing machine, blocking it from view. "You're welcome." She walked toward the door and towed Ann out of the room.

"What is that?" Ann turned her head toward the sewing room, pulled by the magnetic force of something Tammy was obviously hiding.

"Just something I'm working on. Were you able to get your flight changed?"

"Yeah, there's a flight a couple of hours later." She pointed back toward the sewing room. "Something you're working on, like what?"

"Just something."

"Come on, I've never seen you this secretive. Spill."

Tammy dropped her restraining hand from Ann's arm. "Oh, it's a square pillow, if you must know."

"Black? That doesn't seem like something you usually do."

"It's not. I'm . . . well, I'm making this for you. Ethan told me that you preferred black and white, so I was thinking you might want something like that for your home in New York, and I was going to surprise you with it the next time you came, and now you've already seen it so it won't be a surprise."

Ann's throat closed. She threw her arms around Tammy and hugged her as tightly as she'd ever hugged anyone. "I wish I were more deserving of the friendship you've given me. Keith too."

"Sweetie, you need to open your eyes. The rest of us see what you don't—or won't. You are a wonderful woman, made by God to be just the way you are, completely loved and worthy of being loved." Tammy finally pulled away from the hug. "Since you've got a little extra time, let's see if Keith's awake. I know he'd want to see you before you leave."

Tammy walked quietly toward Keith's room and opened the door, then motioned for Ann to come in. Keith was partially sitting, propped up on several pillows, his face pale. He smiled at her. "Hi, Annie."

"Hey, buddy, how are you feeling?"

"I'm all right." He took a couple of deep breaths. "I don't want you to leave."

Ann looked at his sweet face and struggled for something she could say that would make him feel better. Since she couldn't change her mind about leaving, she brought up the one subject she knew would cheer him. "Have your angels been singing to you lately?"

"Yeah." He smiled and closed his eyes.

After a few moments, Ann figured he was asleep and kissed his forehead, then turned to leave.

"Did you hear them in the car?"

"What?" Ann wheeled around.

"In your car. I saw them over there. I thought they must be singing."

Ann looked toward the car through Keith's bedroom window. Then she looked back at Keith. *Angels don't exist*, she reminded herself. *And if they did, then why wouldn't they just make my car start?* It was just Keith's imagination. He'd seen her in the car, the light reflecting off the windshield, that was all. She put her hand on his forehead and ruffled his hair. "I didn't hear them in my car, but if I do, you'll be the first one I tell. Deal?"

"Deal."

She saw the service vehicle pull up in her driveway. "I've got to go. I'll be back in a couple of weeks, okay?" So much for making a clean break here. She felt almost like a junkie who wanted to leave a bad habit. She just couldn't do it.

"'Kay." He was asleep before he got the word out.

Chapter 33

Ann boarded the plane at two thirty. She glanced at her watch for the twentieth time, which did nothing to change the hour. She would land a little before five and make it to her apartment by just after six, assuming everything went smoothly. That would give her half an hour before she needed to leave for the cab ride to the restaurant.

She stared out the window, watching men in blue uniforms loading luggage onto the plane beside hers. There were duffels and suitcases and golf clubs and strollers. Happy people taking happy trips, perhaps going to visit someone they loved, the family they cherished. Ann didn't have any family to cherish anymore. As for people she loved . . . well, it didn't matter. Anyone she'd want to be loved by didn't really love *her*, so what was the point in even thinking about it?

When her thoughts returned to the present, she wondered why the plane hadn't pushed back from the gate yet. She looked at her watch: 2:50. They were scheduled to depart five minutes ago; all the passengers were seated, yet the plane didn't move. Ann pulled a magazine from the seat pocket in front of her and began to flip mindlessly through the articles about exotic destinations and the travel recommendations of several A-list celebrities. She forced herself to read an article about the best restaurants in Paris, although she'd likely never set foot in France. She concluded that *Reynaud's* sounded like a place she'd like to try if she ever did get to Paris.

She put the magazine back into the seat pocket and looked at her watch: 2:55. "Ladies and gentlemen, we apologize for the delay. Unfortunately, we've had to call maintenance about an issue and it may take a few minutes for them to get here. We will keep you updated. Please remain seated with your seat belts fastened, and we will depart as soon as it is possible to safely do so."

A collective groan sounded through the plane. Ann sat back in her seat and closed her eyes, trying to think of anything but being on this airplane. Definitely not about where she was going—or what she was leaving.

The speakers crackled back to life. "The maintenance crew has diagnosed the problem and I'm happy to report they will be able to fix it shortly. Within a half hour we should be under way."

Ann looked at her watch again. She was going to be late for dinner with Patrick Stinson. She pulled out her cell phone, pushed the power button, and nothing happened. Then she remembered the warning beeps earlier in the day. The battery was dead.

Great. Just great. She could imagine how well this was going to go over. As soon as they landed at Newark she'd find a payphone and call. Except . . . Patrick Stinson's number was programmed into her cell phone, which was currently dead. She could call her office from there, she supposed, but didn't want to start any gossip when they found out she was meeting Patrick after hours. If Beka got wind of it, she would know something was going on and would hound Ann until she got an answer, an answer she wouldn't like. And Margaret . . . her sixth sense would be all over the potential future business partnership between Ann and Patrick. No, she wouldn't be able to do anything until she got home and got to her charger.

Of all the times for this to happen, why now? A messed-up plane, a dead cell, and a car that wouldn't start, all in the course of one afternoon. It was as if the whole universe had teamed up against her to make certain that nothing went right. The universe or . . . ? She refused to finish the thought.

Ann arrived at her apartment at seven thirty, half an hour after she was supposed to meet Patrick Stinson. She plugged her cell into the charger and looked for messages. There weren't any, not even a missed call. This hit her as a rather ominous sign.

She punched in his number, which went straight to his voice mail. At the beep, she said, "This is Ann Fletcher. My plane arrived an hour and a half late. My cell phone was dead. I am so sorry I wasn't able to reach you earlier and let you know that I wouldn't make our dinner. I will apologize personally tomorrow morning when I see you in the office. Again, I truly am sorry." She hung up the phone, feeling more relief than regret. For tonight, at least, she wouldn't have to make a decision about the future.

She poured herself a big glass of white wine and collapsed at her table. Then she realized that the night was still early. If he checked his messages, one return call could still move this evening's events forward—even if a little behind schedule.

Ann thought about what was at stake. So many things, so many people, an entire company. Yet was the alternative any better? There weren't easy answers for her. There never had been.

She held up her cell phone, took a deep breath, and pushed the power button. For tonight anyway, her decision was made.

Chapter 34

Ann could see Sarah and knew instinctively that she was watching Sarah's last breath. A giant ball of a shining octopuslike being hovered over Sarah, doing nothing, simply watching. Then the octopus was at Ann's car, once again just watching the disaster unfold. It didn't make sense. If the octopus was at her car, then why wouldn't the car start? And why had Sarah died? Couldn't the octopus do anything? Didn't it have any power to change things? If not, what was his purpose?

Ann jerked awake, still hearing strains of music. Strange, she hadn't heard the song during the dream, but now each note thrummed inside her, despite the fact that it seemed to be coming from far away. It slowly faded and she forced herself to her feet, scrubbing her hands across her face. Time to get up and get going. There was much to be done this morning.

She turned on her cell phone and punched in the number for Patrick Stinson. He answered on the second ring. "Well, my, my, who could this be calling so early?"

"It's Ann." Obviously he already knew that, but the answer popped out. "I'm sorry I missed our dinner last night. My plane

SHEILA WALSH & KATHRYN CUSHMAN

was late, and my cell was dead. It was a perfect storm of every imaginable catastrophe."

The silence buzzed through the phone line as a siren sounded from the street below. "I see. So you're telling me you were more than willing to be there last night, but travel issues kept you away?"

"Yes, it was travel issues."

"Hmm, I see. What do you think we should do about it then?"

Ann walked into her little kitchen and pulled a bottle of water from the refrigerator. "I'm sure we can work something out." She took a sip of water, then looked at the drawings that covered her refrigerator—full of Keith, Ann, and angels. She thought of Keith's comment that the angel had been beside her car. That's when she knew the answer to the questions from her dream.

The angel's purpose—for her at least—had been to keep her from doing something she would've regretted. Well, he'd saved her once, and now it was Ann's turn to decide what she would do with the temporary reprieve.

"I think we should meet at the office this morning as planned, get those contracts signed, and then sit down and discuss whatever it was you wanted to talk about last night. In fact, I think we should do the majority of our meetings at the office from now on."

"Well, where's the fun in that? I like to work with people on a more personal level, and you can't do that in an office."

Ann was trapped, and she needed to decide at exactly what point she was going to claw herself out of here. Not a single person who knew her would ever use the word *prude* in describing her, but she did have her boundaries, and this definitely crossed them. It both surprised and relieved her to realize this. She braced herself for his reaction. She knew it was going to cost her, but while she wasn't a prude, she wasn't a harlot either.

"Mr. Stinson, if casual lunches make it easier for you to work with me, then that's fine, but anything beyond that, well . . . you can count me out."

"I see." He paused for only a second. "All right then. I'm glad to know you feel that way. It's best to know what to expect when starting a new partnership. It's good to get these things settled up front."

Ann stared out her window at the street below, stunned at what she'd just heard. He hadn't even offered an argument, no threats, not even a hint of anger. That really must have been an angel at her car yesterday. Maybe they really were there to help after all. "I think so too. Thank you for being so understanding about last night."

"Don't mention it." He hung up without waiting for a further response.

Ann got to the office early. Margaret was already there, which didn't surprise Ann. She had assumed this might be the case. Margaret walked out of her office and over to Ann before she even had a chance to drop her stuff in her cubicle. "My office. Now."

Ann nodded and followed. She took a seat across from Margaret's desk. Margaret walked around the desk but did not sit. She leaned forward on both her hands. "I got a call from Patrick Stinson this morning." She looked at Ann and waited. The expression on her face did not go well with "and he told me you've worked everything out really great."

SHEILA WALSH & KATHRYN CUSHMAN

Ann shifted in her seat as a growing uneasiness began to gnaw through her gut. "What did he say?"

"What do you think he said? Do you suppose it had anything to do with the fact that you've been plotting behind my back?"

"I've been plotting?"

"I would say asking him to hire you personally instead of using my company would fall under that definition, don't you?"

"Margaret, he's the one who brought that up. We talked about it *once*. Nothing official happened. And I told him that I wouldn't leave Marston until Stinson Towers was completed because I didn't want there to be layoffs."

Margaret stared hard at her. "Well, he's got quite a different version of events, I can tell you that. He's coming by this morning to discuss this with me. He's no long certain he wants to use this company for the job."

"What will we do? Can we survive without this contract?"

"I don't know, but right now, I'm not going to talk about what *we* are going to do. Right now I want to talk about what *you* are going to do."

Ann braced herself for the inevitable apologies and groveling that would be required of her. "And what is that?"

"Clear out your desk effective immediately. Patrick Stinson's due here in a couple of hours, and what *I'm* going to do is whatever it takes to salvage this job."

Ann just stared for a moment, trying to take in what Margaret had said. "Margaret, he is lying. As I said, we talked about me going to work for him *after this project*, and yes, it was something I thought I wanted to do. But there turned out to be too many strings attached . . . and this morning I told him as much."

She leaned forward, mimicking Margaret's body posture. "Think about it. You know that I've been working hard on this project, designing everything around the pieces of furniture that you ordered. I've been doing everything I can to keep this place, *your company*, solvent, including taking a pay cut."

Margaret hadn't moved while Ann talked. Now she sat down and said, "It doesn't matter what *I think* I know. What *I know* is that Patrick Stinson no longer wants to work with you, and this company will go bankrupt unless we keep his business. So you will receive two weeks' compensation as per your contract, but that's the best I can do for you."

Ann stood. "I could take this to a lawyer and have a case filed by this afternoon on the grounds of sexual harassment." She took a breath, trying to pull a new strategy out of the shambles of her mind. She needed to take the offensive. "And that's exactly what I plan to do. Of course, I'll have no choice but to name the Marston Company as accessory."

"I'd think long and hard about that if I were you." Margaret leaned back against her chair, her left eyebrow cocked. "I'm sure Patrick Stinson has a team of lawyers who could drag that out for years. In the meanwhile, no one's going to want to hire you because you'll have a reputation as a troublemaker."

Ann knew there could be more than a little truth in what Margaret was saying, but at this point she was too mad to care. "I guess that's a chance I'll have to take. Are you willing to take that chance, Margaret?"

"A lawsuit would definitely put financial stress on this company. Of course, if that happened"—she dragged a lacquered nail across the portfolio on her desk—"we would have to go ahead with our plans for layoffs. I think you know who would be the first to lose her job in that situation." She paused long enough for the words to firmly hit their mark. "That's not what you want, is it?"

Ann thought of Beka and Gracie, of what they'd already been through and how much worse things could get. She couldn't do that to them. She shook her head. "No." She walked toward the door and stopped before opening it. "I hope you know what you're getting into."

"Good luck, Ann." The flatness in her voice made Ann doubt very much whether Margaret cared what kind of luck she had.

Ann returned to her apartment, grabbed a pillow, then screamed into it for about five minutes.

How could he do this? Taking away his job offer was one thing, but to deliberately get her fired—now that was something altogether different.

What kind of person would do something like that? What kind of mean, nasty, evil person?

The answer was obvious: the kind of person who would get what he wanted at all costs. A person like Patrick Stinson.

The only question that remained now was, what should *she* do about it?

She threw the pillow back onto the bed, opened her bedside drawer, and grabbed pen and paper. It was time to make another plan.

The sensible thing right now would be to get a résumé in order, send it out to as many places as possible, and then get down to Charleston and get the house sold as quickly as possible. It would be hard to get a job in today's market, but if she sold the house, that would give her enough money to keep her solvent for at least a year. And it should give her time to get back on her feet.

The less sensible part of her wanted to return to Charleston and stay for a while. Take some time to revisit her past, hang out with Tammy, Keith, and Ethan. Do some thinking about what was important to her. This wasn't an option, though. She'd sent Ethan packing, and he'd clearly said that he didn't want to be around her. She couldn't afford it anyway. Besides, now was the time to make a clean break from everything in her past that would hold her back.

She flipped open her laptop and began the search for plane tickets. Ouch—$635 if she left tomorrow. If she waited until next week, that number dropped to $350. Okay, she'd wait a week. At this point, she needed to save as much money as possible. This would give her a week to get the résumés in the mail—something she'd better start working on right now. Her portfolio would be an asset, she knew that, but first she had to make the résumé strong enough to get her invited to an interview.

Somewhere during her third draft, she was interrupted by a pounding on the door. She opened it and found Beka, her eyes tinged red. "Tell me what happened."

Ann opened the door to let her friend inside. "First, tell me what you heard."

"When we came in this morning, Margaret told us that you had resigned effective immediately. I know better than that, Ann. There's no way you quit like that, especially without even telling me you were thinking about it. What really happened?"

Ann sat down on a white bar stool and motioned for Beka to do the same. "Did she tell you anything else?"

"No. She's been in a meeting with Patrick Stinson all morning and not allowing interruptions."

"Well, Patrick Stinson . . ." Ann thought better of what she was about to say. If she told Beka everything—well, there was just no reason to do that. "I missed several meetings with Patrick Stinson because of all the time I've been spending in Charleston, and to be honest, my heart just wasn't in the work. It was decided that, under the circumstances, I would likely be happier working somewhere else."

"I see." Beka folded her arms. "Am I to understand, then, that this truly was your decision?"

"It's the best decision for all concerned." And one of those concerned was Beka. Ann made a show of looking at her watch. "Now you'd better get back to the office, young lady. You know how Margaret feels about long lunch hours."

"I would think by now you would realize that you cannot hide things from me. There is more to this story. You're taking the fall for something, aren't you?"

"Your sixth sense has finally failed. I'd think by now your common sense would tell you that 'taking the fall' is something I don't do."

"Mmm-hmm." Beka reached over and hugged her tight. "What are you going to do?"

"I'm heading back to Charleston next week, and I'll likely stay there until the house is ready to list. Meanwhile, I'm sending out résumés here and hoping for something new and exciting."

"I see." Beka clearly wasn't buying it, but she had never been one to push. She'd let it go. For now. "How about dinner tomorrow night at my place?"

"Sure. I think I could use a little therapy right about now."

They both laughed as Beka walked into the hallway. "See you at seven?"

"Sounds good." Ann closed the door, then returned to work on her résumé.

Somewhere during the process, she remembered a conversation she'd had with Patrick Stinson in what seemed like a lifetime ago. A conversation that just might have the answer for her.

She fired up her laptop and began searching the listings for Meredith Radke. It didn't take long to find *Superior Staging, Meredith Radke, head designer.* The contact number was listed, and a few minutes later she had Meredith Radke on the phone.

"My name is Ann Fletcher. We talked a few weeks ago at the open house for your Stinson project."

"Yes, I remember." Her voice wasn't welcoming or harsh.

"Well, it seems that I find myself without a job, and . . . I'm wondering if you have space for another designer."

"That didn't take long, did it?"

"No. No, it didn't."

There was nothing but silence on the line for a few moments. Finally, Meredith said, "To tell you the truth, I am in need of help around here. I was hoping to diversify rather than hire another modern specialist, but why don't you send me your résumé and then we'll talk?"

"I'll put it in the mail today."

"I'll be in touch." The line went dead.

Sometime later Ann pulled a business card out of her wallet and punched in a number. "Hi, you've reached Eleanor's voice mail. Leave me a message and I'll be in touch soon. Thanks."

"Hi, Eleanor, just letting you know I've had a change of plans. I'll be back in Charleston next week. I'm going to spend enough time to get the place ready to go on the market. We need to talk seriously about price point, because I need to sell this place. Fast."

Ann folded a sleeveless white T-shirt into her suitcase, preparing for tomorrow's flight. She still wasn't sure what she was going to do. Meredith Radke had called her in for an interview two days ago. She'd looked through her portfolio, making polite comments, but she hadn't called back.

As Ann zipped her suitcase closed, the phone rang, and before Ann answered, she saw the caller ID: *Superior Staging.* Ann pressed the talk button, prepared for the worst. "Hello."

"Hello, Ann, it's Meredith Radke calling."

Ann held her breath. "Hello, Meredith."

"As I promised I would, I checked your references." She didn't continue.

Ann knew what was coming, it was best to get it over and done. "And?"

"Your former employer wasn't overly complimentary, but then again, given what little I know of the situation, I didn't expect her to be."

"That makes two of us."

Meredith laughed. "I then called several of your clients, and they couldn't say enough good things about you. In fact, they all say they would use Superior for their next staging project if you worked here."

"That's good to hear."

"Yes, it is." She paused. "I wouldn't be able to pay what you were making before."

"I know. I'm willing to take less." All she needed to do was sell the house and she could make it.

"All right. I know you're about to leave town. When can I expect you to start?"

"Two weeks?"

"I look forward to it."

"So do I." Ann hung up the phone and danced around the room. "Yes." Finally, something in her life was working right.

After a light dinner, Ann sat on her balcony and wondered about all of the things that had happened since Sarah's death—the music; the blinking light; Ethan, Tammy, and Keith; the car that wouldn't start; the plane that was delayed. All of it. She stood up and leaned over the rail to do a little people-watching, one of her favorite pastimes in New York City. Tonight, though, she envied the people walking past—couples holding hands, a woman walking her dog—who were leading normal, happy, sane lives.

She looked farther to her right and watched a family make their way across the street. The father held an obviously sleeping toddler on his shoulder. The mother held the hand of an elementary-school aged girl in a dress and tights. A big night at the theater, perhaps?

When she turned her attention below her, she saw the stooped back of someone digging through the trash. That's when she knew what she needed to do. The homeless man who had whistled the angel tune, maybe he could tell her something that would clear things up—or at least prove to her, once and for all, how ridiculous her imaginings had been.

Before she even stopped to think about it, she grabbed a paper lunch bag, stuffed it full of peanut butter and granola bars, then flew out the door. Thankfully, the elevator was on her floor, and in less than a minute she found herself on the street, on the other side of the trash can from the homeless man. "Please, do you mind if I ask you something?"

"Ask me?" The man looked up from his task. He was African-American, probably sixty, with long gray dreadlocks. "Ask me what?"

"Oh, sorry, I thought you were someone else."

"I'll bet. What you got in the bag? You got some booze?"

Ann looked down at it. "Oh no. It's food. You want it?" She held it out.

The man eyed it warily for a moment, then snatched it from her hand. "Who you looking for?" He was already ripping the wrapper off of a granola bar as he asked the question.

"I don't know. I think his name might be Uri. That's what another homeless woman called him. He's a man who comes around here sometimes. I thought that maybe . . . well, I don't know what I thought." Ann turned to go back inside.

"Wait a second. You helped me. I'll see if I can do the same for you." The man had an affable demeanor that made Ann wonder how long he'd been homeless. "What you want to know from this man?"

"It doesn't matter. It's just crazy."

"Crazy's something I do pretty well. Give it a shot." He tossed the remainder of the granola bar into his mouth.

Maybe because he was so nonchalant, or maybe because she thought she'd lose her mind if she didn't tell someone, Ann started talking. "He whistles a tune that I've heard a couple of times before, okay? And, I don't know, maybe there are angels around sometimes when I hear it. I just wanted to know what he knew about it."

He ripped open the second granola bar. "That's an easy one to figure out. Maybe he is one." He took a huge bite, but sort of grinned at her as he chewed.

"One what?"

"An angel."

Obviously this had been a waste of time. Once again, Ann didn't know what she'd been expecting, but this was definitely not it. "I hardly think an angel would walk around like a homeless person in the middle of New York."

"Girl . . ." He slapped his thigh and laughed. "It's obvious you haven't been hanging 'round the right places. Haven't you never read the Bible?"

Ann shrugged. "A little. I've never read anything about angels being homeless."

"'Don't forget to entertain strangers, for by so doing some people have entertained angels without knowing it.' It's from the Bible. Maybe your friend's an angel too. I hope you were nice to him."

"What?"

Again the man slapped his thigh. "Just messing with you, girl. A friend of mine taught me that verse nearly ten years ago. It's one of my favorite angles to play when I'm asking for hand-outs near a church. Reciting it at the right time, well . . . it can be real good for business." He smiled and nodded his head. "Yep, real good. This tune, what's it sound like? I haven't heard that one before; maybe I'll use it next time and see if it helps."

"Oh, never mind." Ann walked over to a bench and dropped

onto it, covering her face with her hands. "You're right—none of that's real."

The man groaned as he came to sit beside her. "Didn't say that exactly. Who knows? When you hear this music, something good happens? Maybe it's real."

"No, usually I hear it when something bad happens. Like my sister dying, or letters I wish I'd never found buried in walls, or my car not starting."

"Car not starting, huh? Didn't sound much like angel work to me neither." The lid of the peanut butter made a swishing sound as he unscrewed it. "Real nice of you to put a plastic spoon in here for this. Most people don't think of little things like that."

"You can thank one of your homeless sisters for that." Ann stared at the dirt between the joints of the sidewalk at her feet. She wondered how many feet had walked over this place just today. How many of those people felt as lost and alone as she did?

"Mmm. This is real tasty." The man made a smacking sound. "When your car didn't start, maybe it kept you from a wreck or something. Or from going somewhere you had no business going."

Ann thought about her meeting with Patrick Stinson. She looked up at the man, his left cheek now smeared with peanut butter. "It sort of did keep me away from something. Of course, when it got started again, I still had to face it."

"You do something different than you would've if your car had started the first time?"

What would she have done? Sent Patrick Stinson packing like the philanderer he was, or gone along with him and landed the career of her dreams? "Probably."

"There you go. Maybe them angels was just giving you a little more time to reach the right decision. They didn't make it for you. They just kind of gave you a little more time to think about it so you could figure it out for yourself."

Ann looked at him and nodded. "Maybe you're right." Now she was agreeing with the reasoning of a homeless man she didn't know? Great. Wonder what craziness was going to happen next.

"Maybe so." The man stood up. "Thanks for this now, hear? I hope I see you again sometime. Maybe next time you'll teach me that tune."

"Maybe so." Ann walked back into the lobby, opposing thoughts pinging around in her brain like a pinball in a machine. When would things ever make sense?

Chapter 35

It wasn't just the landing that jarred Ann as the plane touched down in Charleston. This would perhaps be the last time she ever came back here, and though she looked forward to putting her past behind her, something still hurt.

There wasn't anything worthwhile for her here. She didn't want to be reminded that no one was quite as willing to keep her around as she was willing to be kept around. This town was full of abandonment, and she wasn't going to get caught up in it this time.

When she pulled into the driveway that evening, she looked toward Tammy and Keith's house. She expected Keith to show up at the passenger side window any minute now, like he always did—but he was nowhere to be seen. Surely he wasn't still sick? She glanced toward the house just in time to see the curtains rustling in what she knew was Keith's bedroom.

Seconds later the back door flew open and he was hurrying toward her car. "Annie, Annie. I knew you'd be back soon. I just knew it." He was breathless by the time he rushed over and threw his arms around her, hugging tight.

Ann hugged back, so amazed at the sense of love that seemed to follow this kid. "You did? How did you know?"

"It told me so."

"Your angel?"

"No." He kept his arms tight around her. "My heart did." His breathing still seemed labored.

Ann put her hand against his cheek, willing herself not to cry in front of him. "Your heart was right."

"Yeah, I know." He pulled away then, his smile lighting up the whole world. "Never doubt your heart." He said it as if he were telling her that the sun rises every morning and sets every night.

Tammy had walked across the yard to join them by this time. "Welcome back." She gave Ann a brief hug. "How long you here for this time?"

Ann shrugged. "Couple of weeks."

"Two weeks?" Tammy's voice obviously came out louder than she'd intended because she spoke more softly when she continued. "You've never stayed that long before."

"Well, a few issues came up with my job in New York that gave me some extra free time, and I decided I would come down here and get the house all finished up, tie up as many loose ends as possible." Ann ruffled Keith's hair. "It's good to see you up again. Last time I was here, you had a pretty nasty cough."

"The doctor gave me some medicine."

Ann smiled at him. "That's good."

"And Ethan brought me some of his world-famous chocolate chip cookies. That made me feel *lots* better. You want one?"

Ethan. Just the sound of his name hurt. Ann looked at Tammy and found her staring back, as if waiting for a reaction. Ann could think of several things she wanted to say, several more things she wanted to ask. Finally, she settled for, "How's he doing?"

"Keith, go get Ann one of your cookies, okay?"

"Okay, Mama." He started toward the house, moving fast.

"Walk. You don't want to end up on bed rest again, do you?" Tammy turned toward Ann. "I think he's doing about as well as a man can do when he's got a broken heart."

"A broken heart?" She hadn't expected that. "Right." She sort of laughed the words, trying to play them off as insignificant teasing. "He's the one who didn't want me. I didn't fit into the right mold to be good enough for him."

Tammy turned her face away, her mouth forming a tight line. "Most people I know would kill to have what you keep throwing away with both hands."

Ann opened her mouth to argue. Then closed it. Tammy was right. As with any other chance of happiness she'd ever had, she was building a wall around herself. She didn't want to get close enough that it could hurt her. It was an old habit, and she wasn't sure she could break it, even if she really did want to.

"Here you go, Annie." Keith held the cookie high in the air as if he'd wrestled it free from a throng of cookie mongers. "Here you go."

"Thanks, Keith." Ann reached out and took the cookie from his hand. "This looks terrific."

"It is. You got some milk? Ethan's famous cookies are better with milk."

"I haven't been to the store yet, so I guess I'll have to do without the milk."

"I'll bring you some over. I can do that. Right, Mama?"

"Keith, Ann has been traveling all day. Let's give her some time to herself. Okay?"

"No, I'm all right. Keith, if you want to bring a little milk over, and maybe a cookie and milk for yourself, I think that would be just great."

"Really?" He smiled up at his mother. "Can I?"

"Sure. But don't overstay your welcome."

"Okay, Mama."

Five minutes later Ann and Keith were seated at the kitchen table, each dunking a cookie in milk. "I never knew Ethan could make cookies."

"He can't," Keith said, his mouth full of cookie.

"But you called these Ethan's famous cookies."

"He buys these at the cookie store, but they're real good. So good they're famous."

"I see." Ann tried to puzzle through that one, but wasn't sure she got it.

"I'm glad for Ethan's cookies. And my angel dreams."

"Your angel dreams?"

"Yeah. Sometimes when I go to sleep, I get to be with them. It's real bright and warm, and they play their music—even their wings make music. It helps me forget about sad things."

"What kind of sad things?"

"My dad doesn't want me." He dunked his cookie again. "That makes me sad sometimes."

"What makes you think he doesn't want you?"

"He went away. It's my fault."

Ann reached across and squeezed his hand. "That's not your fault, Keith. It's your father's fault. He's the one who is wrong, and he's the one who missed out on getting to know you. Or having fun eating cookies with you."

"Did your daddy leave you too?"

That question brought up the usual barrage of memories that Ann did not want to face. "Not really, but my mother left me."

"Did that make you feel sad?"

Ann nodded. "Yes."

"That's why God sends His angels to me and you, maybe. So we won't be sad anymore."

"Maybe so."

When Ann finally settled in for the night, sleep wouldn't come. She sat on the couch, then lay down, then sat back up again. She walked through the kitchen, lit only by the moonlight and the soft glow of the streetlights as they shone through the windows. She poured herself a glass of cold water from the fridge and looked out the window toward Tammy's house. She thought about what Keith had said about God sending His angels so that we wouldn't be sad.

She turned her back and leaned against the kitchen counter. "God, if You really are there, if You really have angels that go around helping people, why don't they actually do something helpful? Why didn't they save Sarah?"

Something Keith had said came back into her mind so strongly that she could almost hear him saying it. *"They comfort me like when your mama holds you when you're hurt. The hurt's still there, but you feel better just the same."*

Yeah, well, that wasn't enough for Ann. She wanted someone who could actually *do* something, not just sing a comforting song while it happened. She walked over to her table full of paperwork and dug through the stacks until she found the printouts of the Hagar paintings. She looked at the haughty face of Sarah, her back turned, as Hagar was sent away. Then she turned to the next painting and saw Hagar in the wilderness, crying in despair beside her dying son. Yet the angel was on his way. Help had already been sent. If that was the case, then, in this story, God had probably been watching Hagar the entire time, from even before she got pregnant in the first place.

But why didn't He do something to help before she got to this point? God, if there was a God, was either all-powerful or all-loving, but He couldn't be both. Well, if He didn't have any power, then why did He really matter? And if He didn't love people anyway, then what was the point?

Her mind anxious, she knew sleep was still a long way away. She turned on the television but then remembered she'd had the cable disconnected.

She looked out the window toward Keith's house again, envying his quiet faith, even if it likely was misplaced. "Keith, for your sake I hope there really are angels, and I hope they are over there with you right now." She turned out the light.

As she lay there, thoughts still swirling through her mind, she pictured Keith's golden octopus high above her head. Watching her. Actually caring what happened to her. Willing to intervene, or at least "hold her like your mama does when you're hurt." Was it truly possible that such a creature existed? And was watching her right now? For the first time, Ann kind of liked the idea.

Chapter 36

Ann woke up earlier than usual the next morning, surprised by the silence. Not one single note of music. As much as this should have relieved her—and it did, to some degree—it also left her feeling as though something was missing.

Something was missing, all right, and the medical term for it was paracusia. Maybe she was finally getting over these hallucinations.

Today was the day to get some things done around here. First thing on the list: remove all curtains and replace them with the more modern, white, semi-sheer blinds she'd purchased two trips ago.

Within minutes, the whine of the electric screwdriver filled the house. When Ann removed the curtains from "her" bedroom, she saw a bit of the pewter tankard that hadn't quite been covered up by coats of stark white. Something else she needed to touch up. She put her fingers on the color, remembering how she'd felt that day as she painted the walls something other than her usual. How right its warmth had felt.

It was amazing how far she'd deluded herself. It hadn't taken long for things to return to their usual status quo and pull her right out of that. Just as well. All these delusions needed to stop if she was going to get on with her life.

The doorbell rang. She went to answer it, thinking that Tammy had probably already told Ethan she was back in town. She opened the door, a smile plastered on her face in spite of her herself, and found herself looking into the eyes of Eleanor Light.

"Hi, Ann. I just stopped by to see how things were coming along. Do you think you'll have the place ready for an open house next weekend?"

"Next weekend?" Ann thought of the work she'd need to do before an open house, but what else did she have to do? "Sure, I'll get it ready. I was just changing out the window treatments."

"Ooh, can I see?"

"I haven't got them all up yet, but the bedrooms are done. You're welcome to see the progress."

Eleanor walked in, her heels clicking across the hardwood floor. "These floors sure did turn out nice, I tell you what. That right there is going to be a big selling point." She stopped walking and looked around the living room. "I thought you were painting this another color, something a little warmer."

"Well, I tried it, but it just didn't work."

"Really? This house is so cozy and warm, it seems like a warm color would be the perfect match."

"I tried it; it didn't work, okay?" The loud irritation in Ann's voice surprised even her.

Eleanor took a step back and smoothed an imaginary

wrinkle in the sleeve of her jacket. She continued to smooth it long after the point of uncomfortable silence had been reached.

Ann finally said, "You wanted to see the window treatments in the bedrooms, right?"

"Absolutely." Eleanor made no comment or expression to indicate she'd suffered an offense. She simply followed Ann to the bedroom.

"Oh, these are really pretty." Ann turned to see Eleanor lifting a small section of the just-removed curtains that were lying across the bed. "I can't remember what you had in here before, but these are perfect. Good job."

"Eleanor, *that's* what was in here before. I took them down to add these." Ann unfurled one of the blinds so Eleanor could get the full translucent effect as it hung against the window. Ann loved the way it diffused the sun but did not completely block it. So clean, so modern.

She turned to Eleanor, ready to hear her approval. Instead, she saw her looking from the new blinds to the old curtains, a look of confusion on her face. It took her a long time to say anything, but finally she said, "What gave you the idea to change to these modern shades?"

"The homes I stage in New York are all ultra-modern. I thought it would put a little of me into this house."

Eleanor nodded, her forehead wrinkled in thought. "I don't want to be offensive about any of this—I mean, obviously you wanted the walls white too—but don't you think white walls and white modern blinds are a bit . . . lacking in color? In warmth? This is Charleston, after all, not some high rise in New York."

The words stung. Tammy's similar comments could be dismissed as those of someone ignorant to good taste. Eleanor's . . .

well, she was a professional. Ann took a slow, deep breath and stated in a very calm voice, "I think there are varied tastes in Charleston, just as there are everywhere else."

"That is true. There are some very modern homes in Charleston, where this would look not only beautiful but totally appropriate. This is your home and you can do whatever you think is best, but as your real estate agent, I've got to tell you that, to me, it looks as if this home is trying to be something it's not—like a person putting on a front that says one thing, while deep inside she knows she's something else. That doesn't work for people and it doesn't work in houses." Her phone buzzed and she looked down at it. "I've got somewhere I have to be, but I wish you'd think about it, Ann. Don't be afraid to let people see what's really inside."

"I don't know what you're talking about." But she did know, and that thought terrified her more than anything she'd yet faced.

"Trying to be something it's not." The phrase rang through Ann's mind long past dinnertime. She was not trying to be something that she wasn't; she was trying to be herself. But all of Charleston seemed to be conspiring against her. Well, this was a battle she intended to win. She was strong and independent, able to make her own choices, and didn't need anyone else.

She walked into her old room. *I am my own person. I am not hiding. I don't need this room or anything in it.* She looked toward the wall socket and added, "Or anything that ever once was in it."

That's when she knew what she needed to do. She went into Nana's room and found the rolled paper on the nightstand.

If she was truly going to bid all this nonsense farewell, it was best to get as much closure as possible. She snatched up the roll. *I pulled you out of the garbage last time, but this time, there won't be a second chance.* She got into her car and drove like a crazy woman until she reached the Battery Walk.

The full moon made it easy to watch the intersection of the two rivers as they flowed together, *"forming the Atlantic Ocean."* Remembering Ethan's comment almost made her smile—but memories only caused pain, and it was time to purge as many of them as possible. Excess cargo could sink a ship—or a person. This little memento of her mother would be the first to go. She'd never even read the rest of it, and that was for the best. It was another piece of the past to be cut loose.

Ann extended her hand, watching the moonlight glow faintly on the paper. She began to loosen her grip one finger at a time. It was time to let this go. Let all of it go.

Her fingers seemed frozen in the bent position, in spite of her efforts to straighten them. She looked around, trying to force herself to relax. This was something she needed to do.

The sound of the ocean and the sight of the mansions and the Ravenel Bridge did nothing to make her task any easier. Finally, her pinky finger straightened, and her ring finger slowly began to follow. It was time to give the Atlantic Ocean one more chunk of broken dreams, like the pieces of wrecked ships that once dotted the sandy bottom. Just one more victim.

"Ann, is that you?" Eleanor's voice was suddenly calling to her from farther down the walk. Several people turned Ann's way.

"Hey, what's she doing? Mama, she's littering. Stop her." The high-pitched voice came from a well-dressed family walking her way, including a young girl in a flouncy sundress and huge white hair bow. "You can't drop that into the ocean. It's pollution. Tell her, Mama," the girl said in a nasally, irritating tone.

Ann was so shocked that she couldn't think of how to respond, or even what to do. When she regained her senses, she clutched the paper—and ran. Hard. She didn't stop running until she reached her car, jumped inside. and locked the door.

On the drive home, she began to laugh hysterically. What had that all been about? Like she was afraid of a six-year-old with a hair bow and her thoughts on pollution. And yet, it had thrown her so completely off course that here she was, pulling back into the driveway, letter resting on the passenger seat.

And what must Eleanor think? That Ann was a nutcase, most likely, and one pretending she was someone she wasn't, as they were all so fond of saying.

She took a deep breath and decided to deal with this situation once and for all. Finish reading this letter. *Then* she could put it behind her.

She carried the roll back into the living room, turned on the lamp, and dropped sideways onto the sofa, leaning her back against the armrest and putting her feet up on the cushions. Slowly, she uncurled the paper and scanned down the page to where she'd stopped reading the last time. Only two paragraphs left. She rallied what was left of her courage.

I'm leaving you with Mama. She loves you both to pieces. I don't know how I could bear it otherwise. I just feel like there's this hunger inside me and no matter what I do, it never fills up. The only time the hunger numbs is when I've had a few drinks, or when I'm in a bar and see a man look at me in the way that says I'm something special. I wish I could be satisfied with something, anything, but I'm not. I'm still looking, still hungering. So I'm packing my bags and making a clean break. You'll be better off without me.

Mama will take good care of you. I hope someday you realize how much I love you both. It's just that I'm all broken inside, and I don't have anything more to give you.

All my love,

Lorelei (your mama)

Ann recognized some of her own thoughts in her mother's words. She understood the "clean break" principle. But from this perspective, reading it in her mother's letter, it sounded a lot like quitting. Funny how it felt so much nobler when she was the one making the clean break. Is that what she was doing here? Quitting?

She rolled the paper up and put it back on Nana's nightstand. Retreating to the sofa, she once again lay there wondering if something or someone was actually watching her right now. Someone who actually cared. With questions running through her mind, over and over, she found no relief.

Chapter 37

Ann dug the hole for the last of the petunias, glad to be done with this hot job. Tammy had been over to help, and Keith was lying on a lawn chair in the shade, looking at some of his books. He was coughing again and seemed a little lethargic.

"Ann, can I ask a favor?" Tammy asked. She was covered with potting soil and sweat. There was no way Ann could have refused her anything.

"Sure. Name it."

"Keith and I need to run several errands this afternoon—I obviously need a shower first—but I'd promised Ethan I'd drop some homemade brownies by his house today. I don't think I'll have time to do it, so could I impose on you to deliver them for me?"

Ann hadn't talked to Ethan since she'd arrived. She folded her arms. "You know, if this is your way of trying to get us together, it's not going to work."

Tammy looked at her with an expression of surprise, the

picture of innocence. "I don't know what you're talking about. You can drop them off before he gets home. He'll never even know it was you." She almost smiled, but not quite.

"So, what, should I leave them on the front porch?"

"No, if you don't mind, put them on his kitchen table. The back door opens right up into it, and it'll be unlocked."

"He leaves his back door unlocked?"

Again, Tammy looked a little too innocent. "Usually he does."

Hmm. Tammy was definitely up to something.

"Come on, Keith. We need to get washed up for our trip downtown."

"Okay, Mama. Annie, you want me to leave this book for you? It's a good one. Clifford is just a puppy."

"That is a great one, but I've already read it."

"Really? Is it your favorite?"

"Uh . . ." Ann had a vague idea that Clifford was a red dog, but otherwise she was making this up as she went along. "Yeah, I think it might be."

"Mine too." He put the book into the little backpack he'd brought over with him. "Bye, Annie." He waved and smiled as he left.

About an hour later Ann headed toward Ethan's house. She remembered the day when she and Eleanor had walked by it, and Eleanor had talked about how perfect the place was for him. Only now did it strike her as odd that she'd never seen the inside. She had been so many places with him, but never once to his own house.

She walked up the driveway, thinking how this white house, with green shutters and whale-shaped weather vane atop the chimney, looked as though it belonged in a Kellogg's Corn Flakes commercial. Definitely charming in a down-home sort of way.

She went to the back door. Feeling a bit like a burglar, she tried the knob. It turned in her hand, and the door opened with a light push. Strange that he would leave it unlocked.

But then she saw the inside. A burglar would probably just turn and leave after taking one look. The walls were down to the studs, with rows of insulation showing and the occasional electric wiring. She stepped inside, into what must've been the kitchen. The countertops were missing, as were the doors on the cabinets. At least there was a fridge and stove. To her right, she spotted a plastic-covered table and set the brownies on it.

She walked back outside in a daze. How much time had he spent working on Sarah's house—Ann's house—while his own home went unfinished? He didn't even have a place to cut vegetables in his kitchen, much less make brownies. The realization of what Ethan had done almost took her breath away.

Later that night she walked over to Tammy's and sat down in her kitchen. "I took the brownies over to Ethan's."

"Great. I just couldn't stand the thought of letting him down after I'd promised."

Ann looked around. "Where's Keith?"

"Asleep. Another big day."

"Yeah." Ann tugged at a loose string on the hem of her shirt. "I didn't realize he was doing such an extensive remodel on his house."

"When he bought that house last year, it was in terrible shape, looked like a bulldoze job to me. Of course, to Ethan, it looked like a project. So he dug right in, spending every spare minute working on that place. I thought he was crazy when he first bought it, but seeing what he's doing, I think it'll be something amazing when he's done."

"I'm sure." Ann looked up at Tammy. "Let me guess, he more or less stopped working on it for the last couple of months because he was so busy working on my place."

"Well"—Tammy wiped off a perfectly clean kitchen counter—"you could definitely say the work slowed down over there lately."

Ann shook her head. "I wish I'd known. I wouldn't have let him do that."

"I'm sure he knew that, which is why he never told you anything about it." Tammy rinsed out the blue sponge and set it beside the sink. "He'd do anything for you."

Once again the point was driven home that Ann didn't deserve Ethan.

It was time to do a professional walk-through. What would Ann recommend to the client who owned this house? Of course, the owners would not have been her clients; they would have been Beka's, the traditional decorator of their group. Okay then, what would Beka say?

Ann walked into Nana's room. "Okay, Beka, what would you tell me?"

Doing her best impersonation of Beka's deep voice and Midwest accent, Ann said, "Looks pretty good. Not too cluttered. Furniture is not fancy, but it's appropriate for the house and in pretty good shape."

Ann smiled at her imaginary partner. "Thanks, Beka, that's exactly what I thought."

As she walked from the room, she found herself mumbling in Beka's voice again. "I'm glad you pulled some of those floral pillows out of storage. It was the right thing to do. The blinds are inappropriate, of course. They're trying to make this house look like something it's not."

Ann stopped walking and shook her head. Hard. She'd heard that stupid comment so many times, she was using it in her own imaginary conversations now.

She picked up her cell and punched in Beka's number. After their greetings, Ann explained, "I'm about to have an open house here, and I was just doing a walk-through having an imaginary conversation with you, so I thought I'd call and have a real one."

"Well, I hope I was giving you some good advice."

"As usual, you were questioning some of my choices, but as usual, I showed you the error of your ways."

Beka laughed. "Sounds about right."

"How are things going there?"

Silence. Nothing but a long-drawn-out silence. "Ann, I wasn't going to tell you until you got back."

"Tell me what?"

"The Stinson job, it fell through. Margaret laid everyone off. There's talk that she's filing for bankruptcy, but I don't know for sure."

"That can't be. What happened? When?"

"After you left, it seemed like that whole deal started to dis-integrate. All of a sudden he didn't like any of our ideas, nothing was quite right. I guess it turns out there was never a signed contract—which blows me away. Margaret was always such a stickler about that. So he's not financially obligated in any way. Apparently Margaret had ordered a lot of expensive furniture for him, which she can no longer afford to pay for. I think it's over for her. For all of us."

Ann dropped into a chair. "What are you going to do?"

Another long pause. "I'd like to stay here, of course, so I'll look for a job. But in all reality, I'll likely move back to Wisconsin in the next few months. The cost of living is lower. It's closer to my family."

"Oh, Beka, no."

"It's all right. We're going to be all right; we always are. Now"—there was the sound of muffled sniffling—"tell me about the house. Did you get everything done in time?"

The open house seemed so insignificant now. Still, she knew Beka needed her to be strong. "More or less. You know how it is—there's always something more that could be done. Right now it's time for me to run a dust mop over the hardwood floors and scrub the bathroom one more time."

"Make it spotless."

"I'll do my best." Ann somehow forced herself up from the chair. "I'll call you when I get back next week."

"We'll have you over for dinner."

Eleanor Light arrived, dressed in a white linen suit. "Well, are you ready?"

"I think so."

Eleanor walked into the house and looked around. "You've done an amazing job of getting this place ready, I'll have to say that. You've even managed to provide a homey feel in spite of some of the decorating to the contrary." She looked at Ann then. "Are you sure you want to go through with this?"

"Of course. Why wouldn't I?"

"I don't know, it just seems to me that maybe you'd be happy if you stayed here. Are you sure you're ready to sell?"

"I don't have a choice."

"Ah, that's what people tell themselves, but in truth, you always have a choice."

"Just exactly what—?"

"You'd better get out of here. People will be coming anytime now. Go on, take the day, spend some time visiting the places you love one last time."

Somehow Ann had been ordered out of her house and was now sitting her in car wondering what in the world she was going to do. Well, maybe she would take the advice of all concerned and revisit some of her past. She decided to set out on a quest.

Maybe she hadn't been able to dump her mother's letter into the ocean, but today she would begin the process of saying good-bye to Charleston. Perhaps the best way to do that was to say good-bye to Sarah and Nana.

It didn't seem right to visit the graveyard empty-handed, so Ann stopped at a little florist and bought a dozen roses. She knew that there were more appropriate things to place at a grave, but nothing else could sum up the love she felt better than roses.

She drove toward the cemetery, but along the way, she lost her nerve and turned toward St. Johns Island, deciding that perhaps a little detour might give her time to collect her thoughts.

The summer sun and high humidity had already turned the air into a sticky paste by the time Ann pulled into the parking lot of Angel Oak Park. It felt hard to breathe as she walked toward the massive oak, yet its outstretched branches looked as if they were welcoming her to their shelter. She remembered Ethan telling her that the tree had been severely damaged by Hurricane Hugo. Fifteen hundred years of life, then one big storm almost took it out. Now, twenty years later, her untrained eye could see no evidence that there had ever been a storm. It seemed strong and majestic. Completely unstoppable.

In that moment, she realized that was how people saw her. With the strong, often brash, face she put on, no one could know how thrashed she was inside. She was like that traditional home buried in modern trappings—it was all a lie.

Unable to bear any more soul searching, Ann climbed back into the car. She wound her way through the back roads of the Lowcountry until she drove through the wrought-iron gates of the cemetery. Their intricate design was covered by dots of rust and the warp of too many years in the elements. She parked farther from the graves than was necessary. After a deep breath, she walked over to the final resting place of her sister and grandmother.

"Hi. It's me." She felt kind of silly talking aloud, but she didn't let it stop her. "I just came here to tell you good-bye— I'm going to be leaving soon, and I won't be back." She paused just long enough to work up her courage. "I need to tell you that I didn't keep my promise after all. I'm sorry." Her voice cracked, and it took her a minute to regain control before she continued. "I didn't become a success like I said. Quite the opposite, in fact. I messed up everything." She started to cry. "I don't know what to do. It's all ruined."

She sat beside her sister and grandmother, wrapped her arms around her knees, and rocked back and forth. "I wish you were here, Nana. You would know what to do. So would you, Sarah. You both could help me figure this out. All of it, because none of it makes sense to me." She put her head on her knees.

Time passed, she had no idea how much, but finally the grief inside her began to calm. She began to feel the same peace she felt when Nana would rock her to sleep as a child. She could almost hear her voice. "You know what, Nana? Starting an important business might be great, making it big in New York design would have been so amazing, but not at the price I would have had to pay. That would have been failure of the worst kind. Maybe I did succeed after all, even if I am back at a start-up company working at entry level."

She thought about the new job, the possibilities it presented her. Another path that could lead her toward success. Then she thought about Beka and Gracie and what they were going through. "But there's something else I'm supposed to do. If I'm truly going to be a *success*, I've got another step to take. That's what you would tell me, isn't it?"

Ann stood, only then remembering that she'd left the flowers in the car. She started to walk back to get them but then turned. "You're not really here, are you? Sarah, I'm going to take those flowers to Tammy, brighten her day a little. I'm sure that's what you'd want me to do."

Back in her car, she pulled out her cell phone. Time to take the next step. It was crazy, and it was going to cost everything she had left, but it was the right thing to do. She punched in the number and waited. After Meredith Radke answered, she jumped in.

"Hi, Meredith, it's Ann Fletcher. Listen, some things beyond my control have changed, and I won't be able to take that job after all. I think you were right when you said you were looking to diversify. That would be a better business move; we both know it." She took a breath and looked toward Nana's grave. *Keep going, you've got to see this through.* "I know a very talented designer who is out of work, through no fault of her own. Her name is Beka Simons. Her specialties are traditional and Middle Eastern, and she's amazing. I think she would be a better fit for you."

"Well, I'm sorry to hear that you've changed your mind, Ann." Meredith paused just a minute. "Beka does sound like she could be a good fit. Why don't you have her call me, and we'll go from there."

"You can bet I will." Ann barely hung up before she pressed her speed dial. "Hey, Beka, it's me. I think I might have found something perfect for you."

Ann gave Beka the information she needed but kept the details vague. She didn't want Beka to connect too many of the dots.

By the time she started back to the house, Ann felt the most amazing sense of release. She was sure it was going to work out for Beka, she and Gracie would be okay.

Ann was jobless once again, with no prospects on the horizon, but she'd done the right thing. Maybe she had succeeded, just a little. She'd just have to remind herself of that when she was back in New York, pounding the pavement in her search for work.

As she drove, Ann wondered what kind of turnout there had been at the open house. The place needed to sell soon; she needed the money.

Ann parked her car in the garage and stepped outside into the late afternoon heat, which made it hard to even move. In the distance, the scream of sirens floated through the air, but it seemed as if they too slowed and bogged in this thick summer humidity. She started across the lawn, choosing a path that led from the shade of one tree to another. By the time she was halfway to Tammy's back door, the crank of the sirens had grown noticeably louder. That's when she knew where the sirens were going.

She dropped the flowers from her hand and broke into an all-out run. Without bothering to knock, she flung open the back door and ran inside. "Tammy! Tammy?"

"Back here." Tammy's voice came from Keith's room. Ann skidded to a stop just inside his doorway, already alarmed by the raspy sound of Keith's breathing. His face looked gray. "What's happened?"

The sirens grew louder and louder. Tammy nodded toward the door. "Will you show them the way back here?"

"Of course." Ann raced out into the driveway. The ambulance was still over a block away, but that didn't stop her from waving her hands frantically and screaming, "Over here! Over here!" The ambulance seemed to move slower. Ann waved her hands all that much harder. "Hurry! You've got to hurry!" At last the vehicle pulled into the driveway and the attendants climbed out. "Follow me. Quickly."

She ran back into the house, down the hallway, and into Keith's room, then stood back in the far corner out of the way. As she watched the scene, her mind barely registered the sight of the blue jumpsuits, the gurney, or the clipped instructions traded back and forth. She had shriveled up, retreating somewhere deep inside herself where she wouldn't have to experience this, to feel its hopelessness.

Keith's gurney was being rushed from the room, and suddenly Tammy was standing directly in front of her. "Meet us at the hospital, okay? And call Ethan, let him know what's going on. He'll alert the prayer chain."

Ann nodded numbly. "Sure. Right." Then she watched them all disappear. A blast of sirens and a few flashes of light later, she was alone.

Somehow she managed to stand up and stumble back to her car, where she yanked the cell phone from her purse. She pressed Ethan's name in her contacts list and hit Send. It rang and rang and rang, then finally clicked over to voice mail. "Ethan, it's me." What was she supposed to say? There were too many things, much too many. "Keith's being rushed to the hospital, I don't know what happened, but he was fighting to breathe. Come as soon as you can. Okay?" It was all she could manage. She pushed the button to disconnect the call and started the car. She was halfway down the driveway when she realized she didn't know which hospital.

The smart thing to do would be to go back to the house and make some calls, but Ann was well past the point of acting with any intelligence. She drove toward the Medical University Hospital, supposing that would be the most logical place to take a child. Unfortunately, it was rush hour, and according to radio traffic reports, there was a stalled car and an accident somewhere ahead of her. Traffic was backed up almost to a standstill.

It was an hour later when she ran into the main lobby, found a volunteer to help her, and made her way to the waiting area of the Pediatric Intensive Care Unit. The waiting room had yellow and white walls and chairs in a few cheerful colors. Several people were inside, some talking in groups, one couple standing in the far corner looking worried, but no sign of Tammy. Ann approached the desk where a woman sat, hair stacked high on her head, smile lines etched around her eyes. "May I help you?" she asked before Ann had fully made it to the desk. Ann supposed that in a place like this, she had learned to respond quickly to the urgency most people felt.

"Yes, I think Keith Litton was just brought here. Can you tell me anything?"

The woman looked at some papers on a clipboard in front of her. "And you are?"

Why should she care? "I'm his neigh—" For some reason Ann stopped before completing the sentence and changed course. "My name is Ann Fletcher."

She nodded. "Yes, I see your name right here on the family list. They've just brought him up. Follow me." Tammy had put Ann's name on the family list. Why should things like this continue to surprise her? Ann had no answer as she followed the woman through the double doors.

The PICU was one giant room, with perhaps a dozen alcoves that formed rooms. Ann could see Tammy leaning over a bed in one of the closest rooms. When Tammy looked up and saw her, she extended her left arm to Ann while she continued to hold Keith's hand with her right.

Ann put her arms around Tammy and squeezed. "What happened?" She looked at Keith's face, paler than she'd yet seen it. His eyes were closed. Oxygen tubes, IV lines, and more gadgets than she cared to think about were attached to his little body, and a bank of monitors blinked in the background. It was a stupid question, but asking "How bad is it?" didn't seem appropriate.

At first, Tammy just shook her head no. She took a moment, blinking hard and breathing deeply, then answered, "He was born with a heart problem . . ." She brushed her hand across his forehead. "And fluid sometimes backs into his lungs, which makes it hard to breathe, which makes it hard on his heart. It's a vicious cycle. We've always known that at any time . . ." She put her hand over her mouth, as if trying to hold the sorrow inside. After another minute she said, "His poor little heart just can't keep up with all that love he's got inside anymore."

Ann thought about the truth of that statement. Keith loved more purely, and with more strength, than most people ever would, yet he was so often rejected and misunderstood. Still, none of it made sense to Ann. Why should he be the one to die when there were people like terrorists, and murderers, and that slimeball Patrick Stinson alive? Or when there were people so much less deserving of life—like herself?

Ann put her hand on Keith's arm. "You hang in there and fight, buddy. I need you."

The corner of his mouth seemed to twitch. Likely Ann had imagined it, because it's what she wanted to believe, but she still waited for a sign of recognition, of any evidence of improvement. Anything at all that could give her hope.

They sat in silence at his bedside for hours. The nurses came and went, hanging IV bags, drawing blood, doing whatever it was they were doing. Tammy and Ann simply stood on opposite sides of the bed, each holding one of Keith's hands. Tammy's lips moved silently almost the entire time, and Ann knew that she was praying. Maybe it was time for Ann to give that another try.

God, I know we're not exactly friends, yet, but I have to admit that there is something going on around here that seems to have to do with Your angels. If You really are here, if You really do exist and send Your angels down to watch after us, won't You please send an angel to help Keith?

She found herself straining to listen, and it occurred to her that she was actually listening for music. The song. For the first time, she found herself wanting to hear the song. More than wanting . . . she *needed* to hear it.

Silence.

The nurse came over and injected something into one of Keith's IV lines. She looked up at Tammy. "He's stabilized for now, if you want to go grab a bite to eat."

Tammy shook her head, then looked at Ann. "You should get something, though."

Ann hadn't even thought of food. "Not hungry. But why don't I run to your house and get some things for you? I'm guessing you're going to be here for a few days. You want some toiletries and a change of clothes?"

"Sure. That would be nice." Tammy continued to hold Keith's hand, hardly even seeming to notice that she was speaking.

Reluctantly, Ann stood. She squeezed Keith's hand. "I'll be back. You take care of your mama while I'm gone." She walked out the double doors of the unit and glanced toward the waiting area.

Bent over in a chair, blond hair hanging over his forehead and eyes, elbows resting on knees—there was no mistaking the presence of Ethan. She went over and touched him on the shoulder. "How long have you been here?"

He looked up. "I don't know, a couple of hours. Since right after I got your message."

"Family is allowed back there, you know. You could go on back. I'm sure Tammy put your name on the list."

"She did. It's just that only two people are allowed at a time."

"What?" Ann gasped out the word. "You've been waiting out here because I was in your place this whole time? Oh, Ethan, I'd give anything if I'd known. I would have come out."

"I know you would've. That's why I didn't send word that I was here. It's just as much your place as it is mine. Keith has such a special love for you. So does Tammy. It was right for you to be back there."

Once again, Ann was overwhelmed with the love she felt she didn't deserve. "Well, I'm going to the house to get some things for Tammy, so go spend some time with your best quarterback."

He nodded. "I want to let Tammy know that the prayer chain has been activated. People all across Charleston are praying for Keith right now."

Ann nodded. "I hope it helps." She meant those words more than she'd ever meant them before in her life.

Chapter 38

The pale outline of the For Sale sign in her yard reminded her that there'd been an open house today, something that had seemed so important just a few hours ago.

Ann walked into the house, flipped on a couple of lights, and realized that this place might not be hers for much longer. Not the wood floors she'd spent so much time refinishing; not the rooms where Nana, Sarah, and she had spent so many years together; not the home that her mother had made the final decision to leave forever. This house had never been filled with the finer things. But it had been filled with love. Nana's love. Sarah's love. Ann had spent so much time grieving the loss of her mother's love, though, that she'd never learned to appreciate what was here.

Wasn't she doing the same thing now? With Tammy? And Keith? And Ethan?

Well, she couldn't do anything about that. With no job, and no prospect of a job, she *had* to sell; there was no other choice.

Eleanor's voice came back to her, *There's always a choice.*

"Not in this case, Eleanor. Not in this case." She whispered the words, then shook her head to clear her thoughts. Time to go to Tammy's house and get her things.

When she arrived back at the hospital, she went straight to the PICU waiting room. The woman at the desk recognized her. "Your brother asked me to let him know as soon as you arrived. Just one minute, please."

Ann nodded. Her brother. Since it was immediate family only in the PICU, Tammy had listed both Ethan and Ann as her siblings. "Great. Thanks."

A moment later Ethan followed the woman out of the double doors and walked over to Ann. She extended the duffel bag in her hand. "Here are some things for Tammy."

He didn't reach out to take them. "Don't you want to take them yourself?"

Ann shook her head and stepped closer to him, taking care to keep her voice quiet in the waiting room. "You're always giving up things for me. You left your own house unfinished so you could help me fix up Sarah's. You sat out here all afternoon because I was in your rightful spot."

He put his hand under her chin and lifted it so she had to face him. When she met his eyes, he said, "I don't have a single regret."

"Wish I could say the same . . . Ethan, I'm sorry I—"

"Shh." He lowered his face right in front of hers. "You go in there, spend some time with Tammy and Keith. We'll work out everything else when Keith gets better. Okay?"

Ann nodded. "Okay."

"Take all the time you need."

Tammy's head was leaned against the chair back, her eyes closed. Ann wasn't sure if she was asleep or praying, but she tiptoed just in case. She put her hand on Keith's. His face was bluish, but his breathing seemed more relaxed. *God, if You're there, help him*. It was all she could think to pray.

"How long have you been here?" Tammy stretched her arms, then leaned forward toward her son's bed.

"Just got here. How's he doing?"

"The doctors say it's still touch and go."

Keith gasped loudly, then wheezed a couple of labored breaths. Tammy began to whisper prayers that Ann couldn't quite make out. But she understood clearly because another sound began to fill the space.

She actually felt it before she heard it. A warmth enveloped her entire body. When the music began, it almost seemed to be inside of her, permeating her whole being; then it spilled into the room, faint at first, but growing louder by the second. The harmony was multilayered, and this time it wasn't just instrumental. She heard distinct singing and more than one song. The melody of each song complemented the other, and each voice could be heard distinctly while blending with the others. The sound was beautiful, unearthly . . . pure. Keith started thrashing about in the bed. He was gasping for air, his lungs making a strange wheezing sound as he struggled against the sheets.

The song gained in volume until it overpowered all other sounds. Ann reached across the bed with her free hand and squeezed Tammy's. "He's not afraid. They're here now."

Tammy looked at her, a panicked expression on her face. "What do you mean?" She looked back toward Keith. "Who's here?"

"Listen." Ann looked at Tammy, waiting for the reality to set in.

Tammy simply stared blankly. "What? What do you hear?"

"Tammy, the music. Can't you hear it?" It had grown louder, and chills ran up and down Ann's body from the sheer beauty of it. The voices shimmered with a perfection no human could possibly attain. "The angels are here. They're here with Keith."

"I don't hear anything." Tammy's eyes spilled over with tears. "I don't hear anything. Why can't I hear it?" Keith continued to wheeze, but his thrashing calmed. He wiggled his fingers as if stroking a beloved pet.

"He's all right now. They're here with him so he won't be afraid."

Keith made a gurgling sound. Tammy put her hand over her mouth and took deep breaths mixed with sobs. "Are they still singing?"

The song began to fade. Keith wheezed loudly; then he went silent as note by note the music disappeared.

Keith opened his eyes, smiled weakly at his mother, then closed them again. He squeezed Ann's hand.

It was then that Ann fully realized the incredible gift that God had given her in allowing her to hear what most humans—with the exception of her dying sister, and the most incredible person in the form of a Down syndrome preteen—could not hear. The song of His angels. The song of those in His presence, even when no one else in the room hears it, feels it, or even knows it. He is here. Now. Always.

Chapter 39

"Help. Annie. Please. Help. Annie. Please. Help. Annie. Please."

Ann jerked awake, the memory of Sarah and her last words repeating over and over in her mind. She would never know what it was that Sarah had wanted from her, never know how it was she could help her sister.

She lay back against the arm of the sofa, her heart torn by her inability to help Sarah in her last request. The words still tumbled in her mind; she could still see Sarah's face, the expression of peace as she looked over her shoulder. *"Help. Annie. Please."*

Looking over her shoulder.

Her expression of peace.

Ann jumped to her feet. Sarah had been listening to the angel song. She had been feeling that wonderful, soothing warmth. She hadn't been asking for Ann's help; she'd been asking for God to help Ann. *Help for Ann.*

That's what this had all been about. Sarah had asked the angel to help Ann. That's why Ann had been able to hear the song, why there had been so many coincidences. God had been honoring Sarah's last request. The sheer magnitude of it took her breath away. She rushed into her room and changed into shorts and a T-shirt. There was something she needed to do.

She walked out the front door, half expecting to see Eleanor jogging by in the early morning light. Instead, she saw Ethan's truck parked in Tammy's driveway, and then saw him pulling the lawn mower from Tammy's garage.

Ann knew he was getting the lawn ready for Keith's expected release from the hospital tomorrow. She waved a greeting but continued moving toward her goal.

He came running over to her. "Hey, what's up?"

Ann walked to the For Sale sign and began pulling it up. "You know what? I'm tired of putting on a brave front. I'm tired of hiding from the past. It's time for a new start. In a new—yet old—place. I think it's time I started believing in something."

She stopped pulling and looked at Ethan. "God has been trying to get my attention for a long time, and . . . well, now, let's just say that I know He's there. I told you once that I didn't know how to believe, but you know what? I was wrong."

"Really?" Ethan searched her face for a long second, then nodded. "I'm happy to hear that."

"I thought you would be." She pulled at the sign again, but it still didn't budge. She grunted and said, "I don't know what I'm going to do. It's not like I can afford *not* to sell this place; I've got to pay rent back in New York."

"That's where faith comes in. You trust that Someone bigger than you can handle it, and you learn that it's okay to accept help every now and then instead of always giving it."

Ethan reached over and gave the sign two good yanks. It

came free from the ground and swung loose in his arms. "What do you want me to do with this?"

"I'm going to call Eleanor Light and tell her to come get it. I won't be needing it anymore." Somewhere deep inside she knew that Eleanor's job was done.

Ethan smiled. He leaned over and put the sign on the ground. Then he stood and pulled Ann into his arms. "Welcome home."

"Home," she said. "Tell me more about that."

Ethan looked down at her. "I've got lots to say on that subject."

Ann twined her arms around his neck. "Like what, for instance?"

"Hmm, let me see if I can think of something." He leaned forward and brought his lips to hers.

"Don't ever let me go," she whispered against his cheek.

"I don't plan to, my sweet Ann."

"Call me Annie." She reached up and kissed him again.

Chapter 40

"Hey, Keith, I've got a question about one of your drawings." Annie turned from the box she was unpacking and walked over to her sofa where Keith was resting. She was glad to see the color returning to his face.

"Okay."

Annie held up the drawing of the flattened letter *m*, the angel, and the cylinder. "What is this one?"

He smiled. "That's a garbage can." Keith pointed at the cylinder. "And that's a bird, and that's the angel. His name is Uriel. He watches out for you."

"Why am I handing a bird to an angel?" Then Annie felt her mouth go dry. "Did you say Uriel? As in Uri—the homeless guy?" She remembered the night she'd handed him the food from her dinner with Patrick Stinson. Her leftovers, wrapped in foil, shaped like a swan.

Keith smiled.

Annie remembered the Bible verse she'd learned from the

other homeless man, the one with dreadlocks. She hadn't believed him. She *wouldn't* believe him. But now . . .

"You know, Keith, I think you're right."

"Of course I am. Me and Ethan, we're always right. Right, Ethan?"

"You got it, buddy."

"Sure you are." Tammy laughed as she pinned the hem of the new living room drapes. "I think I could offer a few examples that would prove otherwise."

"There's no reason to get nitpicky. We're right about the important stuff anyway. Keith knows about homeless angels named Uriel, and I know about beautiful women named Annie. Far as I'm concerned, that's all that matters."

"Oh really?" Annie walked over and sat in his lap. "Tell me more about that."

"Ew, gross," Keith said and snickered from somewhere behind them, but Annie didn't care.

Ethan kissed her lightly. "Hope you've got awhile, because I have lots to say on the subject."

"Take all the time you need." She buried her head on his shoulder. "I've got all day."

"I'm thinking something longer term might be necessary."

Annie raised her head.

"Come on, Ethan," Keith broke in. "Let's go play football. This is getting way too mushy." He pulled on Ethan's arm.

"Keith, you may always be right, but your sense of timing could definitely use a little work." He and Annie stood. She watched him start out the door with Keith, but then he turned and looked at her. "Conversation to be continued."

"I'm counting on it."

Acknowledgments

SHEILA WOULD LIKE TO THANK THE FOLLOWING PEOPLE:

Rick Christian: You are so much more than a wonderful literary agent. You are a dear friend and a funny man. It's great to be a part of the "Alive" family.

Lee Hough: I'm so grateful that you are my book agent. You shepherded this project on every level, as a dream became reality. Thank you.

Allen Arnold and the Thomas Nelson Fiction Team: It has been such an amazing experience to work with each one of you. You are truly the best at what you do. You faithfully steward the place of honor and respect that God has given you and it is a joy to be part of your family.

Ami McConnell: You poured yourself tirelessly into this book and your attention to every tiny detail is just one of the reasons that you are so brilliant at what you do. Thank you for a listening ear and an open heart.

Jen Deshler, Natalie Hanemann, and Katie Bond: Thank you for your giftedness, wisdom, care and encouragement.

Mary Graham and the Women of Faith team: Thank you for giving me a platform to share my passion and my call and your forever friendship as we share this journey to the hearts of women.

Barry Walsh: You caught this vision right away and have walked it out with me step by step. Thank you for the hours you spent pouring over the manuscript and keeping us true to Charleston, your home. You and our darling son, Christian, have put a song in this girl's heart!

FROM KATHRYN CUSHMAN:

Lee Cushman—I don't know how I would have survived this past year without your love and support. Thank you for being the man God called you to be.

Melanie Cushman—During the writing of this book I've spent thirty-two days at your hospital bedside, and dozens more days in various doctors' offices, watching you endure more than any sixteen-year-old should ever have to endure. Your courage and upbeat attitude never fail to amaze me.

Carl Parrish—Your courage and sense of humor in the face of cancer give me one more reason to be proud to call you Daddy. Your granddaughter gets it from you.

Ora Parrish—Mom, you've always been my biggest fan, supporter, and best friend. I love you.

Carl, Alisa, Leah, Katy, Lisa—I have the best family in the world.

Gary and Carolyn, Kathleen, Brenna, Kristyn, Judy, Carol, Denice—for the love and support during the darkest of times.

Lori Baur—Friend, neighbor, PR manager.

Carrie Padgett, Julie Carobini, Michael Berrier, and Shawn Grady—my writing and prayer partners.

Jim Rubart, John Olson, Katie Vorreiter, and Jenn Doucette—the Winklings.

Ami McConnell—You are an amazing editor. I don't know how we would have pulled all these divergent ideas into one cohesive story without your guidance.

Jenny Baumgartner—Your attention to detail amazes and inspires me. Thanks for the prayer support, and for all those pats on the back which always seemed to come at just the right time.

Lee Hough—You truly are the ideal agent! You are the calm voice of reason in every situation.

Bill Hogan—Thank you for walking me through the world of Charleston surfing.

Reading Group Guide

1. *Angel Song* is a story of contrasts: North and South, old and new, life and death, natural and manmade, honesty and deceit, weak and strong. How do the authors use these contrasts to deliver the message of the book? Can you think of examples of each?

2. Throughout the book, Ann hears music no one else can hear, while Keith sees beings no one else can see—specifically angels. Have you ever had such an experience? Have you ever sensed the nearness of God or His angels through one of the five senses? What happened?

3. "Eleanor moved closer to the painting of Sodom and Gomorrah. 'Interesting, isn't it, the different jobs that angels have? This one is destroying a city; this one is helping an outcast in the wilderness. A rather diverse job description.'" These are only two descriptions of what angels do. What does the Bible tells us about the nature—and usefulness—of angels?

4. There are many instances when God, through His angels, reaches out to Ann. What do you think was the breaking

point for Ann, when she decided to believe what the angels were telling her?

5. When Keith accidentally breaks Sarah's valuable pitcher, she tells him, "I've been thinking for a long time now that something so beautiful shouldn't be kept up on a shelf where no one ever sees it . . . I've been thinking about breaking it and taking it to an artist friend of mine who makes mosaic tiles. That way I could put it somewhere that I'd see it all the time. It could make me happy every day." This vignette is a parable for what often happens in life: something that seems like a disaster at the time ends up being just the thing we needed to make us see our lives differently. Can you think of a disaster in your own life that was actually a blessing in disguise?

6. Another message is at play when Sarah tells Ethan, "Even something that appears broken, in the hands of a master artist, can be made into something more beautiful than the original." What is the message? Which characters benefit when they learn this message?

7. Eleanor appears at key moments throughout the story: she is at the scene of the wreck, for example, and at the museum in New York. She appears at opportune moments with words of wisdom that make Ann think. What role do you think she plays? Do you think that Eleanor may have been an angel? Why?

8. In a chance meeting on her own street, Eleanor tells Ann, "If there's something you don't want to face, the sooner you get to it, the better . . . And if it looks to be too big to handle, I break it up into smaller pieces . . . But I don't let myself avoid the goal altogether." If you believe Eleanor was an angel, what do you think she was trying to tell Ann?

9. In the hospital, Ethan tells Ann that he just felt in his spirit that he was supposed to help her. He didn't know why, but he felt it so strongly that he kept after her even though she rebuffed him. Have you had a feeling like this? What did you do? What was the outcome?

10. Reading the words *"make a clean break"* in her mother's letter, Ann is startled to see her own thoughts mirrored by the woman who'd abandoned her. *Funny how it felt so much nobler when she [herself] was the one making the clean break*, and begins to reconsider her plans. What's the difference between a clean break and quitting? Have you ever felt you were making a clean break—but then others have accused you of being a quitter? How did you handle that?

11. Arguing with Ethan, Ann says, "See, this is your problem. You're stuck in the old. Old houses, old floors, old ways of doing things. Take a look at what's new around you; it's so much more freeing to be able to live in the moment." Ethan begins to reply, "There's where you're dead wrong. We need the old to—" but he is cut off. What do you think he would have said? Do you agree with him, or disagree? Why?

12. Ethan tells Ann, "Tearing out the old, icky stuff is hard, it's messy . . . And at times it's downright painful. But you've got to be willing to go through the process if you really want to see a true change. Anything less is just a cover-up." He's talking about remodeling homes, but he could just as easily be talking about changing one's life. Do you agree with him? Which characters in *Angel Song* were willing to go through the awkward process of change?

13. A homeless man near her apartment introduces Ann to Hebrews 13:2: "Don't forget to entertain strangers, for by so

SHEILA WALSH & KATHRYN CUSHMAN

doing some people have entertained angels without knowing it." This concept adds to her understanding of angels—and she begins to reconsider everything that's happened to her. How many strangers has Ann met? How many might have been angels? Have you ever met a stranger that, in retrospect, you believe may have been an angel?

14. About her son, Keith, Tammy thinks, *If only everyone could see, they would realize that the one they thought weak was actually the strongest one among them.* What does she mean? What does the Bible say about situations like this?

15. When Ann sees a painting of the dismissal of Hagar, the slave woman who bore Abraham's first son, she is shocked that a young mother would be turned out into the desert wilderness—although the experience of having to make do alone is not unlike her own. Then she notices an angel in the painting. As Ann learns more about Hagar—and angels—she begins to understand the nature of God for the first time. Have you had an experience when you felt completely alone? Looking back, can you say when you realized God had been with you all along?

16. Ann says, "If there is a God, why wouldn't He take better care of the people who actually believe in Him?" This raises the age-old question: why do bad things happen to Christians? Do you think *Angel Song* answers this question for Ann? For you?

Dear Friend,

I have always been fascinated by the power of a good story. Sometimes when it is told just right, you forget that it is a story at all. It's as if you know the characters so well that they have become friends. In those stories, you laugh and cry and feel a little less alone. A good story will do that for you as will a circle of friends. Let me introduce you to my circle.

Over the past fifteen years I have had the privilege of being a part of a team called, "Women Of Faith." As we have travelled from coast to coast, meeting over four million woman one thing had become crystal clear; we all have a story to tell. Each weekend I watch something take place, which is still a mystery to me. As each of my friends gets up on stage to sing or speak or perform a piece of drama I feel the audience lean in and listen. At times you could hear a pin drop, at times the laughter is so intense it rolls in waves. Sometimes as tears flow you know that healing is taking place.

I'd love to invite you to join us one weekend and experience this for yourself. The most common response from women coming for the first time is, "I had no idea!" I understand that sentiment, as that's how I felt after my first weekend in 1997. So check your schedule and gather up some of your circle and join us. I think I'm fairly safe saying, it will be life changing . . . and when you come, find me and let me know what you thought of *Angel Song*, I'd love to know!

Your friend,
Sheila

Since You Appreciate a
Good Story . . .

You'll love the stories our speakers have to tell!

At a Women of Faith two-day event, you'll hear some of the best story-tellers in the U.S. sharing real-life stories packed with humor, honesty, and inspiration. Add concerts by popular music artists, hilarious and heart-wrenching drama, and you end up with a weekend "filled to the brim with friendships, love, and a connection to God and his Word like never before." (Amanda G.)

As Annette M. said, they're *"inspiring, uplifting, introspective, heart- and gut-wrenching, soul-cleansing, and over-the-top fantastic!"*

Join Us and Begin Writing Your Own Women of Faith Story.
Register Today!

Events are scheduled across the U.S. Visit womenoffaith.com or call 888.49.FAITH (888.493.2484) to find a Women of Faith weekend near you.

womenoffaith.com | 888.49.FAITH (888.493.2484)

Follow us on

Women of Faith® is a division of Thomas Nelson.

If you enjoyed *Angel Song*, check out these other great books from gifted Bible teacher and inspiring Women of Faith® speaker Sheila Walsh.

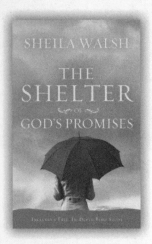

The Shelter of God's Promises
Includes an In-Depth Bible Study

"In these uncertain times, I know 100 percent that I can stake my life on the unshakeable, unchanging promises of God!"
—Sheila Walsh

God Loves Broken People
Includes an In-Depth Bible Study

God intends to wield our failures, our wanderings, and the deep hurt of our lives not only to drive us toward him but also to give us a deeper experience of his grace and healing power.

Available in stores everywhere
March 2012.

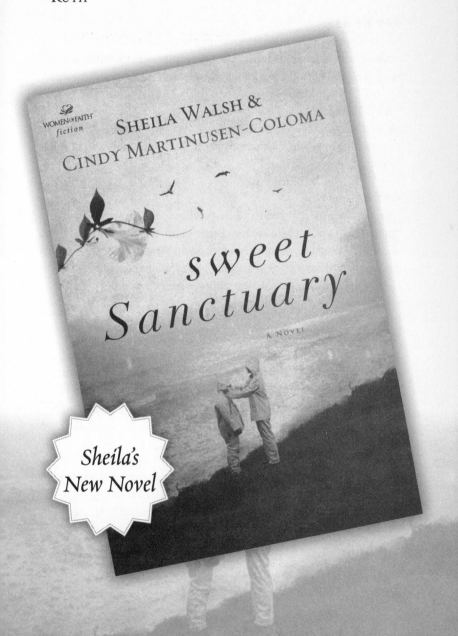

"WITHOUT THE STORM, HOW WOULD WE KNOW THE SWEETNESS OF SHELTER?"
—RUTH

WOMEN OF FAITH
fiction

SHEILA WALSH &
CINDY MARTINUSEN-COLOMA

sweet
Sanctuary

A NOVEL

Sheila's
New Novel

WORLD VISION

WHO WE ARE:
World Vision is a Christian humanitarian organization dedicated to working with children, families, and their communities worldwide to reach their full potential by tackling the causes of poverty and injustice.

WHOM WE SERVE:
Motivated by our faith in Jesus Christ, World Vision serves alongside the poor and oppressed as a demonstration of God's unconditional love for all people.

WHY WE SERVE:
Our passion is for the world's poorest children whose suffering breaks the heart of God. To help secure a better future for each child, we focus on lasting, community-based transformation. We partner with individuals and communities, empowering them to develop sustainable access to clean water, food supplies, health care, education, and economic opportunities.

HOW WE SERVE:
Since 1950, World Vision has helped millions of children and families by providing emergency assistance to those affected by natural disasters and civil conflict, developing long-term solutions within communities to alleviate poverty and advocating for justice on behalf of the poor.

YOU CAN HELP:
Partnering with World Vision provides tangible ways to honor God and put faith into action. By working together, we can make a lasting difference in the lives of children and families who are struggling to overcome poverty. To find out more about how you can help, visit www.worldvision.org or www.theholeinourgospel.com.

Visit these sites to learn more about

Down Syndrome

BAND OF ANGELS
http://www.bandofangels.com/

BETTER UNDERSTANDING OF DOWN SYNDROME
http://www.budsonline.net/

NATIONAL DOWN SYNDROME SOCIETY
http://www.ndss.org/

About the Authors

SHEILA WALSH is a powerful communicator, Bible teacher, and best-selling author with more than 4 million books sold. A featured speaker with Women of Faith, Sheila has reached more than 3.5 million women by artistically combining honesty, vulnerability, and humor with God's Word.

Author of the best-selling memoir *Honestly* and the Gold Medallion nominee for *The Heartache No One Sees*, Sheila's most recent release, *Beautiful Things Happen When A Woman Trusts God*, includes a 12-week Bible study. The *Gigi, God's Little Princess* book and video series has won the National Retailer's Choice Award twice and is the most popular Christian brand for young girls in the United States.

Sheila co-hosted *The 700 Club* and her own show *Heart to Heart with Sheila Walsh*. She is currently completing her Masters in Theology and lives in Dallas, Texas, with her husband, Barry, son, Christian, and two little dogs Belle and Tink.

Visit sheilawalsh.com for more information on Shelia and her products.

KATHRYN CUSHMAN is a graduate of Samford University with a degree in pharmacy. After practicing as a pharmacist, she left her career to spend more time at home with her daughters and has since pursued her dream of writing. She is the author of *Leaving Yesterday*, *Waiting for Daybreak*, and *A Promise to Remember*. Kathryn and her family currently live in Santa Barbara, California.